'A winning combination of high-octane drama and sympathetically likeable heroes'
Big Issue

'A cast of characters who could have come straight from an Ian Fleming novel. The dialogue is crisp, the settings vivid and the pace swift'
CNN Traveller

'Excellent opener from Mr Brownlee'
Daily Sport

Praise for *Burn*:

'Nick Brownlee is on terrific form in his second thriller as he ratchets up the tension'.
Daily Mirror

'In Daniel Jouma and Jake Moore, Brownlee has created a team so different – so compelling – those who pick this novel up will be delighted at how reluctant they will be to put it down again'
Chris High, *Tangled Web/Shots*

'Once again, Brownlee has produced an intriguing story, brimming with action and memorable characters in a fascinating Kenyan setting ... If you enjoy being constantly at the edge of your seat, then get your hands on this!'
RTE Guide

'*Burn* is a fast-paced and exciting novel that brings the dark and dirty streets of Mombasa alive'.
Luke Croll, *Reviewing the Evidence*

Nick Brownlee

MACHETE

piatkus

PIATKUS

First published in Great Britain as a paperback original in 2010 by Piatkus

Copyright © 2010 by Nick Brownlee

A CIP catalogue record for this book
is available from the British Library.

ISBN 978-0-7499-4256-4

Typeset in Bembo by Action Publishing Technology Ltd, Gloucester
Printed and bound in Great Britain by Clays Ltd, Bungay, Suffolk

Papers used by Piatkus are natural, renewable and recyclable
products sourced from well-managed forests and certified
in accordance with the rules of the Forest Stewardship Council.

Mixed Sources
Product group from well-managed
forests and other controlled sources
www.fsc.org Cert no. SGS-COC-004081
© 1996 Forest Stewardship Council

Piatkus
An imprint of
Little, Brown Book Group
100 Victoria Embankment
London EC4Y 0DY

An Hachette UK Company
www.hachette.co.uk

www.piatkus.co.uk

For Georgia, Beatrice, Milly, Tom and Bruce – but not
till you're big.

Acknowledgements

My thanks, once again, to Emma Beswetherick – aka The Tweakmaster – and to Stephanie Glencross, for their calm appraisal of the patient and expert surgery to repair the damage.

But most of all thanks to Janey Brownlee for putting up yet again with the ogre in the attic.

Author's note

The Kenyan Navy was established in 1964, and is unusual in that instead of traditional naval ranks it uses army-style designations. Captains, for example, are referred to as Colonels, Commodores as Brigadiers, Admirals as Generals and so on. I have kept to these designations wherever possible in this book.

'He that will have no trouble in this world must not be born in it.'
Kikuyu proverb

I

1

It was Christmas morning in Mombasa, ninety-five degrees and climbing – and what nine-year-old Jonas Yomo had hoped was a soccer ball under the frosted plastic tree in the living room had, when unwrapped, turned out to be his stepfather's severed head.

The boy, understandably, was struck dumb with shock. He was now in a bedroom of the first-floor apartment in the island's Kwakiziwi district, rocking urgently back and forth on his grandmother's knee while emitting a low, dull moan. His mother, Tabitha, while no longer hysterical, continued to weep silently on the sofa with her head in her father's lap while he softly stroked her hair and made soothing noises.

Paul Yomo's head had been placed in a coolbox and was on its way to the morgue in the back of a police patrol car. The remaining shreds of brown paper in which it had been wrapped had been collected and bagged. Eventually, perhaps in a month or two depending on workload and urgency, it would be examined by the police forensics laboratory in Nairobi.

'What I want to know is what sort of *animal* could do such a thing, Inspector?' demanded Brigadier Charles Wako Chatme.

Tabitha Yomo's father was a tall, broad-chested African of sixty-five, with clipped white hair and a neatly trimmed white moustache. He was the commander of the Kenya Navy dockyard at Mtongwe on the south shore, and even though he was dressed casually this morning in slacks and sports jacket he still looked every inch the high-ranking naval officer. His question was addressed in the stentorian tones of a man who expected an immediate answer from a subordinate.

Detective Inspector Daniel Jouma of Coast Province CID snapped on a pair of white latex gloves and prodded a suspicious-looking stain on the carpet next to the polyurethane trunk of the Christmas tree.

'When was the last time you saw your son-in-law, Brigadier?'

'Last weekend. He and Tabitha came to the house for supper.'

'And what about you, Mrs Yomo?'

Tabitha blinked her dewy eyes. 'He left for work as normal the day before Christmas Eve,' she whispered. 'It was his last day before the holiday.'

'How did he appear? Did he seem concerned about anything?'

'No.'

'Did he mention if he was in any trouble at all? Had he been threatened by anyone?'

'No.'

'Had he *ever* been threatened to your knowledge?'

'No!' Tabitha blurted, and hurried from the room with her hands pressed to her face. Presently, the sound of sobbing came from the bathroom.

'May I commend you on your tact, Inspector,' the Brigadier said acidly.

Jouma sighed. 'In my experience, sir, tact is rarely the most effective way to reach the truth.'

He was wearing the latex gloves because his superior, Superintendent Simba, wanted all scene-of-crime sites to be protected from forensic contamination. It was a futile exercise – the stain on the carpet was dog shit that

4

had been dragged in on the soles of the attending uniformed constable's boots.

Jouma looked across at the Brigadier. 'According to my officer, the ... *item* was left on the doorstep,' he said *tactfully*.

'That is correct.'

'There was no message attached?'

The Brigadier shook his head.

'Who found it?'

'I did. I assumed it was a gift for Jonas. That's why I placed it under the tree.'

Jouma nodded. Before being wrapped in the brown paper, the head had been carefully swaddled in several protective layers of newspaper, the previous day's *Daily Nation* to be precise, presumably to prevent it leaking. It would have looked like a football, especially to an excitable young boy on Christmas morning.

'Then it could have been intended for your daughter?'

'It could have been intended for anyone,' the Brigadier said testily. 'You should be making enquiries as to whether anyone saw the person who delivered it.'

Jouma stood up, knees crackling. 'I can assure you that my men are doing their job.'

'Not that anybody ever sees anything,' the Brigadier grumbled. 'People live their lives with their eyes shut.'

The Inspector nodded, thinking that the Brigadier was most probably right. 'How long has your daughter lived here?'

'Six months. They moved in after they were married.'

The apartment was spacious by the standards of downtown Mombasa, Jouma thought, and certainly bigger than his own in the adjacent neighbourhood of Makupa. Yet Paul Yomo was a thirty-year-old credit officer earning seven thousand shillings a month. His wife, two years younger, was a lab technician on half that wage. Even combined and trebled, their salaries could not have afforded a place this size. It had a well-maintained cleanliness that suggested a maid. The furniture was of a good quality, and there was a modern television in the corner of the living room. Six months they had been here? The apartment could only have been a wedding present.

The door opened and the Brigadier's wife came in. Ellen Wako Chatme was a slim, elegant white woman, as well preserved as her husband. She wore an ankle-length robe made of turquoise silk, with an understated ruby pendant around her neck.

'He is sleeping,' she said softly, closing the door behind her.

The Brigadier stood up. 'A word, Inspector,' he said.

Adjoining the apartment block, separating it from a busy main road, was a small walled garden with a lawn of coarse grass and a couple of well-positioned palms offering shade. Jouma and the Brigadier sat on a wooden bench beneath one of the trees. The Brigadier removed his sports jacket and folded it neatly across his knees. Jouma noted with approval that even the creases in his white, short-sleeved cotton shirt were razor sharp. He appreciated those who took pride in their appearance. There were so few who did these days. The Inspector himself was wearing a blue two-piece suit from Jermyn Street in London, which had cost a great deal of money when new. He was also wearing a tie and his shoes were polished. It cost nothing to make an effort.

'So — is it him?' the Brigadier snapped.

Jouma looked up at him. At just five feet five, the Inspector's head barely reached the Brigadier's shoulder as they sat together on the bench. 'I beg your pardon?'

'The animal who murdered those other two people? Did he kill Paul?'

'It is far too early to—'

'Don't be coy with me, Inspector Jouma! I am not a fool.'

'I would never suggest that you were, Brigadier,' Jouma said. 'But you must understand that it would be irresponsible to speculate about Paul's murder just yet.'

The Brigadier harrumphed, but Jouma could see that he saw the point.

'I read in the newspaper that they are calling this maniac the Headhunter,' he said presently. 'That he leaves the heads on display, as if they were trophies.'

Jouma groaned inwardly. 'I do not write the headlines, Brigadier. And our investigation is ongoing. When I asked your daughter if Paul had any enemies, she seemed to think not. Do you know any different?'

'Why should I?'

'Men will sometimes confide to other men things they would not tell their wives.'

'Paul was a credit officer,' the Brigadier pointed out. 'Do credit officers have enemies?'

'People who are in debt can sometimes resort to desperate measures.'

'Like cutting off my son-in-law's head and leaving it on the doorstep on Christmas morning for his boy to find?' The Brigadier laughed harshly. 'A person who is that creative should not be in debt, Inspector Jouma.'

2

'And a merry bloody Christmas to you, too!' Christie the pathologist said grumpily as Jouma entered the autopsy room in the basement of Mombasa Hospital. He was standing over Paul Yomo's head with a scalpel in one hand and a metal spatula in the other, looking for all the world as if he was about to carve the Christmas turkey.

'I never associated you with the festive spirit, Mr Christie,' Jouma said. 'I thought you would be pleased to be working today.'

Christie, a fittingly cadaverous Englishman with thinning white hair slicked back from a face that rarely saw the sun, gave the Inspector a withering look over the metal autopsy table.

'Just because you Kenyans can't be bothered to celebrate Christmas in the traditional manner doesn't mean the rest of us don't,' he said.

'Mr Yomo's family were celebrating Christmas in the traditional manner,' Jouma pointed out. 'Or at least, that was their intention.'

He thought about the presents under the tree, and how the tree itself had been so carefully laden with tinsel and baubles. He thought about the boy finding the parcel and eagerly ripping it open.

'Yes, well,' the pathologist grumbled.

Yes, well, Jouma thought. To think about that would be to run the risk of regarding the head on his autopsy table as having once belonged to a human being – and that was not Christie's style.

'Let's have a look, shall we?' the pathogist said, abruptly businesslike.

The head was upright, resting on an inch-long stump of neck. The eyes were closed and the mouth was slightly open. Paul Yomo had been a good-looking man, with the strong cheekbones and firm jaw typical of the Kikuyu, Kenya's dominant tribe; but his cheeks were slightly pitted, like the peel of an orange – the result of teenage acne or chickenpox perhaps – and a small scar cut through the close-cropped goatee beard on his chin. His skin was the colour of ash.

'Am I to believe that the head was *gift-wrapped*?' Christie said.

'It was *not* gift-wrapped,' Jouma corrected him. 'It was wrapped in plain brown paper.'

But the idea of someone receiving a head for Christmas had clearly captured the pathologist's imagination. 'I'll be damned,' he said, then shrugged. 'Still, I suppose it beats slippers.'

'The head, Mr Christie. If you please.'

'Well, the first thing to say about it is that it was a good clean cut.' He made a slicing motion with his hand. 'Look.'

He gently laid the head on its side, so the transection of the neck was visible. Jouma, a queasy observer at the best of times, felt the room begin to swim as he saw loops and whorls of muscle, circles of bone and gristle, and the holes where the arteries had been cut. It looked, he thought with a shiver, like an uncooked ham.

'See?' Christie said. 'No burring around the edges of the bone, and no striations in the flesh to suggest something mechanical did this. No, this is the result of a single powerful blow with a very sharp implement.'

'An axe?' Jouma said hopefully.

'Axes are notoriously unreliable, old man. It's the

9

length of the things, you see? Did you know that it took a professional executioner two attempts to chop off Mary Queen of Scots's head? And even then it was still attached to the poor old bird's neck by a length of gristle—'

'For goodness sake, Mr Christie!' Jouma exclaimed. 'Will you *please* get to the point?'

'I'd say machete.'

'Machete?' His heart sank.

''Fraid so,' Christie said, tapping Paul Yomo's head with his finger. 'Of course, you could be in luck. This could be nothing more than your average run-of-the-mill Kenyan decapitation. And of course I won't be able to confirm anything until I have completed a full and thorough examination.'

'Of course.'

'But I have to say straight away that the similarities to the other two cases look more than coincidental. I also hope you realise that you have spoiled my Christmas by calling me in at such short notice.'

Jouma could not imagine anything less cheerful than Christmas at the pathologist's gloomy bungalow on the north shore, where Christie eked out the solitary hours between shifts in this white-tiled hell.

'That said, I've got rather a nice bottle of sherry in my office,' Christie said. 'Gift from the cleaning staff. I could open it – if you happened to be at a loose end, that is.'

The Inspector gaped. Was the misanthropic pathologist being *sociable*? If so, it would be the first time in the fifteen years the two men had worked together. The Mombasa detective found himself at a loss for words – and in that moment of awkwardness Christie's shutters came clanging down again.

'It's cheap stuff, probably not worth drinking,' he said, swiping Paul Yomo's head from the autopsy table and turning his back to place it in a steel dish on the bench behind him. 'I'll do the full examination as soon as possible.'

Jouma opened his mouth to speak, but Christie was already snapping off his gloves as if they were an offending layer of skin. In the few seconds it took to deposit them in a waste basket, all trace of seasonal goodwill had disappeared. The Inspector felt oddly relieved that the old Christie was back. The brief hiatus when the pathologist's veins were filled with the milk of human kindness had been unsettling in the extreme.

'Season's greetings to you, Mr Christie,' he said, heading for the door.

'And to you. Oh, and Jouma!'

Jouma turned. 'Mr Christie?'

'That friend of yours. The English chap from Flamingo Creek. How is he?'

For a moment Jouma didn't know who Christie was talking about. In all the excitement he had forgotten all about Jake Moore.

'I believe he goes home today,' he said.

'Really?' Christie said, impressed. 'They must breed 'em tough in the north-east of England. After what he went through, that bugger is bloody lucky to be alive.'

3

Images. Splintered memories. Or were they hallucinations?

At one point a gull had been circling high above him, narrow white wings outstretched against the blue of the sky to catch the sun's heat reflected back off the ocean.

Perfect circles in a perfect sky.

A perfect day to die. How easy it would have been just to let the warm water close over his head and sink to the bottom.

Jake Moore came awake to the sound of his own head rattling against the passenger window of the Land Rover, as the ancient vehicle careered along the dirt road that ran along the south bank of Flamingo Creek. Its shot suspension offered little protection from the ruts and potholes and its driver couldn't care less about avoiding them.

Harry Philliskirk squinted at the road ahead from beneath the brim of his baseball cap like some myopic hobgoblin, his long bony nose almost pressed against the grimy windscreen. He uttered a colourful oath as another king-sized crater sent a juddering impact through the Land Rover's chassis and threatened to jettison both men through the roof.

'What's the hurry?' Jake asked him.

Harry glanced over and frowned with disappointment. 'I was hoping to get back to the boatyard before you woke up.'

Jake was about to say something, but thought better of it. He had known his business partner long enough to know that there was logic in there somewhere. Instead, he braced himself for the rigours of the last half-mile of the journey and hoped that he hadn't survived an assassin's knife in his belly and six hours floating in the Indian Ocean only to have Harry wrap him around a palm tree.

He remembered little of what happened that day in the cockpit of *Yellowfin*, when a female killer known as the Ghost had tried to murder him. Her preferred method of assassination was to thrust a stiletto blade into the base of her victim's neck, severing the spinal cord and causing immediate death – and, had Jake not reacted instantly as she ambushed him, smashing the back of his head into her face, it was how he too would have died.

There was nothing he could do about the six inches of steel the Ghost plunged into his guts, though.

He remembered the pain. He would never forget it. Six years ago he had been shot and had felt nothing but a mule-kick impact. The sensation of the Ghost's blade tearing into his innards was like nothing he could have ever imagined – a ripping, searing agony that literally sucked the breath from his lungs. She had come for him again, face impassive, knowing that he was dying, a predator closing in on its kill. And that was when he had tumbled backwards from the stern rail, because he was damned if he was going to die on his own boat.

'Well, here we are, old boy,' Harry said. For some reason he seemed almost embarrassed.

The Land Rover came round a bend in the road and there was the boatyard. Except it wasn't the decrepit flea-pit Jake had last seen six weeks ago. The scummy breezeblock walls of the workshop had been given a lick of whitewash and the corrugated-iron roof had been scoured of the accretions of five years' unchecked vegetation, rust, and bird and monkey shit. The words *Britannia Fishing Trips Ltd* had been carefully stencilled on the metal in three-foot-high red-painted letters.

'Christ,' Jake said.

A banner had been tied between two trees and someone had daubed *Welcome Home Jake* on it using the same paint as they'd used on the workshop roof. There were clusters of balloons hanging limply from the branches. And as they drew nearer Jake saw there were people gathered in the yard.

'Harry—'

'Suki Lo insisted,' his business partner said hurriedly.

Suki Lo owned a bar three hundred yards further along the creek road. She was a diminutive Malay with teeth like rotten wooden pegs and now she was coming across to the Land Rover with a bottle of Jack Daniel's raised above her head and a smile on her face that looked like the gates of hell.

'Honey boy!' she squawked, flinging herself at Jake as he gingerly climbed down from the cab. 'I so fuckin' please to see you!'

'Easy, Suki,' he winced, fending her off the way he might discourage an over-excited puppy. 'I don't want to burst my stitches.'

'You know I came visit you,' Suki said earnestly. 'In the hospital. Many times.'

'Harry told me.'

'They tell Suki you gonna die. I say, "Not Jakey! Not my brave boy! He no fuckin' die!"'

The narrow slits of her eyes filled with tears. She was looking at him, and he knew it was not a pleasant sight. Jake had gone into hospital with the build of a six-foot, fifteen-stone rugby player; he had come out of it looking like a survivor from a Japanese POW camp, cheeks sunken, muscles wasted away, eyes hollow.

14

'Well, I didn't die, Suki. Now what's all this?'

He stooped to kiss the top of her head and glanced across at the small crowd gathered outside the workshop. He smiled to himself. The grizzled clientele of Suki's bar, mostly game-boat skippers and mechanics, never looked comfortable out of their natural habitat. Most of them looked like they were still suffering from the night before. In fact, they looked, Jake thought, as if they were the ones who had spent six weeks at death's door, not him.

'Amazing what the promise of free booze can achieve,' Harry said cheerfully, coming round from the driver's side. 'Although, believe it or not, one or two of them *were* concerned about your welfare.'

'I probably owed them money,' Jake said. He walked towards the workshop, grimacing again at the sharp pain in his abdomen whenever he moved too quickly. Then he stopped.

Something was not right.

Looking across towards the wooden jetty and the sluggish brown water of the creek, it took him a few moments to realise what it was.

'Where's *Yellowfin*, Harry?'

4

When Jouma married his wife Winifred, her bridal price
was set at thirty-five cows and two dozen goats. This was
high, very nearly exorbitant – but then Winifred was a
beautiful girl and her father was a village elder who
knew how to strike a hard bargain.

'You had better provide me with strong grandsons,
Daniel,' Jouma's father had muttered after emerging
from the negotiations. In order to have his son marry
the elder's daughter, he had just agreed to hand over a
quarter of his herd.

Times had changed in the thirty years that had passed
since that day. In fact, sometimes Jouma thought that his
marriage to Winifred was the only stable factor in a world
that had gone steadily insane. And if their union had
failed to produce the grandchildren his father had longed
for, Jouma still looked at his wife each morning across the
breakfast table and wished that the old man was still alive
to see that his investment had indeed been a bargain.

Paul and Tabitha Yomo had been married six months
earlier in a Roman Catholic service at the Holy Ghost
Cathedral in central Mombasa. It was a grand affair, as
befitted such a prestigious venue. There were over a
hundred guests gathered for the official photograph
taken on the steps outside the vast whitewashed edifice
on Nyerere Avenue. It was, Jouma thought as he held
the silver frame, like a photograph from the society
magazines the switchboard operators at police headquarters were always reading: the bride in a stunning

16

white dress, the groom in a pale-pink morning suit, Brigadier Charles Wako Chatme resplendent in his naval dress uniform, his wife Ellen like some exotic bird of paradise with multicoloured plumage sprouting from her wide-brimmed hat.

And there was Jonas. The boy looked awkward in a suit and a wing-collar shirt that looked three sizes too big for his thin neck. He was holding hands with the man who had just become his stepfather, smiling shyly at the camera.

'Jonas was Paul's best man,' Ellen said sadly, staring at the photograph from behind Jouma's elbow. He hurriedly replaced it on the mantelpiece. 'Paul thought the world of him.'

They were in the lounge of the Wako Chatmes' villa in the prosperous north shore suburb of Nyali, where Tabitha and Jonas had been moved after the horrors of Christmas morning in Kwakiziwi. A cool sea breeze was blowing through open French windows that led out to a large well-tended garden.

'I have heard that children sometimes find it hard to bond with their step-parents,' Jouma said.

Ellen sashayed across to an ox-blood leather sofa and sat down. 'Paul and Jonas were thick as thieves the moment they met.' She smiled sadly.

'Where is the boy now?'

'Charles has taken him to the dockyard to look at the ships. We thought it best to try to take his mind off things.'

Jouma cleared his throat. 'Mrs Wako Chatme—'

'Ellen, please.'

'Is there any reason you know why someone might want Paul dead?'

She thought for a moment. 'Paul was simply wonder-ful,' she said.

It was no answer — but then, ever since she had let him over the threshold, the Brigadier's wife had proved expert at deflecting Jouma's questions. She did it with the deftest of touches, of course, just enough to set them off on a different and less turbulent course — but it was just as effective as if she'd answered him with silence.

Jouma sighed. It was not even Ellen he wanted to talk to. But in the few short hours since he had last seen Tabitha at the apartment, the girl's parents had formed a seamless protective barrier around their daughter. And if the Brigadier was an immovable object, then his wife was an irresistible force.

Tabitha, she told him, was resting in her room. The girl was still devastated by what had happened and was not receiving visitors. However, Ellen was sure that, when the time was right, she would answer any of his questions. Meanwhile, was there anything *she* could help him with?

Jouma had tried.

How did Paul and Tabitha meet?

At a church social function.

Did Paul ever talk about his past? His background?

Paul was a very private person. But I believe he was brought up in the Rift Valley. He came to Mombasa to study at the polytechnic.

You never thought to find out more about your prospective son-in-law?

We did not hire private detectives, if that is what you mean!

Did he have family?

His parents sadly died a few years ago. He was an only child.

Did Tabitha ever mention any concerns she might have had about Paul?

No.

Did you and your husband set them up at their apartment in Kwakiziwi?

Are you married, Inspector? Then you will know how difficult it can be for a newly wed couple to get their feet on the ladder.

What of Jonas's natural father—?

'Young girls are impulsive, Inspector. They often do things that later they regret. Lord knows I did! Now, would you care for some more tea?'

Jouma felt he had been worked over in the boxing ring by a professional fighter whose fists were too fast to see. He was astonished to see by the brass submarine clock on the wall that he had been there for an hour. It seemed that time flew when you were achieving absolutely nothing.

5

Jake was sitting on the jetty, looking out at Flamingo Creek. The last of Suki's regulars had tottered away and, although he appreciated the sentiment, he was glad to see the back of them. As far as he was concerned allowing yourself to get knifed in the guts was no cause for celebration, even if you had lived to tell the tale.

Harry knew it too, because he had learned to read his partner's moods as surely as if they were an old married couple. Running a seat-of-your-pants concern like Britannia Fishing Trips Ltd every day for five years had that effect. And he could tell that more than anything Jake was pining for his boat.

'Where's *Yellowfin*?'

Those had been his first words after he woke from his coma in the intensive care unit of Mombasa General. He had undergone sixteen hours of surgery during which his heart had stopped four times. Even the surgeons who had rebuilt his shredded innards said they were amazed he had pulled through. But then they were astonished Jake was still alive when he'd been hauled from the Indian Ocean by a passing dhow after six hours in the water. They reasoned the cold water, coupled with the relatively narrow entry wound caused by the stiletto blade, had helped staunch the bleeding.

But the main reason the Englishman was still alive was his sheer determination not to die.

'I've just been in touch on the ship-to-shore,' Harry said, sitting down beside Jake in his canvas director's

20

chair. 'Ralphie says he's just about to turn into the creek.'

'Does he know to drop Sammy at Jalawi?'

Harry nodded.

'Five minutes, then.'

Jake fixed his gaze at the headland downriver where *Yellowfin* would shortly appear. He looked, Harry thought, like an anxious parent waiting for his child to return from its first sleepover.

The murderous bitch who stabbed Jake had hijacked the thirty-footer and sailed her north up the coast and dumped her in a backwater half a mile up the Sabaki Estuary. It was fortunate indeed that *Yellowfin* had been spotted by a passing skipper from nearby Malindi who recognised the name; little short of miraculous that the boat had not been stripped to the bare bones by opportunist local scavengers. As for the Ghost – well, she was still out there, somewhere. And despite the lame reassurances of the FBI agents on her tail, Jake knew they would never find her. Not unless she broke cover to finish what she had started, in which case he was a dead man. For now all he could do was try to put that thought out of his mind. He had not clung to life only to spend the rest of it looking over his shoulder.

'Here she comes,' Harry shouted. 'We gave her a damn good clean-up and a lick of paint where required. I think you'll approve.'

As *Yellowfin*'s familiar lines materialised around the headland, Jake stood. His heart was pounding because Harry was right – his boat seemed to shimmer in the sun. She was *beautiful*.

Fifty yards out from the jetty, the boat performed a brisk about-turn so that she faced downriver. A pot-bellied figure emerged from the shade of the flying bridge tarpaulin and climbed down the metal connecting ladder to the cockpit on hairy white legs. As Jake watched, he teetered along the starboard rail to the prow and secured the boat to a mooring post that jutted from the water. Also attached to the post was a single-engine launch. The man jumped down into it with a heavy thump, started the motor and guided the launch towards the jetty.

'So that's the legendary Ralphie, is it?'

'That's him all right,' Harry said, looking oddly sheepish. 'My big brother.'

Jake shook his head. 'Two Philliskirks on one continent. God help us all.'

6

Twelve hours after its discovery, Paul Yomo's head remained, literally, on ice at the Mombasa Hospital morgue.

'We've been having some problems with the generator that powers the refrigerators,' Christie said grumpily. 'The bloody thing cut out entirely for two hours today while every bugger was out at lunch. By the time we managed to get some ice shipped in from the dhow harbour, a number of our longer-term residents had passed their sell-by date. We had no choice but to cremate them before they stank the place out.'

'I hope the head survived your meltdown, Mr Christie,' Jouma said, shivering against the pervasive chill.

The pathologist grinned. 'That's where the gods smiled on you, Jouma.'

He led the Inspector past the rows of metal lockers containing the remaining cadavers and into a small galley kitchen near to the autopsy room. He opened a mini-fridge on the counter next to the kettle and Jouma recoiled when he saw Paul Yomo's head inside.

'This is where we normally keep the milk and the butter,' Christie explained. 'But as soon as the generator went on the blink I thought it prudent to put our friend in here for safekeeping.'

He reached inside and carefully removed the head. It was resting face up on its metal dish, the skin and the exposed stump covered in a fine layer of frost.

'If it wasn't for all the palaver over the generator I

would have expected to have had it boiled down by now. As it is, I've only just finished my general examination. Can I get you a cup of tea, Jouma?'

Jouma looked at him, appalled. 'No – no, thank you. I would rather know your conclusions.'

'My initial examination was pretty much on the money,' Christie said. 'The neck was severed with a single blow from a sharp implement. An *extremely sharp* implement. And again, I would emphasise the unusually clean nature of the blow. Clean as a whistle.'

'The same as the others,' Jouma muttered.

Christie's eyes narrowed. 'Not quite.'

'What do you mean?'

'Well, it may be nothing – but you will recall that, with the first two heads, the damage to the cervical vertebrae suggested a left-to-right blow.' He made a horizontal movement with his hand, then gestured at the head on the table. 'This, on the other hand, shows evidence of frontal splintering. In other words, Jouma, the blow was front-to-back.'

'Is that important?'

'That all depends on whether you regard *how* the killer despatches his victims to be important,' Christie said. 'It strikes me as odd that he should change his *modus operandi*. I would have thought any self-respecting serial killer would have been extremely protective of his methods. His *signature*, if you like. But then again, it may be nothing.'

'You're saying someone *else* killed Paul Yomo? That there's a copycat out there?'

'I'm saying nothing of the sort, Jouma,' Christie retorted. 'That's your job.'

Yes, Jouma thought, *it was*. Which was why, right now, his spirits were sagging. One machete-wielding maniac was bad enough in Mombasa – but two?

'Chin up, old man,' Christie said. 'At least it'll keep you busy.'

Jouma nodded. 'That is what concerns me. I had hoped Paul Yomo might lead me to the Headhunter – now I just hope it was the Headhunter who killed him.'

II

7

'You know,' Jake said, 'all those weeks I spent in hospital, the only thing I could think of was a 16oz sirloin steak, medium rare, cooked to perfection, the blood bubbling out of it as I stuck my fork in it. And beer – ice-cold beer in a fucking great schooner glass, with the sides all misted up with condensation. And now,' he sighed glumly, 'I'm sitting here at last with my steak and my beer, and I can't face either of them.'

Jouma looked at him sorrowfully. 'I expect it is natural to experience a loss of appetite, my friend,' he said. 'Do not forget that your internal organs have been through a great deal of trauma. Here – would you care for some chickpeas?'

The two men were having lunch at their favourite Algerian café down by the dhow harbour in Mombasa. It was the first time they had met since Jake had been discharged from hospital and Jouma was shocked at how much weight his friend had lost. He couldn't help thinking that the Englishman looked like he'd been released from a prisoner of war camp instead of a hospital ward.

'I know what you're thinking, Inspector,' Jake said, and Jouma realised to his embarrassment that he had been staring. 'And you're right. I look like shit.'

Jouma winced at the term. 'You are lucky to be alive, my friend,' he reminded him.

Jake prodded his steak unconvincingly. 'Yeah, well—'

'It will be difficult to readjust.'

'I was trying to remember what it was like after I was shot back in England, how I felt after I got out of the hospital, because I'm sure it was never like this. I feel – I dunno – *pointless*? Someone else is driving my boat, I'm getting on Harry's nerves, and, well, I've got nothing to do all day except hang around the boatyard like a spare prick at a wedding.' He shook his head. 'Christ, I'm sorry, Inspector. The last thing you need right now is a wet blanket crying over your chickpeas.'

Jouma smiled and poured himself a glass of water. 'Believe me, Jake, your human frailty makes a refreshing change. Lately I have been thinking that the world has gone mad.'

'The Headhunter, right?'

'Not a term I prefer to use, but an accurate one, nevertheless.'

'I read the papers,' Jake said. 'The guy sounds like a 24-carat nutcase. Do you have a link between the victims?'

'No. Apart from the fact that they were all male, of course.'

'You think that's important?'

'Possibly. But I have no idea why. It really is most baffling.'

'Serial killers don't always think like you or me, Inspector,' Jake pointed out. 'Dennis Nilsen killed fifteen men, most of whom he just picked up in bars or off the street. There was no motive, no link – nothing that would make sense to any sane person, at least. Nilsen told the police he couldn't even remember killing them.'

'How did they catch him?'

'He chopped up the bodies and flushed the pieces down the toilet. Unfortunately for him, they ended up blocking the drains.'

30

Jouma stared balefully at his plate of chickpeas and decided he no longer wanted them. 'Fifteen, you say?'

'There were probably more. Nilsen wasn't a fastidious record-keeper.'

'My God.'

'Yeah. So right now your Headhunter wouldn't even get a mention in the Psycho Hall of Fame.'

'For some reason I do not find that reassuring, Jake.'

Faisal, the pot-bellied café owner, came out and stared quizzically at their untouched plates.

'Something wrong with your food?' he demanded.

'I'm sure it's fantastic as always, Faisal,' Jake said. 'But I'm just not hungry.'

Jouma nodded. 'I, too, have lost my appetite, Faisal.'

Faisal swept up the plates with a single dismissive movement. 'Maybe you prefer Tamarind?' he said sniffily, gesturing at the north shore and the popular restaurant situated on the headland. He strutted back into the kitchens before they could reply.

Jouma watched him go. 'I suppose all problems are relative. It would be nice to be running a café instead of a murder investigation.'

'Don't be fooled,' Jake said. 'I came to Kenya for the quiet life – and look what happened.'

For a moment the two men fell silent. Lunch had been a pleasant interlude – but it had served only to remind them of the sour realities that existed beyond Faisal's café.

That morning, Jouma had risen early, kissed his wife and set off across town in his ancient Fiat Panda to the heart of Mombasa's commercial district. It was quiet; many of the European-owned businesses were shut for the Christmas holidays – but there was still enough traffic on the main thoroughfares to make a journey of less than three miles last thirty minutes.

Paul Yomo worked for a company called Exciting Prospects Credit Agency. Its office was above a launderette on the first floor of a crumbling concrete building in Kombo Street. The name was written beneath a buzzer connected to a door at street level and in peeling stencil along the window above. As he stared up from the pavement, Jouma saw a shadow move across the ceiling tiles. Ignoring the buzzer, he pushed open the door and climbed a flight of steps.

At the top of the stairs was another door with two plastic chairs outside. Jouma turned the handle and went in. There was a wooden counter with a bell. Behind it was a room with three desks and a number of filing cabinets. A large poster had been thumb-tacked to the back wall. It showed a young African couple standing in front of a new three-bedroomed house. A smiling man in a smart suit was handing them a set of keys. *Unlock Your Dreams* it said in bold letters underneath.

And pay them off at forty per cent interest for the rest of your life, Jouma thought uncharitably. He struck the bell with his palm.

A woman was standing at one of the filing cabinets with her back to him. A dark skirt and blouse strained against her hefty build. 'We are closed,' she said without turning.

'My name is Inspector Daniel Jouma of Coast Province CID.'

The woman slammed shut the cabinet door so quickly she risked jamming her fingers. 'Police?' she said. She had piggy little features that seemed out of proportion with the rest of her face.

'And you are?'

'Mrs Judith Ogalo. I am the office manager.' She smiled unconvincingly. 'How may I be of assistance?'

'You have an employee named Paul Yomo?'

'That is correct.'

'I regret to inform you that he is dead.'

Mrs Ogalo blinked again. 'Dead?'

'He was murdered sometime between December 24 and 25.'

When he told her how, Mrs Ogalo made a strange noise in the back of her throat and began to list ominously to one side. Jouma lifted the counter hatch and hurried across. He manhandled her into a chair just as she was about to smash into one of the desks.

She looked at him. 'Beheaded, you say?' she said weakly.

'That is correct.'

Her eyes widened. 'You don't think—?'

So she had obviously heard about the Headhunter. But who hadn't? The ghoul was rapidly becoming a national celebrity.

Jouma fetched her a cup of water from a cooler in one corner of the office. An electric fan on one of the filing cabinets stirred the sluggish air. He put it on the desk and aimed it at her.

'How long had Mr Yomo worked here, Mrs Ogalo?'

'Eighteen months.'

She explained that Paul Yomo's official job title was Senior Credit Analyst. What that meant in practice was that he sifted through the piles of loan applications, selected the most promising – or rather the least risky – then passed them on to Mrs Ogalo for final approval.

'May I see his desk?'

It was scrupulously tidy. Pens and pencils were stored in plastic tidies, paperwork neatly stacked in trays. There was a photograph of his wife and stepson in a wooden frame. They were smiling. Jouma opened the drawers. They contained fresh notepads, boxes of staples, erasers and unused loan application forms. There was also a cheap, leather-effect diary. The detective checked to see that Mrs Ogalo was not looking and quickly skimmed its pages. Like most diaries, Paul Yomo's had started out in January full of good intentions – appointments, birthdays, anniversaries all dutifully logged. But by March the entries had almost completely dried up, and from May onwards it was empty. He replaced it and closed the drawer.

'You are the only people who work in this office?' he asked her.

She nodded. 'Our head office is in Nairobi.'

'Have any threats been made against you or Mr Yomo? People who have been refused a loan, perhaps?' he suggested.

Mrs Ogalo shrugged. 'What purpose would it serve to threaten us? We just deal with the paperwork, Inspector. The paperwork is passed to our head office in Nairobi. It is they who make the final decision. It is they who have the money.'

'May I ask what are you doing here today?'

'I came in to sort through a backlog of paperwork,' she said. Then she started to blubber again. 'Paul is *dead*? But he was such a sweet-natured boy. He had no enemies, Inspector.'

So everyone kept telling him, Jouma thought. He had heard the same thing about the Headhunter's previous victims. But the fact remained that all three men had been decapitated – and, however deranged, there *had* to be a reason why.

Jake's problems that day had all been in his mind. Specifically the fact that it would be the first time he had been on *Yellowfin* since the day the Ghost had tried to kill him. He hadn't thought it would be a problem, of course. He'd never once thought of himself as the type to suffer psychological jitters. But until now he'd sat on the jetty and stared across the water at the thirty-footer and all he had been able to see was that *bitch* coming towards him with a stiletto knife in her hand.

There was mist on the river, and *Yellowfin* looked like a ghost ship as he stepped into a rubber dinghy and paddled steadily towards her. It was an effort; every stroke wrenched his damaged stomach muscles, and he'd not realised how out of shape he was after six weeks in a hospital bed. For several minutes after hauling himself aboard he sat on the cockpit deck with his back against the rail and waited for his limbs to stop shaking.

Made it, he thought.

He looked at the fighting chair, the outrigger booms and the tackle boxes. He reached out and touched the cold metal ladder leading to the flying bridge. He ran his fingers across the smooth wooden decking. Everything was as he remembered it – and yet it was somehow *different*. The familiar blemishes had been removed. The scuffs and scrapes on the paintwork, the beer stains and cigarette burns on the deck, the grimy fingermarks and the wear and tear of a thousand feet – all gone. Scoured of his blood, *Yellowfin* had been stripped of her past.

As he sat there and tried to make sense of it all, the cabin door opened and Ralph Philliskirk shambled out. Harry's elder brother was in his early fifties, short and fleshy, the opposite of his rangy grasshopper of a sibling. Yawning and scratching his balls through a pair of voluminous orange boxer shorts, he blearily crossed to the starboard rail and pissed copiously over the side. He turned, manhandling his cock into his drawers, and jumped when he saw Jake staring at him from the other side of the boat.

'Jesus!' he exclaimed. 'I never saw you there.' Then he winced as his headache kicked in.

The brothers had been drinking at Suki Lo's long into

the night. Jake had heard them singing 'God Rest Ye Merry, Gentlemen' as they staggered back to the boatyard as dawn was breaking over the Indian Ocean.

'Good night?' he asked.

Ralph rolled his eyes. 'I should say so. That little Oriental woman runs some place there, doesn't she?'

'I wasn't expecting to see you till this afternoon.'

'No such luck. Got to pick up some Ernies from Kikambala at nine.'

Ernies! The term was Jake and Harry's nickname for the holidaymakers who chartered *Yellowfin* for a day's game fishing. Harry said it was because they were all deskbound, landlocked Europeans who fancied themselves as Ernest Hemingway. To Jake it seemed bizarre to hear it coming from the lips of a stranger – even if the stranger was Harry's brother.

Then again so was the idea of Ralph skippering Jake's boat.

But Ralph, as Harry kept reminding him, was an experienced seaman.

'I thought he was a hedge fund manager,' Jake had said. 'Or at least he was until Lehman Brothers went bust.'

'He's been sailing since he was a kid,' Harry soothed. 'He's got all the qualifications, he's won trophies at Cowes—'

'The Solent is not the Indian Ocean,' Jake reminded him.

Harry frowned. 'Exactly. It's *twice* as treacherous. And I might remind you, Jakey-boy, that your only qualification when you took this job was that your old man was the skipper of a North Sea fishing trawler. In any case, you should be bloody grateful Ralphie's here. We'd be scuppered without him. *And he's not getting paid for this, you know.*'

Jake had to concede that it was a fair point. As usual

36

with Britannia Fishing Trips Ltd, what it boiled down to was that beggars could not be choosers. Jake might have his misgivings about Ralph Philliskirk skippering *Yellowfin*, but there was no one else to do it right now – least of all him. The doctors had told him it would be at least a month before he would be strong enough to take the wheel, not to mention deal with the physical requirements of looking after paying customers whose only experience of game fishing was watching the Discovery Channel.

Jake, of course, considered that to be medical bullshit. Lying in his hospital bed, he had imagined he would be able to resume his life as soon as he returned to Flamingo Creek. But that was before he'd discovered to his surprise that he barely had the strength to heave himself over *Yellowfin*'s stern rail.

Ralph had gone into the cabin to get dressed. When he returned a few minutes later, he had two bottles of Tusker clamped expertly in the fingers of one hand.

'Hair of the dog,' he said with an uncertain grin. 'I understand this is the form among you grizzled game fishermen.'

Jake took one, but only because he didn't like to admit it was the last thing he wanted at seven-thirty in the morning.

'This beer cracks me up.' Ralph chuckled. 'Did you know it was named after the elephant who trampled to death the chap who founded the Kenya Brewery? You'd think they'd call it *Fucking Jumbo*.' He giggled again and lifted his bottle. 'Anyway – here's to you, old man. It's good to have you aboard after all you've been through.'

'Thanks.'

'And I just want you to know I'm no cuckoo. *Yellowfin*'s a beauty all right, but she's your boat, Jake. I'm just minding the shop for my kid brother, that's all. Soon as you're up to it, I'm out of here.'

'I appreciate it,' Jake said. He meant it. There was more than a touch of the dissolute about Ralph — but in the short time Jake had known him it seemed that, just like his brother, his heart was in the right place. And Harry was right, of course: without Ralph the business would have gone to the wall. Which was why there was no point acting like a kid whose favourite toy had just been snatched — even if that was how he felt.

But don't get too attached to her, Ralphie, he thought as the first sour mouthful of beer hit the back of his throat. *Because I don't intend being an invalid for ever.*

8

The Honourable Justice Banda had been Coast Province's leading circuit judge for more than twenty years and, although he was less than five days away from well-earned retirement, he was determined to put the same effort into his last case as he had his first – which was why he was on the veranda of his well-appointed home overlooking the ocean, studying legal precedent, while the rest of his large family, who had gathered for the holidays, were playing Wii tennis on the other side of the house.

The judge paused from his work and sat back in his leather captain's chair. He picked up his glass of wine and held it up to the light. Beyond the wooden deck was a large garden that stretched to a low wall a hundred yards away. Beyond that was the private beach. The wall, which formed the perimeter of the property, was the judge's only concession to security, although a child could vault it. His neighbours all had state-of-the-art security fencing, CCTV cameras and hair-trigger alarms that would bring gun-toting *askari* speeding to their assistance at the slightest suggestion of an emergency. But Justice Banda had always eschewed such protection. What purpose did it serve other than to send the message that he was either superior to the people over whom he sat in judgement – or frightened of them?

The slatted door to the house opened behind him and a small girl wandered on to the veranda. She was four years old, her hair braided with beads that matched her purple Sunday-best dress.

'What are you doing out here, *Babu*?' the girl demanded, using the affectionate Swahili term for grandfather. 'Why aren't you playing tennis?'

The judge smiled and extended his arms. 'Come here, little Jemima, and I will tell you.' The girl ran across and the old man lifted her on to his knee. '*I am looking for Guji Men*,' he whispered conspiratorially, pointing at the sea.

The girl's eyes widened. 'What are Guji Men?'

'Guji Men have three legs and two heads. Sometimes they are very tall, but mostly they are very small. They swim ashore when nobody is looking and dig up lawns looking for buried treasure left by pirates many centuries ago.'

The judge tried hard not to laugh at his granddaughter's face as she tried to assimilate this information.

'And what do you do when you see them?' she said.

'You must always tip your hat and say, "Good morning, Mr Guji Man. How are you this fine day?"'

Again the girl's brow furrowed as she absorbed what her grandfather was telling her.

'*Babu*,' she said presently.

'Yes, my child?'

'Are *those* Guji Men?'

The judge swivelled his chair so that he could follow the direction of the girl's outstretched hand – and his heart almost stopped. A small engine-powered skiff had appeared from nowhere and landed on the beach. Three men had jumped from it and were now walking purposefully across the sand towards the house. They were scruffily dressed in jeans and sleeveless vests, and each sported lank dreadlocks and shades. They made no attempt to disguise their appearance as they vaulted over the low perimeter wall, which was strange as two were carrying Kalashnikov assault rifles and the other an automatic handgun.

'Go and get your father,' the judge said firmly.

'But *Babu*—'

'*Go*, child!'

The girl needed no second bidding. She could tell from her grandfather's voice that he was being serious.

She was barely through the door when the first of the men reached the veranda. Banda stood and backed away as the intruder raised his hand and swept aside the chair and the pile of law textbooks beside it.

'You are the judge?' he said, his voice harsh, the gun pointed at Banda's head. He was wild-eyed and his lips were dry, a look the judge had seen before many times in the faces of defendants crazed by the twin evils of *bhang* and *chang'aa*.

'I am Justice Banda. What is the meaning of this?' His voice was firm despite the terror he felt inside.

A second man stepped forward and whacked the old man across the temple with the barrel of the Kalashnikov. The judge fell to the floor without a sound. The two men with rifles slung them over their shoulders, grabbed the judge's arms and dragged him off the veranda as easily as if he was a sack of sorghum.

'*Papa!*'

The shouting was coming from inside the house. One of the judge's sons burst on to the deck, but stopped in his tracks as the intruder with the handgun aimed it directly at his head.

'The Headhunter wishes you all a very good day,' he said. 'But if you resist I am ordered to kill you and everyone in this house. Do you want to die today? Do you want me to kill every member of your family?'

The son shook his head.

The gunman lowered the weapon. 'Good,' he said.

With that he turned and sauntered back across the garden to where his colleagues were continuing to haul the dead weight of Justice Banda towards the beach.

9

Mombasa was a hectic place, too hectic at times, which was why, over the course of his thirty years as a police officer in the city, Jouma had established a number of boltholes to which he could escape for a few minutes of blissful peace to think. After his lunch with Jake he walked the short distance to the Old Town central cemetery on Biashara Street where he now sat, savouring this oasis of death at the heart of the living city.

He watched an old woman trudge up to one of the graves, place a meagre bunch of fresh flowers in a jar against the headstone and trudge away again. He had seen her here before, many times. Always the same weary trudge, always the same cheap flowers. Whoever lay under the ground – husband? son? daughter? – was long dead, yet still she came to keep their flickering memory alive. Was there someone to do the same for her? he wondered. Did the same thought ever cross *her* mind when she came here?

Jouma stared out across the headstones, the marble and the cement and the wood. Even in death there was inequality, it seemed. Then he shook his head. Now was not the time for sentimental rumination. He needed to cleanse his thoughts and focus them on the business at hand.

Three beheadings. The first two identical in style and method, the third so subtly different that only the expert eye of a pathologist could tell.

But did that mean there were two killers?

Jouma knew the only way to be certain was to find

out *why* the three men had been targeted, to try to identify a common link between them. But he also knew that so far his investigations into the first two victims had failed to dredge up a single connecting factor. The murders of Gordon Gould and Eric Kitonga were, it seemed, as random and senseless as that of Paul Yomo.

Jouma reached for his briefcase and withdrew a bulky case file. He placed it carefully on his knee, then opened it and flipped through pages of densely typed reports and photographs, all of them so familiar to him that he almost knew them by heart.

Gordon Gould was a sixty-three-year-old Australian with a mop of thick white hair framing a full and jolly face latticed with broken capillaries. He had once been a sub-editor with a daily newspaper in Sydney, but that was a long time ago. Now, largely to keep him out of mischief in his retirement, he wrote and maintained a popular website called *Jambo* from the garage of his house on the north shore. The site was aimed at the ex-pat community and was filled with stories about hotel owners bagging holes-in-one, charity balloon rides and gossipy updates on society fundraisers and social events. It was extremely popular, and so was Gould. He was described as a bear of a man with a booming laugh and a passion for golf and game fishing. Nobody could think of one single reason why anyone would want him dead.

The same was true of Eric Kitonga. He was fifty-four years old and from humble beginnings as a stevedore at Kilindini port had, over thirty years, assiduously built up a thriving business running a small fleet of dhow freighters between Mombasa and Zanzibar. He was hard-nosed when it came to business, but, unusually for the traders who worked out of the harbour, he was universally liked and respected. He was wealthy but affected no airs and graces; he and his wife still lived in the same Old Town apartment they had moved to when they first married, he was devoted to his three daughters and eight grandchildren, he paid his men well and campaigned for better working conditions for those who did not work for him.

Gould was last seen alive shortly before nine o'clock on the evening of December 15, putting the final touches to the latest online edition of *Jambo*. The last person to see him was his wife Jackie, who put her head round the door to tell him she had taken a sleeping pill and was going to bed. The pill did the trick; Jackie was still out cold at eight-thirty the next morning when the housemaid went into the garage to find it had been the scene of an almighty struggle – papers scattered everywhere, furniture upturned, a large, fist-sized dent in the metal filing cabinet, the computer hard drive lying smashed on the carpet. Of Gould there was no sign, and it would be another twenty-four hours before his head was delivered to the house, neatly packaged in a cardboard box and impaled on the silver-plated copy spike he had been presented with on his retirement three years earlier.

Five days later, on the night of December 20, Eric Kitonga vanished while walking home from a Moroccan restaurant on Makadara Road where he had been dining with business acquaintances. His head was found the next morning nailed by the right ear to the mast of one of his dhows.

There were no notes, no telltale signatures except for two unavoidable similarities: both men had been killed by a single left-to-right blow of a sharp implement, the heads neatly separated as if by a surgeon's scalpel.

And now there was a third. Paul Yomo, murdered on or around December 25. Were the five days between the killings significant? Did they prove that Paul had been killed by the Headhunter? Would there be a fourth murder on New Year's Eve? That was only three days away.

There was, of course, another consideration to throw in the mix, one that filled Jouma with even more dismay: *what if the Headhunter was not working alone?* It was simply assumed that the killer carried out his atrocities on his own, yet the evidence – the struggle at Gould's house, the ease with which Kitonga had been abducted off the street – suggested otherwise. Was it possible that the Headhunter was in fact a *collective*?

Jouma rubbed his temples in the vain hope that it would help him to see clearly. But all he could see was fog. Someone else was making their way across the cemetery now. A young African woman in her mid-twenties, professional-looking in a powder-blue linen jacket and jeans, hair teased into fashionable, finger-length dreadlocks. She seemed so incongruous that Jouma did not recognise her until she was almost upon him – and by then it was too late.

'Season's greetings, Inspector Jouma!' she announced. 'You are a hard man to track down.'

Jouma winced. Her name was Katherine Rapuro, and she was the Mombasa bureau reporter for the *Daily Nation*, Kenya's leading national newspaper.

'I have nothing to say, Miss Rapuro.'

'A man decapitated? His head delivered to his own doorstep on Christmas morning? Oh, come on, Inspector! Where is your Christmas spirit? I have a deadline to meet.'

'I am afraid that is your problem. You should refer all enquiries to our press spokesman, Mr Boswinga, at police headquarters.'

'Mr Boswinga's vocabulary consists of two words,' the

reporter said. '"No" and "Comment". I prefer to get my information from the horse's mouth.'

'Then you will have to find another horse.'

'Is it the Headhunter?'

Jouma stood and began walking towards the cemetery gates. 'I have nothing—'

'Give me a break,' Katherine Rapuro said. 'Please. A simple yes or no will suffice.'

Jouma paused. 'The simple answer to your question is I don't know, Miss Rapuro,' he said. 'And, if you have any respect for the family of Mr Yomo, you will wait for confirmation before you print your story.'

He turned away and started walking again.

'Three murders in as many weeks, Inspector Jouma,' she called after him. 'People will be wondering if you are ever going to stop this killer. They are wondering who is going to be next.'

Jouma kept on walking, but the reporter had just put into words his exact thoughts.

Who *was* going to be next?

And *why*?

10

Jake's time with the Flying Squad had coincided with the last days of the hard-drinking, sixty-a-day copper, the sort whose hours were spent on the street and in the pub. By the time he quit, the Yard had been well and truly infiltrated by a sinister new breed – the Evian-sippers who ate sushi in the squad room and held gold card membership of the Metropolitan Police fitness club.

Although he was young enough to have been one of the latter, Jake had always nailed his colours to the former's mast. As a result he was a trusted member of the old guard, the sort who gathered in the Cheapside Club each night, licking their wounds, getting drunk – and most importantly looking after their own. He knew full well it was no coincidence he had risen rapidly to the rank of detective sergeant, because back then the senior officers all drank there too, and they believed in prolonging the species.

But deep down they all knew that extinction was inevitable. Had his career not been ended by a bullet fired by an East End toe rag, Jake would have undoubt-edly been sidelined to some inconsequential recidivist backwater by now, or found himself tottering round the local municipal golf course, unemployable and suffering early-onset cirrhosis, arteriosclerosis and emphysema.

Jake was now thirty-five – and, as time went by, he had come to believe that fate had done him a favour that day, because getting shot and getting out of the rat race had allowed him to be reborn. Kenya was so off the map in terms of European sensibilities it was more like another planet than a foreign country. Here it was possible to live your life the way you chose.

Now, six weeks after the Ghost had jammed a stiletto blade into his guts, Jake was beginning to wonder if *she* hadn't done him a similar favour – because every time he watched Ralphie Philliskirk chugging downriver in *Yellowfin* he realised how he had come to take his existence here for granted. And it made him even more determined to get his life back.

In the scrub behind the workshop he had created a makeshift gym. Cement blocks on either end of a metal bar were dumbbells for bench presses, water-filled oil cans doubled as free weights, and the low bough of a mangrove tree had become a pull-up bar. Every day for an hour he forced himself to complete a two-mile run along the creek road followed by a punishing weights circuit. Every step was agony, and his muscles screamed surrender – but whenever he felt the urge to quit he thought about Ralphie on *Yellowfin*'s flying bridge, drinking his supply of Tusker.

On his return from Mombasa he pulled on his running shoes. This time the circuit took him fourteen minutes, which was shit compared to Roger Bannister but two whole minutes faster than yesterday. When he had sufficiently recovered he went over to his homemade bench-press apparatus. Lying on his back, he stared up at the clear blue sky beyond the treetops and steeled himself. He was about to reach up and grip the metal bar suspended on its wooden cradle above his head when he heard a familiar voice so utterly incongruous to the Kenyan jungle that at first he thought he was hallucinating again.

'Fuck me – it's Rocky Balboa!'

He sat up, narrowly avoiding braining himself on the bar. A thick-set man was leaning against the mangrove tree, arms folded, a huge grin visible under the dark, heavy matting of his moustache.

'*Mac?* What the hell are you doing here?'

Former Detective Inspector Mac Bowden, late of the Metropolitan Police Flying Squad, would be in his late forties now. He had always had the physique of a weight-lifter, and even though it was starting to run to fat around his middle, and his black hair and trademark moustache were streaked with grey, he had hardly changed since that day five years ago when he'd shaken Jake's hand at Heathrow Airport and wished him good luck in his new life.

'I heard a rumour you were dead, *kimosabe*,' he said. 'Just goes to show I can't let you out of my sight for a minute.'

11

On the instructions of Superintendent Simba, the old wooden door to the CID offices at Mama Ngina Drive had been replaced with a heavy steel door fitted with a CCTV camera and security lock which could only be activated with a swipecard. This laminated strip, which also carried a head–and–shoulders mugshot of the holder, doubled as an ID card and was supposed to be worn around the neck on a thin metal chain at all times.

This, as far as Jouma was concerned, was an abomination. Not only was he highly suspicious of any form of modern technology – he was the only detective in the department who didn't have a cellphone – as a man who took great pride in his appearance, he also resented having what was to all intents and purposes an ugly plastic medallion hanging around his neck. His recalcitrant attitude had already led to one confrontation with Simba, who had threatened him with a week of deskbound duties if he refused to wear his card. By way of a compromise, Jouma had agreed to carry it in the top pocket of his shirt. As usual, the card was in a shirt that was at the bottom of Winifred Jouma's washing basket.

Upon his return to the office from the cemetery, Jouma strode up to the door and, with a gesture of exasperation aimed specifically at the security camera, pressed the communication button to alert the department that he was there.

There was no answer, and after several more attempts to attract attention Jouma realised with a sinking feeling that the skeleton crew of detectives on duty today had by now scattered to the four winds, keeping a low profile under the pretence of meeting contacts until their shift ended.

Grumbling to himself, he set off around the perimeter of the building, peering on tiptoes through windows in the vain hope that somebody might actually be doing some work. But the squad rooms and offices were deserted. Most had their blinds down. Eventually he came to his own office where to his relief he saw that the window was slightly ajar. Heaving himself up on to the sill with trembling arms, he managed to squeeze inside, whereupon he tumbled into the room and ended up in a heap on the floor.

Five minutes later, when Detective Constable David Mwangi sauntered back into the office from the lavatory at the other end of the corridor, he found Jouma sitting at his desk with a thunderous look on his face.

The Inspector's expression did not change when the young detective explained where he had been.

At twenty-four, Mwangi had only recently transferred to Coast Province CID, his university education and early promise in the Fraud Squad at Nairobi earning him a fast-track promotion to homicide in Mombasa – but already he was accustomed to the blackness of his senior officer's moods. And ever since he had taken charge of the Headhunter case, Jouma's moods had been black indeed. Mwangi recognised the signs and knew when to keep his own head down.

He went to his desk and fired up his laptop computer.

Presently Jouma peered across with suspicion. 'What are you doing with that contraption?'

'I was hoping to try out some new software I have downloaded.'

'What?'

'It is an algorithmic program designed to identify integer similarities. I am hoping it may isolate correlations in the victims' SIM cards.'

'In *English*, Mwangi!'

Mwangi looked up from his laptop to see Jouma staring at him with a look of utter incomprehension, and he almost laughed.

'I took the liberty of impounding the cellphones of the two victims as evidence, sir. By removing the SIM cards and uploading the data, it is possible to access the individual contact books of Mr Gould and Mr Kitonga.'

Jouma still looked at him blankly.

'The software program should be able to identify if there were any contacts common to both victims. It may help to provide some sort of link between them.'

Jouma rubbed his nose thoughtfully. 'A good idea, Mwangi,' he said grudgingly. 'But you forget there are now three victims.'

'Of course, sir.' Mwangi nodded. 'But, as far as I am aware, Mr Yomo's cellphone has not been found.'

'A pity indeed,' Jouma said. 'But perhaps I have something more relevant.' He lifted a ring-bind folder that was thick with documents. 'I borrowed this from the credit agency where he worked. It contains the details of every loan application declined by Paul Yomo since he began working at the Exciting Prospects Credit Agency eighteen months ago.'

Mwangi's face fell. 'Really, sir?'

'Yes, Mwangi. I would very much like you to cross-check these names with the contact books of the other two victims.'

'They aren't stored digitally? I mean – the agency has no computer system?'

'Only for applications that have been approved.'

'Then you want me to—?'

The phone rang.

'Every one.' Jouma nodded, picking up the receiver. 'It's called the old-fashioned way, Constable.'

As Jouma took the call, Mwangi carried the heavy file across to his desk. *The old-fashioned way, indeed!* One of these days the Inspector might just catch up to the twenty-first century. By then, of course, the rest of the modern world would already be in the twenty-second.

Jouma put down the phone. 'Leave the file, Mwangi,' he said, his voice strangely distant.

'Is everything all right, sir?'

'No,' Jouma said. 'No, it isn't.'

12

On a grey Wednesday afternoon in winter, on the grubby floor of a sub-post office in Canning Town, East London, Mac Bowden had saved Jake's life.

Mac would never admit to anything so melodramatic – but while the rest of the Squad flapped and panicked and screamed for paramedics, and his partner just lay there with blood frothing from a bullethole in his side, the senior man calmly went behind the counter, helped himself to a roll of parcel wrap and jammed a six-inch strip over the wound.

'Parcel wrap?' Harry said.

Mac smiled bashfully. 'My basic medical training kicked in. They say that with a bullet wound nine times out of ten it's the shock that kills you. Once I'd sealed the hole it was just a case of talking bollocks to him until the ambulance arrived.'

'That wasn't difficult,' Jake said.

'What really saved Jake's life was the fact that the scumbag with the gun was such a lousy shot. How anyone can miss a vital organ from five feet is beyond me.'

'Believe me, Mac,' Harry said, 'they could have shot Jakey-boy through the middle of the forehead and still missed a vital organ.'

Both men grinned at Jake across the table, and he flipped them the bird. Behind the bar Suki Lo took this to mean he wanted another round and immediately began opening three more Tuskers. When the beers arrived Jake did not argue. His fitness regime had gone up in flames today, but he had long since overcome his guilt. He had also forced himself to overcome his sudden and disturbing aversion to beer. Fortunately, it had taken just one chilled bottle to restore his thirst. Drinking capacity, he had decided, was a far more reliable barometer of a man's health than bench presses – and if he could keep up with Harry and Mac Bowden over the course of an afternoon session then he was in better shape than he dared to have hoped.

It was late afternoon and apart from the three Englishmen the only other people in Suki's bar were a couple of surly mechanics who had just been laid off from a yard downriver and were more interested in their whisky bottle than the conversation from the other table.

'I take it you're no longer running around chasing armed robbers?' Harry said.

Mac nodded. 'Jacked it in last year. Or, rather, I went before I was pushed. I was old school. My profile didn't fit the new, all-inclusive regime at the Met. Anyway I'm knocking on fifty – thought I might as well cash in the pension early, look for something a little less hazardous to do for a living. I always envied old DS Moore here, living the life of Riley in the back of beyond. I thought I'd come and see what all the fuss was about.'

Harry raised an eyebrow. 'Don't tell me you came all the way to Kenya to see this reprobate?'

'Yes and no,' Mac said. 'I'm actually here on business.'

'Business?' Jake laughed. 'In *Mombasa*? You used to get a nosebleed if you went outside Essex.'

'It's consultancy work. Short-term contract, fucking good money.'

'What sort of security work?' Harry asked.

Mac shrugged. 'I guess I'll find out when I meet my man. The guy runs a hotel at a place called Shanzu. Says he wants to beef up security for his guests.'

'Security consultant!' Jake chuckled. 'If I had a quid for every ex-copper who has gone into that line of work I'd be a rich man.'

'Me too. But beggars can't be choosers. And in any case, I could do with a little excitement in my life. There's only so much daytime TV a man can watch before he loses the will to live.'

'Hear, hear to that,' Harry said, standing uncertainly. 'Television is the devil's own invention. Now excuse me while I take a piss.'

Mac smiled as Harry tottered across to the toilets. 'He's quite a character. How the hell did you meet him?'

Jake explained how he had answered an advertisement in the classified pages of a Sunday newspaper looking for someone to help run a fishing business, and with a few grand to invest as capital.

Mac nodded. 'It's one way of spending your police pension.'

'Yeah – well, things haven't been quite as stress-free as I'd hoped. But this is my life now, and I couldn't ever imagine going back to England.'

'Don't blame you for that, *kimosabe*. The old country's going to the dogs.'

'It must be if you're here,' Jake said. '"Security consultant"? Don't give me that shit. What the hell are you *really* up to, Mac? Have you got a woman stashed away over here or something?'

'It's true,' Mac protested. 'Honest, gospel, cross my heart, all that crap.'

'In Kenya?'

'I got a tip from a friend of mine back in London. Said he knew of an outfit that was looking to recruit people with experience.'

'What sort of experience?'

Mac grinned. 'You know: the sort that twenty years in

the Flying Squad gets you. Like changing the plug on an intruder alarm. Listen – it's a short–term contract and good money. Twenty grand for a month's work.'

Jake whistled. 'That *is* good money.'

'And I need it. The boys are growing up fast and Shirley's giving me all sorts of earache about the maintenance payments. I'm down to the bones of my arse. She's fucking cleaned me out.'

'How old are the boys now?'

'Simon's seventeen and Danny's fifteen.'

'Christ. That makes me feel old.'

'Yeah, well think how I feel.' Mac swigged some beer. 'Listen – what I said before, about how I envy you. I meant it, you know. You got out at the right time.'

Jake looked at him. 'What – before the corruption inquiry?'

'There was no fucking corruption,' Mac said angrily.

'Taking bribes from Russian villains in exchange for looking the other way? Come on, Mac.'

'In our day it was known as Standard Operational Procedure. But the Met's a different place these days. I wasn't the only one to take the fall: Stevie Morrison, Eddie Ward, Stick Murphy – they all got their marching orders same time as me.'

Jake shook his head. 'You silly bugger – another couple of years and you could have walked away with a full pension.'

'Yeah, well. What's that they say about hindsight?'

Harry was coming back now. Mac drained the rest of his beer and stood up.

'Got to love you and leave you, I'm afraid,' he said.

Harry's face fell. 'Do you really have to go, Mac? Why don't you stay tonight? I was rather looking forward to putting the world to rights.'

Mac shook his head. 'I'd love to, Harry. But I've got

to meet my man in Shanzu at the crack of dawn tomorrow. And I can't afford to piss this one against the wall by turning up with the hangover from hell.'

'I'll walk you back to the boatyard,' Jake said.

'Wouldn't dream of it. Stay and finish your beer. I'll be fine.' The two friends shook hands. 'I take it the local fuzz aren't as pernickety about drink-driving as they are back home?' he said. 'Only I think I'm over the limit.'

'Everybody drives like they're pissed round here,' Jake told him. 'You'll fit in just fine.'

13

It was a scene that was becoming wearyingly familiar: sobbing women, stunned-looking men, a sense of numbing disbelief and horror. Justice Banda's living room looked exactly like those of Gordon Gould and Eric Kitonga and Paul Yomo. It was less than an hour since the judge had been taken. And, despite all his words of encouragement and hope to his distraught family, Jouma knew that the judge would not be coming back.

Not in one piece anyway.

But at least this time there was *something* to grasp on to.

'They were young, no more than seventeen or eighteen I would say. Wild eyes? I don't know. One of them pointed a gun at me. Told me he would kill me. Kids, Inspector Jouma – they were just kids.'

The speaker was one of the judge's sons, a tall, handsome man in his thirties who ran a dental practice near Lake Victoria and was visiting his father with his family for Christmas.

'And you say they took your father on to a boat?'

'After they hit him,' the son said. He gestured at a drying pool of blood on the sanded wooden planking of the veranda. In the middle of the blood lay the upper row of the judge's false teeth, where they had been dislodged by the blow.

'What sort of boat?'

'I don't know – a launch, I think. You know, the inflatable sort.'

'With an engine?'

'Yes. A big engine.'

Jouma asked him a few more questions then thanked him and went outside into the garden. Mwangi was approaching the house from the direction of the beach.

'Anything?'

The constable shook his head. 'The tide is coming in. If there were any footprints, they have been washed away.'

Jouma stared at the low perimeter wall. How simple it must have been for the judge's abductors to gain entry into the grounds of the house. There might as well have been a large welcome sign on the beach.

'The son seems to think there were three of them,' he said.

'Then perhaps it was not the Headhunter, sir. It could be an unrelated kidnapping.'

It was possible. But Jouma said nothing; the information he had gleaned today merely confirmed what he had suspected all along – that the Headhunter was not acting alone.

'The judge's son said his father was due to hear a case next week,' he said.

Mwangi nodded. 'A fraud trial. A car-hire operator from Malindi accused of fiddling with the odometers on his vehicles.'

It was not what Jouma wanted to hear. If the case had involved some high-powered crime boss, rather than a crooked car-hire operator, there might have been some faint glimmer of a motive for taking the judge out of the equation. But even then it made no sense, because judges could be replaced.

'When we get back to the office I want you to look back over every case presided over by Justice Banda in the last five years,' he told Mwangi.

Mwangi nodded earnestly. 'I have already been in touch with the central court, sir. They are preparing the files.'

Jouma turned and looked back at the house. It was a low, colonial-style building of whitewashed stone, framed by palm trees and casuarinas and pretty as a picture in the sunlight. The garden was bordered by high hedges of blindingly bright bougainvillea, hiding the houses on either side. Even if the judge's neighbours had been in their own gardens they would have been unable to see the intruders who took him.

He wandered down the beach. The sea had risen to within twenty feet of the perimeter wall. The sand was white and clean, except for a circle of black charcoal where a fire had been built. He imagined the judge walking here in the early morning, listening to the rush of the ocean and watching the sun rising over the horizon. It seemed so peaceful.

As he looked out at the breakers thundering against the reef in the distance, Jouma felt something tugging at his trousers. He looked down to see a small girl with braided hair – the judge's granddaughter.

'Will the Guji Men bring *Babu* home again?' she asked.

'I hope so, my dear,' Jouma said. 'I sincerely do.'

But the detective had already seen enough of the Headhunter's handiwork to know that they wouldn't.

14

Bound and blindfold, Justice Banda had been pinned to the bottom of the launch by a foot between the shoulder blades and encouraged to remain there by a gun to the head. He'd lain in an inch of oily saltwater and it was all that he could do to keep from drowning in it. The journey seemed to take an age, but there was no respite when the engine finally spluttered and died. He was hauled up and dragged over the side, then forced to wade through waist-deep water and thick mud before finally they threw him to the ground.

'*Get up! Get up!*'

Blows rained down on him as he staggered to his feet, and his captors continued to kick and punch him as he was led like an animal through what he assumed was jungle. Thorns and branches tore at his skin and face and on several occasions they let go of him so that he crashed into trees. It seemed to amuse them greatly. Presently he was manhandled through a door, and when the blindfold was snatched from his eyes he saw that he was standing in a wooden hut lit only by a couple of candles stuck into the dirt floor. The acrid stink of rotting vegetation was almost overpowering, almost enough to mask the smell of *bhang* and the cloying, antiseptic reek of crudely distilled liquor.

'What is the meaning of this? You realise the penalty for kidnap is—'

Something hard smashed into the back of his legs and he roared with pain as he sank to his knees.

'I am aware of the penalty,' a voice said.

A figure moved from the shadows into the gloomy light. He seemed unnaturally tall and at first Banda blamed it on his scrambled vision. Then he saw that his eyes had not deceived him: the man *was* a giant, a freak standing fully seven feet tall, the top of his head brushing the tar-paper roof of the hut. He was naked, his hairless body gleaming like polished ebony.

'Who are you?' Banda asked.

The man lifted his chin imperiously. 'I am Athi, son of Ngai, the Divider of the Universe and Lord of Nature.'

'*Who?*'

The freak smiled, revealing small teeth that had been filed into points. 'I understand the apostates call me the *Headhunter*. You may be familiar with my work.'

Banda was indeed familiar with the Headhunter's work. His bladder emptied involuntarily.

'I have a wife,' he said, his voice little more than a whisper. 'Children. Grandchildren.'

'You are an apostate – and Ngai has selected you for sacrifice. You should be grateful. Soon all your mortal frailties will be gone.'

The Headhunter reached over his shoulder and there was a dull hiss as he withdrew a foot-long machete blade from the sheath on his back. The steel was polished like a mirror, the handle was of notched ivory. He looked at the weapon with reverence, then drew his thumb slowly down the edge of the broad blade.

Suddenly an apparition appeared from the corner of Banda's vision: it was a second man, dressed in the garb of a tribal witchdoctor, his headdress made of cowhide and feathers and hung with tiny gourds, his face daubed with lurid colours. He was holding a cage made of cane and dried grass. Inside it a scrawny chicken was frantically beating its head against the bars. The witchdoctor's

63

eyes closed as if in prayer and a deep, reverberating moan came from his open mouth that seemed to grow in volume as he slowly circled the room. Banda watched with mounting but helpless panic as the Headhunter held the blade in front of his own face, relishing its deadly sharpness. He raised it up above his head and held it there until the wailing of the witchdoctor, coming from behind Banda now, was almost unbearable.

Then it stopped. Rough hands clamped the judge's arms to his sides, preventing him from moving. The Headhunter's eyes snapped wide open – and, in the split second that their gaze met, Banda thought about little Jemima, and about how much he loved her.

How much he loved them all.

In a single fluid movement, as graceful as a dancer, the Headhunter's left hand brought the machete down on Justice Banda's neck. The blow was so clean and quick that the severed head remained balanced on the stump of neck for several seconds until the force of the blood from the severed arteries toppled it on to the ground.

The Headhunter was breathing heavily through his nose, the machete still held out in front of him, his hands rock steady. Then, slowly, as his breathing subsided, he raised the weapon up to his face again.

'Dispose of the body,' he instructed the witchdoctor. 'Then bring the head to me.'

He watched the smear of blood on its silvered blade coalesce into a single scarlet reservoir, then, almost reverentially, he brought it to his open mouth and ran his tongue along its length.

The blood was still warm. It tasted sweet. *Nourishing.*

15

In a large ornate room in Mombasa's State House, the city's Mayor peered through thin-rimmed spectacles at the crowd of expectant faces and waited for the hubbub to die down. He had no love of reporters, in fact he thought they were parasites. But on this occasion they more than served his purpose. He leaned forward towards the thicket of microphones on the desk in front of him so that his papery voice might carry to the back of the packed room.

'A vicious killer is on the loose, and one of this city's most repected citizens, Justice Banda, may have become his next victim,' he announced gravely. 'But *I* will not allow Mombasa to become a city of fear. As your elected Mayor, *I* will not stand idly by while you, the citizens who put your trust in me, lie awake in your beds at night wondering who will be next. *I* will see to it that this killer is apprehended. It is *my* duty. It is *your* right.'

A flurry of hands shot into the air – and, as the Mayor began fielding questions, less than half a mile away at the headquarters of Coast Province CID, Superintendent Elizabeth Simba jabbed a TV remote-control button and killed the sound.

'As subtle as ever,' she said. She looked at Jouma, who was sitting on the other side of her office, still staring at the Mayor's doughy face on the screen. 'You know what this is really about, don't you, Daniel?'

Jouma nodded. He knew all right. It was about the

Mayor getting his own back on Simba, Jouma and Mombasa CID. It was about the humiliation he had suffered when his plan to stamp his authority on the division by installing his own man to oversee a major murder inquiry had gone disastrously wrong.

In the end, as ever, the Mayor had survived the debacle, while the hapless Detective Inspector Oliver Mugo and others had been sacrificed on the altar of political expediency. But Simba and Jouma both knew that he had been wounded; and, like a poisonous snake, he would remain coiled in his lair until the opportunity arose to strike again.

'If we catch the Headhunter, he will claim all the credit,' he said. 'If we do not—'

'He will have *our* heads,' Simba said emphatically. 'He has engineered himself into a situation in which he cannot lose. Which is why we must ensure that *we* do not lose, Daniel. What do we know about Judge Banda's abduction?'

'He was taken by three armed men in a motor launch. I say men, but from what I have been told they were little more than teenagers.'

'Has the boat been found?'

Jouma shook his head. 'They took off in a northerly direction. We are liaising with the coastguard to check inlets within a twenty-mile radius of the house.'

'Good.'

What he didn't tell Simba was that within that twenty-mile radius there were more than two hundred inlets, and that finding a single-engined skiff would be a miracle – assuming, of course, it hadn't made rendezvous with another vessel.

'Are we sure that the Headhunter is behind this, Daniel? Might it be related to one of the judge's old cases?'

'The leader of the kidnap gang mentioned the killer specifically. Of course we cannot be sure – but I have men keeping watch on the house in case . . . well, in case of unusual deliveries.'

Simba nodded thoughtfully. 'Is it possible that one of these three men could have been the Headhunter himself?'

'It is possible. But they were young.' Jouma looked down at the floor sheepishly. 'Dr Lutta believes the Headhunter is probably in his late twenties or early thirties.'

'Ah, yes,' Simba said, her tone betraying a distinct air of cynicism. 'Your pet criminal psychologist from the Kalami Secure Mental Hospital. I forgot about him. What did you say his name was?'

'Lutta. Nicholas Lutta.'

'I thought Dr Klerk was in charge up there?'

'He is, ma'am. It was he who suggested I speak to Dr Lutta.'

'And what is so special about Dr Lutta?'

'He specialises in the treatment of serial psycho-pathic offenders, ma'am. His work within the field has earned him quite a reputation within the criminology community.'

'Is that so?' Simba peered at him over her glasses. 'I have to say I am still not convinced that all this psychobabble has any bearing on the success of the investigation.'

'As I explained, ma'am, I think any form of profes-sional evaluation could be helpful. And Dr Klerk has been very cooperative in the past.'

'He has? I was not aware you were a *regular* visitor to Kalami, Inspector.'

Jouma shuffled his feet uncomfortably. 'I am not, ma'am. But sometimes circumstances—'

Simba waved her hand impatiently. 'No matter. What

exactly does this illustrious criminal psychologist say about our killer?'

'Dr Lutta is very interested in his *modus operandi*. The decapitation, the way the heads are subsequently displayed. He thinks there may be some sort of symbolic ritual involved in the act of beheading.'

'Isn't that what *all* criminal psychologists say about serial killers?'

Jouma sighed. He knew this would not be easy. 'As I say, ma'am, Dr Lutta's is merely a professional opinion.'

'Yes, well – I hope you are not paying for this professional opinion.'

'Of course not, ma'am.'

'Good, because thanks to *him* my budget is barely large enough to pay for the opinion of the man on the street.'

She jabbed her finger at the TV, where the Mayor's mouth was moving silently as he addressed the ranks of reporters attending the press conference.

Relieved that the subject seemed to be dropped, Jouma also turned his attention to the Mayor. So plausible, he thought, so much a man of the people – it never failed to amaze him how career politicians were so unlike the rest of the human race. It was as if, in order to grab power, they had to evolve into a different species entirely.

'If he knew we were consulting criminal psychologists . . .' Simba muttered. Then she looked at Jouma again and her demeanour softened. 'Listen, Daniel, if you value the opinion of Dr Lutta, then by all means continue to seek it. But for goodness sake keep it to yourself.'

'Of course.'

'What is the current status of the investigation?'

'Detectives Buna and Fugogo are coordinating the search

for Justice Banda, and I have Tana, Wachile and N'Opo following leads on the Gould and Kitonga murders.'

'And Paul Yomo?'

'I am looking into that personally, ma'am.'

Simba seemed surprised. 'Personally?'

Jouma told her about the pathologist's report, and how Paul Yomo's decapitation differed from those of the previous two victims.

'You did not mention this to me before. Do you think it is a different killer?'

'I don't know,' Jouma admitted. 'But I am aware that manpower is an issue, especially now that Justice Banda is missing.'

A hint of a smile appeared on Simba's face. 'And you think you can get to the bottom of this quicker on your own, is that it, Daniel?'

'I have already started enquiries, ma'am.'

'Then carry on. But if it is clear that Yomo's murder is not related, you will pass it across immediately. I want your full attention on the Headhunter, understand?'

'Of course, ma'am.'

He went to the door, grateful that the inquisition was at an end.

But then Simba said, 'What about Mwangi?'

'Mwangi, ma'am?'

'What is he doing?'

Jouma suppressed his irritation at the question. Simba had been responsible for Mwangi's transfer to Mombasa, and sometimes the Inspector got the impression she was almost maternally protective of him.

'He is helping me with the Yomo investigation,' he said. 'Checking records.'

'He is a bright boy, Daniel. Perhaps this is a good opportunity to give him some more responsibility.'

'Responsibility, ma'am?'

71

'You say Detective Fugogo is coordinating the search for the judge. I think even you would admit that Fugogo's best days are behind him. Why not give him the records to check and send Mwangi out into the field?'

'Forgive me, ma'am – but Fugogo has twenty years' experience in the homicide division. Mwangi has three months.'

Their eyes locked across the room, but it was Simba who capitulated.

'Very well, Daniel,' she said icily. 'You are chief case officer. But I want the Headhunter caught – or else the Mayor will ensure that this maniac will make victims of us all.'

Yes, I am chief case officer, ma'am, Jouma thought as he strode angrily from the Superintendent's office. But it wasn't the slur on his judgement that annoyed him so much as the fact that Simba regarded Detective Fugogo as being over the hill. Fugogo was only forty-three years old, for heaven's sake! And if *his* best days were already behind him, then where did that leave Jouma?

He stormed into his office, ready to give the sainted Mwangi a totally undeserved and vindictive earbashing. But the detective constable was not in and, as he sat down at his desk, Jouma reflected that it was probably a good thing. Simba was right – Mwangi *was* a bright boy, and Jouma could see in him the makings of a first-class detective. Indeed, he secretly enjoyed the younger man's energy. He was certainly far more engaging company than the wretched Fugogo, whose conversation rarely strayed beyond how many years were left before his retirement.

Still, all great detectives had to start somewhere, Jouma consoled himself. Which is why, when Mwangi returned, there would be a fresh pile of papers for him to sift through.

16

Had David Mwangi been experienced in the ways of policework, he would have known that when a telephone is ringing in an empty squad room the very last thing you should do is answer it. But he was not, and he did – which was why he was now heading north across the Nyali Bridge to the Sandpiper Ocean Club Hotel in Shanzu.

As he drove he felt a knot of apprehension in his stomach that had nothing to do with the incident. What worried Mwangi was that he was supposed to be running background checks on the three Headhunter victims – four, if the abduction of Justice Banda turned out, as anticipated, to be the work of the machete-wielding serial killer. Jouma would not be pleased to discover he had broken off from a multiple murder investigation to attend to what appeared to be a case of aggravated assault. In fact, Mwangi knew the Inspector would be furious.

But what was he supposed to do? He was a homicide detective, wasn't he? This was a case of attempted murder, wasn't it? He could not simply dump the case without at least making a thorough report of the incident; that would fly in the face of everything he had been taught. It would be unprofessional.

By the time he arrived at the hotel the victim, Frau Maria Klinker, was already on her way to Mombasa Hospital and the English hotel manager was washing down a fistful of Tylenol with three fingers of neat whisky.

'Detective,' he said, swiping his mouth with the back of his hand. His name was Alec Standage. He was a stocky man in his forties with a large head and a sweeping fringe of sand-coloured hair. 'Thank God you're here.'

As the two men walked from the main building towards the rows of sun-loungers overlooking the beach, Standage explained that he'd only recently taken the position after five very successful years running an all-inclusive hotel in Diani.

'You think you've hit the big time. A bit of class for a change. And then the shit hits the fan. It's supposed to be *Christmas*, for God's sake!'

They were standing over Frau Klinker's lounger now. It had been positioned slightly away from the others and was shaded from the sun by the broad leaves of an adjacent palm tree. The lounger was of a sturdy wooden construction, with the head end raised at an angle of thirty degrees. Like the others it had a two-inch-thick white mattress – except this one was stained a deep red with Frau Klinker's blood.

'What time did it happen?' said Mwangi.

'Just before seven,' Standage replied. 'When it happened to Mr Wuyns, we all assumed a coconut had fallen out of a tree. There was one lying a few yards from his lounger.'

Mwangi looked up from his notebook. 'This has happened before?'

'Three days ago,' the Englishman said shamefacedly.

'And you did not report it?'

'Like I say – we thought it was an accident. That's why I immediately ordered the trees to be harvested. The grounds staff should have done it as a matter of course. Suffice to say they are no longer employed here.'

Mwangi looked up to the top of the palm tree. Where

normally there would be clusters of coconuts, all that remained were jagged stumps of fibre where the fruit had been hacked off.

'The first victim's name was . . .?'

'Wuyns. Alfred Wuyns. A Dutch gentleman.'

'Where was he sitting?'

'Not far from here. Maybe a little nearer the beach.'

'Was he alone?'

'His partner was in the pool.'

'His partner? You mean his wife?'

Standage cleared his throat self-consciously. 'Mr Wuyns was on holiday with his *gentleman* friend.'

Mwangi rolled his eyes. 'So he didn't see his attacker?'

'He was asleep.'

'None of the other guests saw anything?'

'No. But it was early. Mr Wuyns and his friend liked to be out early. Before the rush.'

'Where are they now?'

Standage's face fell. 'They left. They were very upset, as you might imagine.'

Mwangi pointed his pencil at a couple of uniformed hotel guards patrolling purposefully along the edge of the beach 'What about the *askari*? Did they see anything?'

'No.'

'And I take it they didn't see what happened to Frau Klinker either?'

'No,' Standage said, the low menace in his voice suggesting that for certain members of the hotel security staff this was to be their last day of employment. 'She was on her own, reading a book. Herr Klinker – her husband – was in the restaurant having breakfast. The next thing we know, he found her just lying there with blood pouring out of her head.'

'Where is Herr Klinker now?'

'He went with his wife to the hospital. He was very worried.'

'I expect you must be worried as well, Mr Standage,' Mwangi said. 'Guests at five-star hotels can usually afford good lawyers.'

17

At one-thirty the heavy security gates at the front of Brigadier Charles Wako Chatme's house opened and his wife Ellen drove away in a silver Mercedes convertible. As the vehicle roared past, Jouma sighed with relief as he ducked down beneath the dashboard of his decidedly proletarian Fiat Panda. With Ellen gone and the Brigadier at work, the only person now left in the house was their daughter Tabitha.

It was the moment he had waited the best part of two hours for.

But even as he opened the car door the electric gates squealed open again and this time a yellow VW Beetle came hurtling out on to the main road. Jouma ducked back inside in time to see Tabitha behind the wheel, her face set. He cursed and, as he fumbled to start the engine of his car, he wondered if he was destined never to speak to the infernal girl alone.

The Beetle was easy to follow, and when it crossed Nyali Bridge on to the island Jouma assumed that Tabitha was heading for her apartment in Kwakiziwi. To his surprise, she kept on going across town until she came to the broiling Kingorani slum south of Moi Avenue. Here, within sight of the huge twin tusks that spanned the main thoroughfare, she parked her car and hurried inside its corrugated-iron perimeter. Jouma parked a hundred yards away and followed her on foot.

To the uninitiated, the claustrophobic dirt thoroughfares

of the slum, hemmed in by tightly packed houses, stalls and drinking dens, seemed to have no design or purpose. Only the emaciated dogs and goats that roamed the streets appeared to know where they were going, and usually that was in the direction of the large, open-air refuse tips that marked its boundaries. Yet to those who knew it, there *was* a strange sort of order to the place. Jouma, who had been here many times, likened it to the whorls and cul-de-sacs of his own thumb. Close up it made no sense, yet taken as a whole it had a certain meaningful symmetry. Not that the Inspector was in any way seduced by the organic charm of the slum. Far from it. Every time he came here it was to investigate a murder – and he usually had cause to visit at least fifteen or sixteen times a year.

And one thing he never got used to was the stink of nearly 60,000 people living in squalor in an area little bigger than a football pitch. On hot days like this the stench consumed even that of the cloying exhaust fumes of the cars and lorries.

What was she doing here?

Tabitha seemed to know precisely where she was going. She walked with a determined, head-down posture, ignoring the whistles and lascivious jeers of the men stoned on *bhang* and *chang'aa*, and the suspicious looks of the women hanging washing on lines between the shacks.

Presently she came to a single-storey building constructed from scaffolding, concrete mesh and breezeblocks that had clearly been stolen from a building site. She paused, seemed to catch her breath, then went inside.

Jouma grabbed the nearest person he could find, a toothless old woman with a goitre the size of a melon growing in her neck.

'What is that building?' he demanded.

The woman looked at him dumbly. With a sigh he handed her fifty shillings. She examined the money carefully before secreting the bills in the folds of a grubby sarong.

'Well?'

The woman spat on the ground. 'That place, sir, is where you go when *kagunyo* got you,' she said. Then she smiled, exposing wizened gums. 'Though when *kagunyo* got you, he got you forever.'

Jouma stared at her with disbelief.

Kagunyo. The worm.

Slum slang for the AIDS virus.

18

Frau Klinker was fifty-eight years old and from Stuttgart. She and her husband, a retired engine designer with BMW, had been married for forty years. They had been coming to Africa for the last ten and during that time had only ever stayed at the Sandpiper Ocean Club Hotel. But now she was in the intensive care unit of Mombasa General Hospital, wired to machines and drips, her head almost entirely swathed in bandages.

'It does not look good, Constable Mwangi,' admitted the consultant neurologist. 'As you can see, the blow inflicted substantial damage to the upper cranial area.' He pointed at an X-ray of Frau Klinker's skull clipped to a lightbox on the wall of his office.

Mwangi's first-class degree from Oxford was in mathematics, but even he could tell that the fist-sized indentation in her head did not bode well.

'As soon as the patient arrived I performed an emergency craniotomy,' the consultant explained. 'Ideally I would prefer to carry out a decompressive craniectomy as well, but I'm not convinced by the integrity of the skull.'

'I am not a doctor,' Mwangi said. 'If you please?'

'The first procedure involves drilling a small hole in the skull to relieve the build-up of pressure. That's not a problem. However, the second is when I remove a section of the skull itself to allow the brain to swell without impediment. But I am concerned. You see that the bone did not shatter, but rather it was depressed

80

on to the brain itself. This, I suspect, is the only reason the patient is still alive. If it were to fragment ... Well, I'm not sure it's worth the risk.'

'What are her chances?'

'No more than ten per cent.'

'And if she were to recover, how long would it be before she was lucid?'

'Lucid? I doubt she will ever be lucid. Even if she survives, the trauma to the frontal and parietal lobes of the brain is such that she will have little or no cognitive faculties. She will be, to all intents and purposes, a vegetable. If I may be blunt, in cases like this it is often better if the patient dies.'

'But you will do your best to keep her alive, I trust?'

'My job is to keep people alive.'

'Good — because at the moment she is my only witness.'

Mwangi went across to the lightbox and peered again at the X-ray. It was strange, but there was almost a pleasing symmetry to the dent in Frau Klinker's skull. It was almost perfectly circular.

'One more question. Could this injury have been caused by a falling coconut?'

The consultant looked at him with surprise. 'Not unless the coconut was made of lead, Constable Mwangi.'

19

Tabitha's visit to the Kingorani slum was brief. Ten minutes after Jouma had watched her enter the building, she returned to her car. When he put his face to the open window, she yelped with surprise.

'I think we need to talk, Tabitha,' he said.

They went to a café on the other side of the main road and Jouma ordered a pot of tea.

'Are you infected?' he asked her.

Tabitha's eyes bulged. 'You *followed* me?'

'Tell me, girl – *are you infected*?'

She bristled with indignation. 'Of course I am not! What sort of a person do you think I am?'

'I don't know,' Jouma said. 'What sort of person goes to a slum clinic selling HIV drugs to whores and drug addicts?'

'This has nothing to do with you,' she said.

'Until I find your husband's killer, it has everything to do with me.'

She blinked with surprise at his vehemence. This was no longer the sympathetic, deferential little policeman she had been used to. There was steel in Jouma's voice and a harsh look in his eye.

'They lend money,' she said presently.

Now it was Jouma's turn to be taken aback, especially when Tabitha explained that, with HIV rampant in the slums, there was a healthy black market for cheap retroviral drugs. These were the sorts you didn't have to register for, the sorts that weren't really retroviral drugs at all but synthesised placebos that contained just enough heroin to keep the addicts coming back for more. And of course the money from these drugs funded many things, including high-interest loans to drug addicts to pay for their habit.

'And *you* go to these people for money?' He stared at her, trying hard to understand how she could possibly have found herself involved with such a sordid trade.

Her eyes flared again at the suggestion, but then she looked down at the teacup on the table in front of her and shook her head. 'Paul had a gambling problem,' she said. 'It was before I met him, and he had kicked his habit − but he owed these men some money.'

'How much money?'

'One thousand dollars.'

Jouma whistled. Such a sum would have been the equivalent of two or even three months' wages for a lowly credit officer like Paul Yomo.

'Were these men threatening your husband?'

'They had no need, Inspector. He was paying them off regularly.'

He looked at her sadly. How naïve she was about the nefarious nature of man. 'Believe me, Tabitha, moneylenders *always* have need to resort to threats. And sometimes to murder.'

'But you don't understand,' she said. 'That was why I was there today − to give them the last instalment. Twenty-five dollars.'

'The debt was repaid in full?'

'My husband was a debt counsellor, Inspector Jouma. He knew the importance of keeping up his payments.'

Jouma stared at her. There was a fierce defensiveness in her eyes, as if she dared him to say something derogatory about her dead husband.

'Do your parents know about this?' he asked her.

Tabitha shrugged. 'Why should they? It is none of their business.'

'It seems to me, Tabitha, that they have made your life their business. What do you think they would say if they knew about Paul's gambling?'

'It doesn't matter what I think, because they will never know.' She glared at him. 'Unless you plan to tell them, Inspector?'

Jouma leaned forward. 'That all depends on what you tell me.'

For the first time uncertainty crept into her expression. 'What do you mean?'

'I asked your mother about Jonas's father. She refused to tell me who he was.'

'That was a long time ago. Why do you need to know?'

'I need to know *everything*,' Jouma said.

There was a pause while Tabitha stared out at the relentless lines of traffic moving along Moi Avenue. 'His name was Billy,' she said. 'Billy Kapchanga. He was from Kingorani. A musician. We were only together for a couple of months.'

'Where is he now?'

'I don't know. I have not heard from him since Jonas was born.'

Jouma nodded. 'I see.' It was a story he had heard a million times: the feckless father disappearing rather than face up to his responsibilities. 'Well, it is probably better for you and the boy that he is no longer around.'

Again her eyes flared with indignation. 'Billy and I were in love, Inspector! We were engaged to be married. When I told him I was pregnant he said it was the happiest day of his life.'

'Then what happened?'

'I don't know. One day he was there, the next he was gone.'

'Gone where?'

'Just gone. His house was empty, his possessions gone.'

'Sometimes the responsibility of fatherhood can be too much for a man,' Jouma pointed out. 'You have not seen or heard from him since?'

'I don't even know where he is, Inspector. Every day I used to hope that I would receive a letter from him, but there was nothing.'

Jouma lifted his teacup. 'You must have thought a great deal of him.'

'I still do,' Tabitha said. 'He is the father of my child.'

20

Jake's run that day took him along the creek road, beyond Suki Lo's bar and the handful of boatyards nearby, almost to the mouth of the river itself. Here he stopped, sucking in lungfuls of sea air, savouring the burn in his legs and the thump of blood in his ears. He felt good, better even than he had before he'd been stabbed. And with every passing day the attempt on his life seemed to be fading into the distance; like the shooting six years ago, which now felt as if it had happened to someone else.

He jogged down to the riverbank, where some kids were fishing in the shallows for baitfish with rudimentary cane poles. He watched for a while, enjoying the simplicity, thinking about the days when he and his mates from the Meadowell estate used to spend hours hanging rods off Tynemouth pier, clinging on to the metal barriers for dear life as the North Sea smashed great spumes of pure white spray against the thick concrete walls. Sometimes he would be there when the fishing fleet came home, and he would watch the rusting metal boats slowly chugging upriver towards the fish quay at North Shields. His father's boat would always be at the front, looking battered and weary after a week at sea, the crew busy preparing to unload the fish holds while his old man guided the vessel through the navigation channel, eyes narrowed against the smoke from his cigarette.

It was a hard, unforgiving life, and it was assumed that

Jake would follow it like six generations of his family before him. But even then he could see the writing on the wall – the dwindling fish stocks, the crushing bureaucracy, the constant struggle to make ends meet. He saw it in the fissures in Albie Moore's face, smelled it on his boozy breath when he eventually staggered home after long hours at the Low Lights Tavern, felt it in the beatings his old man would administer when the drink could no longer deaden the frustrations of his life.

One of the kids had a coconut, and Jake watched him deftly slice off the top with a machete blade.

'You want some, boss?' he called out to Jake, offering its warm sweet milk.

Jake smiled and shook his head. 'You have it,' he said. 'You've earned it.'

The boy grinned and brought the green husk to his mouth. When he had drunk he wiped his lips with the back of his hand and handed the coconut to his friends. Jake laughed wistfully to himself: at Tynemouth pier the only refreshment was a litre bottle of Coke and maybe a couple of bags of crisps. Coconuts? You only ever got them from Spanish City amusement arcade up the coast at Whitley Bay, wizened brown shells with a lining of dry white flesh that tasted like plaster.

He looked out at the ocean and his heart jumped as he saw *Yellowfin* turning into the mouth of the creek. Ralph was up on the flying bridge and Sammy the bait boy was swabbing the cockpit. In a few minutes the boy would dive off the side and swim across to his village at Jalawi on the far bank – although Jake hoped that Ralph would be throttling back on the boat's turbos before then. *Yellowfin* must have been doing more than twenty knots as it settled into the navigation channel and headed upriver, too fast for either Ralph or Sammy to see him waving.

Jake hurried back to the path and began running in the direction of the boatyard. Racing his own boat would be a stern test of his fitness. As he picked up speed he heard the shrieks of the kids behind him as *Yellowfin*'s bow wave struck the bank, knocking them off their feet and into the warm brown water of the creek.

It was no contest. By the time he reached the yard, sweating and gasping for breath, *Yellowfin* was already at anchor and the launch was moored at the jetty. Jake approached the workshop, but stopped at the sound of raised voices coming from inside.

'Don't bloody deny it, Ralph,' Harry was shouting. 'You were *seen*, for Christ's sake!'

'What do you mean I was seen?' Ralph said indignantly. 'I don't even know what you're talking about, H.'

'Mombasa's a small place, and the Old Town is even smaller. Believe me, chum, I know *everyone* and they know me.'

'Bully for you, Harry. You want me to fill out a form telling you where I'm going now, is that it? Do I need your permission?'

'You said it wouldn't happen again,' Harry said. 'You *promised*, Ralphie.'

'And I promise it didn't, old man. Cross my heart and all that.'

Jake stepped into the office and the two brothers immediately stopped bickering.

'Not interrupting anything, I hope?' he said cheerily.

'Not at all,' Harry said. 'Ralphie and I were just having a little difference of opinion, that's all.'

'Didn't sound like it to me. I thought if I didn't step in you might start hitting each other.'

'Brothers!' Ralph exclaimed. 'We always were at each other's throats, even over the smallest thing. Isn't that right, H?'

Harry smiled at him, but Jake saw the embers of fury in his eyes. This was no fraternal squabble over nothing. Something was going on between Harry and Ralph Philliskirk.

'How was it today?' he asked Ralph.

The elder of the two Philliskirk brothers looked relieved that the subject had been changed. 'Terrific! We hit a bloody huge pod of tuna out near the banks, and then to cap it off we ran into a couple of humpbacks. Two highly satisfied Ernies – so satisfied they've booked us again tomorrow.'

'Great.'

'I take it they paid?' Harry said icily.

Ralph produced a roll of bills from the pocket of his shorts. Harry took it from him and began counting it – which Jake knew from experience was a very un-Harryish thing to do.

21

His mind churning after his encounter with Tabitha, Jouma barely noticed that Mwangi was still absent from his desk and that the stack of paperwork he'd left for the young detective was untouched.

There had always been, at the back of his mind, a gnawing suspicion that all was not as it seemed with the Yomo case. There was just something too *perfect* about the family, that there were gaping fissures hidden behind that veneer of respectability and solidarity.

Well, now he knew that all was *not* as it appeared. Paul had a gambling problem that had left him in hock to some thoroughly disreputable characters in the Kingorani slum.

Characters like Davey Cav.

Cav was a surprisingly affable young African who had been christened David Cavikikoi, but who now went by a streetwise moniker that was more in keeping with his attire of vest, baggy jeans, reversed baseball cap and rolls of jewellery. And, as he pointed out, he ran a perfectly legitimate moneylending concern – that just happened to be funded by the illegal sale of Class A narcotics to desperate, HIV-ravaged addicts from the Kingorani slum. When Jouma pointed out this anomaly, and the ability he had to make Cav's life a misery, the shark was all too happy to cooperate.

'What can I say, Inspector?' he said. 'Mr Yomo was a most valued customer. He paid his weekly instalments promptly and I never once had to resort to penalties.'

'By penalties I take it you mean breaking legs?'

They were sitting in a windowless, airless room at the back of the building Tabitha had visited earlier that day. Cav sat at a desk made from a length of chipboard balanced on two maize-oil drums. Perhaps, in another life and in other circumstances, he might have been a bank manager or an insurance salesman. Mind you, Jouma thought, he would have been on a fraction of the salary he was currently earning.

Cav laughed. 'I have never had any problems with Mr Yomo and, when his delightful wife came to see me personally today to pay the outstanding balance on his account, I was very sad. In fact, I offered her a new loan at a most preferential rate.'

'I see. And what rate of interest was Mr Yomo's original loan?'

'I believe it was our standard fixed rate of sixty per cent.'

'That strikes me as very expensive.'

'Other financial institutions are available.' Cav smiled. 'But perhaps Mr Yomo's circumstances meant his choices were limited.'

'And what were his circumstances?'

'I do not know the details. But a respectable man like that? With a good job and prospects? He should not have been coming to me for money.'

It was a fair point, Jouma conceded. Why would anyone go to an extortionate loan shark unless they had been refused more reasonable credit elsewhere? And, as Tabitha had pointed out, it was not as if Paul didn't know his way around the industry.

'Is there anything else I can help you with, Inspector Jouma?' the shark said. 'A loan, perhaps?'

'You have been very helpful, Mr Cav,' Jouma said. 'Which is why I will wait one hour before calling my colleagues in the drug enforcement division to inform them about your activities here. That will give you time to make yourself scarce.'

Cav looked indignant. 'I hardly think that is necessary.'

'Then there is perhaps one thing you can do for me.'

'Name it, Inspector! I am at your service.'

'I need to find a man named Billy Kapchanga. He lived here in Kingorani several years ago. I understand he was some sort of musician.'

Cav's eyes narrowed. 'I have never heard of him.'

'Somebody will know him. And because you are a man with his ear to the ground, Mr Cav, I am confident you will be able to help me.'

This seemed to please the loan shark. 'I shall make enquiries.'

'Please do.' Jouma handed him a business card. 'And *when* you find anything out, please do not hesitate to give me a call.'

He doubted the phone would ring, though. Now, as he sat in his office, Jouma wasn't even certain it would make any difference if it did. Loan sharks? Absentee fathers? What did it all mean? More to the point, what relevance did it have to the Headhunter case? *If only he could be sure. If only he could close the file and hand it on to another detective, as Simba suggested.*

But he couldn't. Not yet.

He looked at the files on his desk. Gordon Gould and Eric Kitonga. Respected, popular professionals. Happily married, law-abiding citizens. Financially secure and personally content. Hundreds of man-hours of diligent policework had so far failed to uncover even the faintest suggestion of a skeleton in their cupboards. Every time he tried to dig his claws into either man, Jouma found they simply slid off. It was infuriating, baffling – and, although he would never admit it to Simba, for the first time in thirty years as a detective he was utterly stumped.

At least Paul Yomo's increasingly seamy double life gave him *something* to cling to. It made him feel at least a little better about himself; that his day, unlike that of Detective Fugogo, had not been and gone without anything to show for it.

Fugogo. Jouma picked up the telephone and made a call of his own. After several connections the veteran detective came on the line.

'Where are you?' Jouma demanded.

'At the coastguard headquarters.'

'Any news on the judge?'

'No,' Fugogo drawled. 'The search helicopter has just returned. What do you want me to do?'

'Keep looking, Fugogo,' Jouma snapped and slammed down the receiver.

Keep looking. Even if it is a waste of time. Jouma was in no doubt that Justice Banda was already dead. In fact, the terrible truth was that he was impatient for the discovery of the head, because at least it might offer a chink of light to show him the way. But what if it did not? What if the judge was as squeaky clean as Gould and Kitonga? What then? Must he wait for another victim? And another after that?

Where will it end, Daniel?

The office door opened and Mwangi came in. He seemed unusually shifty, and when Jouma asked him where on earth he had been the detective constable told him about the assault at Shanzu.

'I am sorry, sir. I should have waited for you to come back.'

He seemed almost shocked when Jouma gave him a wry smile. 'You did the right thing, Mwangi.'

'I did?'

'You are a detective, are you not?' Jouma said. 'Is it not your job to investigate crimes?'

'Yes, sir.'

'Then you were doing your job.'

'I – I thought you would be angry.'

'Why?'

'Because I am supposed to be concentrating on the Headhunter case.'

'Sometimes it is good to take a step backwards, Mwangi. A change is often as good as a rest. And, as you will see by the paperwork I have left on your desk, you will be working long hours tonight.'

Mwangi looked at the pile of papers with relief. 'Of course, sir. I will get right on it. However, there was something in the last bundle that might be of interest.'

'The last bundle?'

'The loan agreement forms from the credit company Paul Yomo worked for.'

He picked up a sheet from his desk and brought it across. Jouma studied it closely. *Yes*, the Inspector thought. *This was indeed interesting. Details of a particular loan arrangement that suddenly cast new light on his investigation.*

Mwangi returned to his desk. 'Is there any news about Justice Banda?'

'None.'

'Then there is still hope.'

'Yes, Mwangi, there is still hope,' Jouma said distantly, his eyes still fixed on the loan agreement in his hands. 'And whatever happens we should never forget that.'

22

Stella Binns was in love: mind-spinningly, heart-flutteringly, head-over-heels in love. Not only that, but she was engaged to be married and Jai, her fiancé, the love of her life, was smiling at her with his strong white teeth and twinkling jet eyes. Stella smiled back and wiggled her plump fingers coyly, in case any of the other visitors to the Ngomongo Villages tourist attraction should see their little exchange.

Not that she had anything to be embarrassed about. Far from it. But Stella was not stupid; she knew what people thought about an overweight white woman in her mid-forties carrying on with a black African in his early twenties. *Silly bitch*, they thought. *Sad, lonely, silly bitch, making a fool of herself with a bit of local rough, thinking he only had eyes for her.*

Yes, Stella knew what they thought all right. And, as far as she was concerned, they could all fuck off. Stella and Jai were in love, and that was that.

The attraction, which was situated in an old lime quarry on the outskirts of Mombasa, consisted of a half-mile-long trail through thick jungle dotted at regular intervals with huts representing the various indigenous tribes of the region. Stella had come here this afternoon with a party from her hotel, and, while a few eyebrows had been raised when Jai was waiting for her at the reception hut, British politeness won through and nothing was said. Right now they had reached the Kikuyu hut, which, like all the others, was occupied by a single glum-looking extra in tribal robes. But while the rest of the group gawped and took photographs, Stella found herself gazing at Jai once again and experienced a sudden, pleasant stirring as she remembered how it had felt to have that lean, muscular body driving between her thighs like a piston. She giggled at the sheer *sordidness* of it all. *You filthy cow*, she thought. What would they say back in Wrexham, those nosy bitches from the supermarket checkouts when she turned up to the next works night out with her own *bona fide* Bantu warrior in tow?

'It will not be easy,' he had warned her in his treacle-thick African accent that sent shivers down her spine. 'Obtaining the relevant paperwork will cost much money, and it may be several months before I can join you. If, that is, you wish to take me . . .'

'Oh, Jai!' Stella had exclaimed, her eyes filling with tears. 'I do! *More than anything else, I do!*'

Which was why, that morning, she had cashed in eight hundred pounds of traveller's cheques as a first instalment of the two thousand pounds Jai said it would cost for him to come to Wales. The money was in an envelope in her handbag.

The rest of the party had moved on along the track through the trees towards the Kalenjin hut. The Kikuyu extra, with ten minutes before the next group was shepherded through, had disappeared into a Portakabin behind the trees to count up his tips and smoke a cigarette.

Stella looked at Jai. They were alone. *At last.* She lunged for him greedily, pulling him into the vacant hut, her breath rasping with the need to feel his hard body against her hot skin.

'God, I want you,' she grunted, pushing his head down between her breasts as they fell on to the earth floor.

'You have the money?' he muttered.

'Oh yes ... *yes* ...'

With a thrill of ecstasy, she felt his eager fingers working at the elasticated waistband of her panties, easing the skimpy material down over her thighs. And then he was on top of her, moving slowly and easily, building up tempo like a steadily charging engine, and Stella could feel the heat building inexorably within her until it seemed that her entire body was ablaze.

And then he stopped.

Stella looked up to see the Bantu staring with wide-eyed horror at something over her exposed left shoulder.

'Fackin' hell!' he screamed, in a broad Cockney accent. '*Jesus fackin' Christ!*'

'What? *What?*' she wailed, utterly bewildered by the African warrior's sudden terror and by the string of East End expletives unexpectedly pouring from his mouth. She tried to move, but, in his hurry to get to his feet, Jai pushed his hand into her face, smacking the back of her head against the baked earth.

By now, the Kikuyu tribesman had run to see what all the commotion was about. What he saw when he burst into the hut was a fat white woman, her knickers around her knees, trying to stand up, and Tony, the Englishman with whom he had a lucrative arrangement – ten bucks to look the other way while he gave his latest dupe the 'tribal experience' in his hut – being violently sick.

The reason was plain to see: there, resting on the skin of a traditional Kikuyu war drum in a corner of the hut, was a human head, its eyes rolled back and its mouth agape. The tongue had been pulled so far out of the mouth that it was connected only by a strand of tendon, and a single wooden nail had been hammered through it and into the skin of the drum. At first the tribesman thought that its black skin was moving, almost as if the head was somehow still alive – but as he moved closer he realised that in fact it was covered in a thick layer of flies that were feasting greedily on the rancid flesh. He reached out, and as he did so the swarm lifted from the head with a furious buzzing, and it didn't matter how hard he swatted at them because they were already in his eyes and filling his own open, screaming mouth.

IV

23

Mahmoud was seventeen years old. He had grown up in the slums of Mombasa, where his mother was a glue addict who earned money to feed her habit by scavenging for plastic on the vast garbage mountains. The money to feed her eight children came from whatever her eldest daughters, who were twelve, ten and nine respectively, could earn from prostitution, and what Mahmoud could make from petty theft in the bazaars and market places, and the occasional mugging of a tourist in the parks after dark. There were those who said Mahmoud's father was the devil himself, but he didn't care. Despite what the missionaries and the churchmen told him, there was no God in the slums, which was why he believed only in easy money and good *bhang*, in that order.

He didn't care how he got either. And it was for that reason he would make an ideal recruit.

When the stinking rag blindfold was removed from his eyes he saw that he was standing in the centre of a circle of wooden stakes. Impaled on each stake was a human skull, and each skull glowed eerily from the candle stuck to it. Mahmoud smelled pungent *bhang* smoke and the ripe stench of human sweat.

A man was sitting naked and cross-legged on a rock opposite, his shaven head bowed low so that it hung down almost to his bare feet. His limbs were thin, emaciated almost, as if the glossy black skin had been simply painted over his bones. He looked to Mahmoud, who was considerably under the influence of strong hallucinogenic weed, like an enormous insect.

'Do you know who I am?' the man rumbled without looking up.

In front of him was a thick wooden block with a narrow channel carved down the middle. On the ground, directly beneath the lip of the channel, was another skull. The top of the cranium had been removed.

Mahmoud shivered again, although the night air was almost unbearably humid. For the first time since he had met the old man in the slum drinking hole that afternoon, he was beginning to have second thoughts about this whole arrangement. *I am looking for recruits*, the man had told him, his voice low against the drunken babble and the thump-thump of the jukebox. *One job, two hundred dollars, no questions asked. Are you interested?*

Was he interested? What sort of a question was that? Mahmoud would have slit his own mother's throat for two hundred dollars. Which was why he did not think to ask what the job was, even as the blindfold was applied and he was bundled first into the boot of a car and then into the back of a motorlaunch. *I apologise for the discomfort*, the old man had told him.

But Mahmoud didn't care, not with the weed the old man had given him still exploding in his brain.

Now, though, the effects were beginning to wear off – and, as they did so, Mahmoud's unease began to grow. Where was he? Where was the old man?

'*Do you know who I am?*' the creature on the rock demanded.

'No – no, sir,' Mahmoud stammered, suddenly feeling very scared and very alone.

The man slowly sat up and Mahmoud saw that cradled in his arms was a goat kid, no more than a few days old. It was sucking eagerly on his little finger as if it was a teat.

'I am Athi, son of Ngai, the Divider of the Universe and Lord of Nature,' the Headhunter said.

As if responding to an unseen signal, a second figure materialised from the darkness, and Mahmoud almost gasped with relief. It was the old man — although for some reason he was now wearing the garish robes of a tribal witchdoctor, with pieces of carved wood and bone fixed to the leathery flesh of his nose, earlobes and mouth. His demeanour had changed also: the bonhomie of earlier that day had gone, replaced by an expression of solemn self-absorption. When Mahmoud tried to catch his eye, he found himself studiously ignored.

The Headhunter handed over the kid and then stood up — and Mahmoud could not help but catch his breath when he saw how tall he was. *Seven feet?* He could also see now that there was some sort of leather strap across his chest.

The Headhunter slowly took his own penis in his fingers. The witchdoctor handed him a gourd and he urinated into it until it was half full of frothing yellow liquid. Then, carefully, he poured a small amount on to the wooden block. The urine quickly moved along the carved channel until it began to dribble into the skull.

Now the witchdoctor brought the kid. Sensing it was in imminent danger, the animal began bleating frantically, but the Headhunter grabbed it by the scruff of the neck in his right hand and held it at arm's length. His left hand reached back over his shoulder and, from a concealed sheath, withdrew a gleaming foot-long machete.

This time Mahmoud gasped audibly — but the killer's eyes were closed. When he opened them, there was a sudden movement, a glint of metal, and the goat's innards spilled out of its freshly slit belly. With another expert jab of the machete's tip, he removed the thumb-sized bag of the animal's stomach from the gaping cavity and presented it to the witchdoctor on the flat of the blade. The old man burst it open with his thumbnail and deftly turned the stomach inside out so that its rippled lining was exposed. He returned it to the Headhunter who, with small, sharp teeth, gnawed off a chunk of the rubbery tripes, chewed it to a pulp, then spat it into the skull.

Mahmoud watched the ritual with horrified fascination. *What was this?*

But it was not yet over.

'Come here, boy,' the Headhunter said, dropping the still-twitching body of the goat on to the dirt floor. His voice was friendly, paternal even. But the machete was still gripped in his hand and for a split-second the boy was paralysed and unable to move. 'There is nothing to be afraid of.'

Mahmoud felt the witchdoctor's hands like slabs of pumice on his shoulders, gently propelling him towards the wooden block, and suddenly the reason for his own nakedness became clear and he began to cry.

'Strength, boy,' the old man whispered into his ear.

His forefinger and thumb closed around the tip of the boy's foreskin and gently pulled it to its furthest extent across the block.

The machete blade struck once. Mahmoud felt no pain, not even an impact. The steel cleaved through the stretched sheath of skin as if it was made of air. Only when he saw the shrivelled tube lying on the wooden block and his own bright-red blood gushing into the channel did he realise it had been done. And that was when he fainted.

When he came to, the throbbing pain in his groin made him cry out. He was sitting on the ground, his back against the witchdoctor's chest. When he dared to look down, he saw the end of his penis had been wrapped in leaves.

'The pain will soon go,' the old man muttered. He was holding the skull in both hands like a chalice in front of Mahmoud's face. 'You are a brave boy. A worthy disciple of Athi. But there is still one more ritual to be performed.'

He brought the skull to the boy's mouth. It was full to the brim with a rich, terracotta liquid. Mahmoud recoiled at the stench.

'Drink it, boy,' the witchdoctor hissed.

Mahmoud felt the skull against his lips. The urge to gag was almost impossible to resist.

'*Drink . . .*'

He felt the thick liquid in his mouth now, tasted its warm bitterness as it slid like mucus down his throat.

'*Drink . . .*'

Mahmoud finished the contents of the skull and, retching, fell back against the witchdoctor.

Coiled on his rock, the Headhunter nodded his approval. 'You are a disciple of Athi now,' he said. 'Your strength comes from Ngai, the spirit of the great white mountain, *Kirinyaga*.'

Mahmoud swiped the foul slop from his chin and was sick again.

The Headhunter raised his head and sniffed the air. Then he turned and looked at Mahmoud, a half-smile playing at the corner of his mouth. 'Soon you will go to work with your brothers. You will obey the will of Ngai and bring the chosen apostates to the living god for sacrifice. So sleep now. Mortals need to replenish their strength. And there is much that needs to be done.'

24

On her way home from the *Daily Nation* bureau office in downtown Mombasa, Katherine Rapuro had purchased a bottle of wine and a microwave chicken jalfrezi from the local convenience store and was looking forward to a night watching TV and doing nothing. She would never admit it to her newsdesk in Nairobi, but she was exhausted. The discovery of Justice Banda's head in a hut in the Ngomongo Villages had confirmed the fact that he was the Headhunter's fourth victim, but it had also resulted in a frenzy of activity – press conferences, door knocks, interviews and, because the newsdesk had got it into their heads that the killer had once appeared before the judge, acres of background checks on Banda's previous cases.

But it looked like the newsdesk was barking up the wrong tree as usual. The judge had locked up some pretty dangerous characters in his long career, but none with a history of chopping people's heads off. In any case, Banda was just one of four victims that included a website editor, a dhow owner and a credit officer. What about them? How did they fit into the equation? No – the Headhunter's motives were far more complex than simple revenge. They had to be.

But these were thoughts Katherine was careful to keep to herself. She had no wish to antagonise her superiors in Nairobi, because they could just as easily turn round and replace her. And now that Kenya's biggest murder case in a generation had landed in her lap, she was damned if she was going to give it up. She had worked too hard on the case – and, besides, she was owed a crack at a decent story for a change.

During the bloody post-election uprising of 2007, when the world's press flooded into the Rift Valley and the tribes obligingly set about killing each other in the most graphic ways possible, Katherine had waited patiently for the riots to spread to Kenya's second city. When it became clear that the unrest was going to be confined to Nairobi, she demanded to be reassigned – but her news editor had told her to stay put.

'It's wall-to-wall shit and misery up here,' Larry Gazemba told her. 'We're going to need a little froth on the inside pages.'

So it was that, while the rest of her profession gorged themselves on the biggest news story to break in Kenya since the Mau Mau rebellion fifty years ago, Katherine was under orders to produce a stream of good-news stories about charity events, football matches and tourists who had caught record-breaking marlin.

She'd never forgiven Larry. Furthermore, she'd vowed that she would never again allow herself to be on the periphery when the big story broke.

And the Headhunter was a hell of a story. The succession of front-page by-lines had also been suitably gratifying. But cranking the story up non-stop for the last month had been gruelling. Katherine had no idea how many hours she'd spent criss-crossing Coast Province in her car looking for new angles to keep the story fresh. Now she was due a night off. And, as she put the key in the lock of her modest apartment, she was damn sure she was going to enjoy it.

But she knew she was not alone as soon as she smelled the whiff of expensive cologne. A man was sitting in her living room. He was smartly dressed and Katherine recognised him immediately.

'Good evening, Miss Rapuro,' the Mayor said. 'You will forgive me for intruding, but I wanted to see you in private – and you know what Mombasa is like for gossip.'

Trying to remain calm, Katherine placed her shopping on the kitchen counter. 'How did you get in here?'

'I have security staff trained in such matters.' He saw her looking around. 'They are outside. I expect you walked straight past them.'

She began casually unloading the shopping bag, trying hard not to let this whole situation creep her out. 'Would you care for a glass of wine?' she said, holding up the bottle of cheap Frescobaldi.

'That would be most pleasant.'

She unscrewed the top and foraged for a couple of tumblers, embarrassed at her lack of sophistication. The Mayor, she suspected, was a man accustomed to drinking fine wine from crystal glasses. *Well, to hell with him!* she thought defiantly as she poured. *He* had broken into *her* house.

'What can I do for you?'

The Mayor sipped the wine and if he found the taste revolting he made no indication.

'I wanted to talk to you about the story you are working on,' he said.

'The Headhunter?'

The Mayor looked pained. 'I prefer to call him a murderer, but I understand you are in the business of selling newspapers.'

'You have information about him?'

'Perhaps.'

Now she was interested. 'What sort of information?'

The Mayor sighed. 'I was born in this city, Miss Rapuro, and I care very deeply about it. This current crisis is like a knife through my own heart. The thought of people living in fear of this *monster* is almost too much for me to bear.'

Katherine looked at him suspiciously. What the hell was this all about?

'I am very anxious that the citizens know that I share their concerns,' he continued. 'That I am doing everything in my power to restore normality.'

'That's very touching, but I don't—'

'Between you and me, it grieves me that the press coverage has portrayed both myself and my office in a negative light regarding this situation.'

Katherine smiled into her glass. So *this* was what he wanted.

'I can assure you that everything I have written has been balanced,' she said. 'I attended your press conference the other day.'

'*One paragraph*, Miss Rapuro,' the Mayor pointed out. 'At the bottom of a sixteen-paragraph story in which local people expressed their fears that this so-called Headhunter might never be caught. I would hardly call that balanced reporting.'

Katherine shrugged. 'Like you say, Mr Mayor – my business is selling newspapers.'

'Of course.'

'And to be honest, a mayoral press conference in which precious little of interest was said is hardly going to make the front-page lead.'

'I understand that. Of course I do. Which is why, tomorrow morning at ten o'clock, I will be paying a visit to the dhow harbour in order to unveil a plaque in honour of the late Mr Kitonga in recognition of his services to the Mombasa economy. And why, later that day, I will be having lunch with the widow of the late Mr Gould – in appreciation of the sterling community values he promoted through his website. And why, Miss

Rapuro, I would be most appreciative if both you and a photographer could be present to record these events for your newspaper.'

Katherine nearly spat her wine at the sheer brass neck of the Mayor.

'I'm afraid the news agenda of the *Daily Nation* is not dictated to by your office,' she said.

He smiled. 'Of course. I would not dream of such a thing. Which is why I would like to offer you a *quid pro quo*. A little *exclusive* that may give your Headhunter coverage the edge over your rivals – in return for a little coverage of our own.'

She was interested now. 'What sort of exclusive?'

The Mayor opened a slim leather wallet and waved a manila envelope at her. 'These are the post mortem reports on the bodies of the four victims,' he said. 'They make for very interesting reading.'

Katherine eyed the envelope greedily. She knew that the contents were gold dust – every request for them had been turned down by the police. But she did not take it.

'Where did you get these? How do I know they are genuine?'

'Miss Rapuro, the Mayor is the second most powerful man in Coast Province behind the Provincial Commissioner. I get to see *everything*. Trust me – the reports are genuine. And believe me when I tell you there is plenty more information about this investigation to which I have access.'

'Won't this compromise the police investigation?'

He shrugged. 'What police investigation? It may have escaped your notice but this killer has struck four times and the police are no nearer to solving the crime.'

'They will want to know where I got them.'

'And you, of course, will tell them that a journalist never reveals her sources.'

110

'I could go to jail.'

He laughed. 'You don't seem to understand who runs this city, Miss Rapuro.'

Katherine thought for a long time before she spoke. 'I'm sorry, sir – but I don't do *quid pro quo* deals.'

The Mayor looked at her long and hard. Then he shrugged. 'Then I am sorry also. But might I suggest you think about it? I am well aware that a reporter – even one who works for the esteemed *Daily Nation* – is only as good as their last story.' He placed his glass on the table and stood. 'And if I may give a little further advice – white wine is always best served chilled, even the cheap stuff.'

25

The Kalami Secure Mental Hospital, hidden away in a valley west of Malindi, is an imposing building constructed from imported Scottish granite and Lakeland slate from the north-west of England. It was built by the British at the turn of the twentieth century as a prison to house and torture Kenyan nationalists perceived to be of a particularly high security risk to the colonial administration, and was especially busy during the Mau Mau insurgency of the 1950s.

Fifty years later, its inmates were still regarded as high security – and with good reason. Kalami was home to the criminally insane, those deemed too dangerously unstable even for maximum security prison, those who had been convicted of cannibalism, bestiality, mass murder, paedophilia and sodomising rape.

The building, Jouma thought, was still redolent of its colonial prison past: functional, imposing, the thick stone walls of the corridors painted drab cream and olive green, the air heavy with the smell of antiseptic and boiled vegetables. Most of the inmates – *patients* as the chief criminal psychologist, Dr Cyrus Klerk, insisted on calling them – were kept in a block reminiscent of a castle keep, with cells arranged along a walkway sixty feet above a central well. Each cell had its own metal door with a grille for the guards to look in, and a letterbox-style slot through which food could be passed. A net was strung between the walkways, presumably to prevent inmates from flinging themselves to their deaths on the concrete floor far below.

The clinical staff were housed in a modern annexe on the other side of the compound. Klerk had established a five-strong team of psychologists, of which the newest recruit was Dr Nicholas Lutta, who had been with them for just over twelve months.

Lutta was twenty-five, Mombasa-born of Indian extraction but Yale-educated and regarded by the paternal Klerk as something of a rising star in the field of criminal psychology − although to Jouma he looked anything but. Skinny, with a thatch of unruly black hair and a prominent, hook-shaped nose, he looked like a crow that had come off worse in a fight. His appearance was not helped by his dress sense, which to a man with Jouma's high regard for sartorial elegance was non-existent. Perhaps he was wrong, but Jouma could not imagine an institution as venerated as Yale encouraging its alumni to be seen publicly in holed jeans, scuffed baseball boots and stained T-shirts.

Yet, despite his reservations, he liked Lutta. Beneath the scruffy exterior was a razor-sharp mind capable of swift and cogent analysis, yet allied with an easy-going, totally uncondescending manner that immediately put Jouma at his ease. They had met only once, shortly after the murder of Eric Kitonga, when Jouma's desperation at the lack of clues had driven him to contact Dr Klerk for help. Klerk had immediately recommended Lutta − and, although he'd had only patchy case notes and photographs to work with, Lutta had been able to construct a plausible profile of the Headhunter.

And, for Jouma, having a picture of the killer in his mind rather than some nebulous, evil presence was supremely comforting.

'Good afternoon, Inspector,' Lutta said, his mouth full of food, half-standing, brushing crumbs from a threadbare woollen pullover. 'Please take a seat. I apologise for the mess.'

His office was windowless and small and packed with books and files, half-eaten sandwiches and bottles of soda. There was barely room for Jouma to sit, but he was able to perch on the edge of a chair stacked with densely typed sheets of A4 paper.

'I'm writing a paper for the *British Journal of Psychology*,' Lutta explained apologetically. 'It's on Kernberg's theory of malignant narcissism. A modern-day appreciation of it, if you like. You are familiar with—? Essentially he argues that – well, no, I – perhaps not now.'

'You read the report I sent you, Dr Lutta?'

Lutta nodded. 'Yes . . . Yes . . . The judge . . . Terrible, absolutely terrible.' He rummaged in a stack of papers until he found what he was looking for. Jouma recognised it as the concise report he had sent to Kalami prior to his visit. 'But interesting, nonetheless. From a purely clinical point of view, of course,' he added hurriedly.

'In what way?'

Lutta scanned the report. 'The judge – he was abducted from his home by three men, is this correct?'

'According to witnesses, yes.'

'And these men were young?'

'Teenagers, possibly. Why?'

He picked up a pen and began drumming it against his cheek. 'Only that it is unusual that he should have accomplices. Most serial psychopaths tend to lead a solitary existence. Their whole motivation is anti-social. They regard themselves as alien to society – or at least what we would call society. *Mmmm*. Yes. This would suggest some sort of *sect* mentality.' Lutta looked across at Jouma's baffled expression. 'What I mean to say is that perhaps these people are not accomplices so much as

114

followers, Inspector. The killer is their *leader*. He has some sort of psychological hold over them.'

'A witness at the judge's house seemed to think that these men may have been under the influence of narcotics.'

Lutta nodded. 'Yes, yes – that would make perfect sense. Sectism is often associated with narcotic influence. Tribal shamen have traditionally used natural psychodelics in order to induce a transcendental state in themselves and their followers.'

'Tribal shamen? Are you saying that the Headhunter is a witchdoctor?'

'It would be disingenuous to make such an assumption, Inspector. The term "witchdoctor" has become something of a cliché. I have no idea what motivates this man, but if he does believe himself to be some sort of spiritual entity, if he does have a retinue of disciples, for want of a better word, then perhaps it sheds some light on his actions. The removal of the heads, I mean. It would lend weight to the hypothesis that the decapitations are indeed part of a mass ritual.'

'Well, that should make him easier to find,' Jouma said hollowly.

But Lutta was still reading. 'I see from the pathologist's report that the method of decapitation was—'

'The same as the first two victims. Decapitated with a single left-to-right blow.'

A light seemed to gleam in Lutta's eyes. 'The first two, yes. But not the third. The third was decapitated with a front-to-back action – which of course raises the question of whether it was the same killer.'

Jouma was impressed. The young psychologist didn't miss a trick. Not for the first time he found himself thinking that Lutta would make a brilliant detective.

'I was hoping you might be able to shed some light

115

on that, Dr Lutta. In your opinion how important is the *coup de grâce* to the Headhunter?'

Lutta shrugged, dislodging another shower of crumbs from his sweater. 'Very. At least it is for most serial killers. Again it goes back to the ritualistic nature of the act. The actual murder is less important than the reasons for it, and certainly less important than the means by which it is committed. Am I making sense, Inspector Jouma?'

'If you are telling me that the Headhunter did not kill the third victim, then I'm afraid I may have already reached that conclusion.'

'Not necessarily. It may be the case that the third victim was in some way *different* to the others.'

'Different?'

Paul Yomo was certainly different to the other three victims.

'Perhaps he fulfilled a different criterion to the others,' Lutta said. 'One that warranted a different method of execution.'

This was a possibility Jouma had not considered. He leaned forward, wondering if perhaps his investigation into Paul Yomo's background was not a waste of time after all.

'Serial killers do not necessarily have a single fixation,' Lutta continued. 'Their psychotic delusions can be many-faceted. You say the method of execution was the same?'

'A single blow from a sharp implement.'

'And the autopsy details have remained classified?'

'Only myself, the pathologist and certain senior officers have seen the reports. And you, of course, Dr Lutta.'

Lutta nodded enthusiastically, and it seemed to Jouma that he looked even younger than his already tender years. 'Then in theory there is nothing to preclude the third killing being committed by the same man.'

Jouma exhaled, relief mingled with the knowledge

that he was still no closer to understanding the Headhunter's motives.

Lutta looked at him quizzically. 'Is that good news, Inspector?'

'Only if it means I am hunting one madman and not two, Dr Lutta.'

26

Mac Bowden had been in Kenya just over a week, but from what Jake could see his old Flying Squad boss had fitted into the ex-pat lifestyle as if he'd been born to it. Here he came now in his bush shorts and corporate polo shirt, striding across the air-conditioned lobby of the Sandpiper Ocean Club Hotel like he owned the place, a broad grin already in place beneath the thick moustache.

'*Jambo, kimosabe!*' he said, extending his hands. 'That's what they say round here, isn't it?'

'The Swahili's not bad. Lose the Cherokee and you'll fit in just fine.'

Mac laughed. 'Did you come here by boat?'

'Harry's Land Rover.'

'You came here specially to see me?'

'Believe me, I've got nothing better to do.'

'Must be driving you nuts being a landlubber. When do the docs think you'll be shipshape?'

'Another couple of weeks. But I'm thinking of defying medical opinion. The thought of Harry's fat brother having all the fun is hard to take.'

'Come on – I'll buy you a beer.'

They walked through the atrium and past the pool, beyond the lawns full of sunbathing guests to a thatched bar manned by a smiling African. The two men perched on stools as the barman poured their drinks.

'Mineral water?' Jake said, looking with surprise at Mac's glass.

'Give me a break – I'm on duty. I shouldn't even be taking time out to talk to you.'

Now that they were away from the hotel, Mac seemed suddenly less ebullient. In fact, Jake thought, his old friend looked decidedly preoccupied, as if there was something on his mind.

'How's it going?' he asked.

Mac shrugged. 'OK.'

'What's the new boss like?'

'Standage? He's all right, I suppose. Bit paranoid, though.'

Mac leaned forward to wipe the condensation from the sides of his glass, and as he did so Jake noticed a bulge in the small of his back beneath his shirt.

'Christ, Mac! Are you carrying a——?'

Mac glared at him and shook his head. 'Come on,' he said. 'Let's walk.'

'When I first got here, Standage told me he was keen to beef up security,' Mac said as they followed the surf towards the low wooden fence that marked the boundary of the Sandpiper's beachfront. 'CCTV installation mainly, and an idea of where the perimeter was vulnerable. Typical Brit paranoia, I thought. My job – or so I thought – was to scope out the lay of the land and then give him my expert opinion on where I thought things could be improved. For a few days everything was going swimmingly. Money for old rope, I thought.' He picked up a stone and threw it into the sea. 'Then things changed.'

'How?' Jake asked.

'One of his guests got hit over the head by an intruder while she was sunning herself in the grounds. Turned out it was the second time it had happened.'

Jake laughed. 'That's a good start.'

'Hey – I'd just arrived,' Mac said, raising his hands

defensively. 'I'd barely got my suitcase unpacked. But that was only the start of it. I'd thought Standage was a nervous wreck then — but you heard about that judge who got killed? The one who got his head cut off?'

Jake nodded. 'There's a serial sicko on the loose.'

'Yeah — well, as soon as Standage heard the news, it was like someone shoved a red-hot poker up his arse. And all of a sudden my job description is changed. Instead of overseeing improvements to the hotel's security, he wants me as his own personal bodyguard.'

'That's why you're packing a gun?' Jake said.

Mac discreetly lifted his shirt to reveal a 9mm automatic nestled in a holster in the hollow of his back. 'Said he would up my pay to forty grand to wear it. Like I say, the guy's fucking paranoid. I'm pretty sure he hits the bottle for breakfast.'

'You're not a bodyguard, Mac,' Jake said. He didn't like this one little bit.

'I know. I told him the last time I'd fired a 9mm was at the range at Hendon,' Mac said. 'But he wasn't having any of it. And forty grand is double what I signed up for.'

Jake stopped and looked at him. 'I know you're just looking out for Shirley and the boys — but this is a different ballgame altogether, Mac. If you're carrying a weapon he's going to expect you to use it.'

'Like I say, *kimosabe*, he's just spooked by everything that's been going on.' He checked his watch. 'Anyway, I'd better be heading back. The boss will be getting anxious.'

Standage was waiting by the pool. He looked dreadful — ashen-faced, dark circles under his eyes, the telltale puffiness of too much booze. When he saw Mac and Jake approaching the hotel from the beach, he made a beeline for them, his expression thunderous.

'Where have you been, Mr Bowden?' he said, giving Jake only the most cursory of glances. 'I paged you five minutes ago.'

'An old friend from my Scotland Yard days came to see how I was getting on,' Mac told him pointedly. 'I was just showing him around. Mr Standage – this is Jake Moore.'

The fact that Jake had police connections seemed to interest the hotel manager. He proferred a sweat-sodden hand. 'Alec Standage. Did Colin Ryeguard send you, too?'

'I—' Jake began, but Mac cut him off.

'Jake has run a game-fishing boat out of Flamingo Creek for the last five years,' he explained. 'He's not in my line of work.'

'I see,' Standage said. He seemed disappointed.

'Mac tells me you've been having a few security problems, Mr Standage,' Jake said.

'Nothing we can't get on top of,' Mac said, in a voice that Jake knew of old. It meant he wanted him to shut the fuck up. 'You still need to go into Mombasa, Mr Standage?'

'Yes,' Standage said absently. 'Yes, I do.'

'Then I'll go and get the car and bring it round the front.'

'Good. Thank you, Mr Bowden.'

'Everyone calls me Mac, Mr Standage.' He took Jake by the arm and began to lead him away towards the hotel building.

'Nice to meet you, Mr Standage,' Jake said. But Standage was lost in his own thoughts.

'Who the hell is Colin Ryeguard?' Jake said as they crossed the atrium once again.

'Just some fixer back in London.' Mac shrugged. 'Sorts out old lags like me with security jobs like this.'

'I thought Standage was paying you?'

121

'He pays Ryeguard. Ryeguard pays me – minus his commission, of course. But the extra for the bodyguard duties is coming out of Standage's pocket.'

'Twenty grand's a lot of money.'

'Then I'd better make sure I keep him alive.' Mac grinned. 'Anyway – I'd better get to work.'

They had arrived at the hotel car park, beside Standage's hulking SUV.

'Bulletproof?' Jake said, tapping the tinted windows.

Mac grinned. 'That dickhead wouldn't know a bullet-proof window if one smacked him over the head.' But he could see Jake's concern. 'Listen, *kimosabe*, if I thought for one minute I was in any sort of danger I would tell Standage where to shove his 9mm. But the guy has obviously been watching too many horror movies. As long as he stays scared until my contract's up, I won't complain. And more importantly, neither will Shirley.'

I'm sure she won't, Jake thought, as he watched the SUV roll up to the hotel entrance and Standage hurry inside as if he was some world-famous celebrity trying to dodge the paparazzi.

27

The vultures were flying high today, their wings spread on the thermals, their eyes scouring the Headhunter's lair for carrion. On the warm stones of an exposed rocky outcrop overlooking his kingdom, the killer addressed his small band of disciples. He told them of his father Ngai, the creator and giver of all things, the Divider of the Universe and Lord of Nature. He spoke of how Ngai's spirit flowed as one through him and him alone, and how the apostates who denied him would be rent asunder by a great cataclysm.

Sitting cross-legged on the ground, naked save for a loincloth and his skin daubed with pigment, Mahmoud listened intently as the words sloshed around in his drugged brain like driftwood on the ocean. He felt strange, but not unpleasantly so. Colours exploded like fireworks and sometimes he thought he heard the wind speaking to him; but he felt secure. He felt that he *belonged* here, in this place, with these people. His fear was gone.

His fellow disciples sat beside him, staring with rapt attention at the Headhunter, their mouths open and their lips dry. There were three of them; young men like him. And like them Mahmoud now shared their wonderment and sense of purpose.

What he yearned for was their *experience*.

In the small hut they shared on the other side of the outcrop he had listened to their stories; how they ventured out to take those who had been chosen by

Ngai for sacrifice, how the apostates had screamed and begged for mercy, how they had beaten them into pathetic submission – and how they had watched as Athi removed their heads with his ivory-handled machete.

At first they had scared him. But, as the days melted into one seemingly continuous blur of hallucinogenic colour and sound, more than anything he wanted to *join* them.

'Soon, boy, your time will come,' the old man had told him. 'Athi, the living god, has a great mission for you and your brothers.' And, as he spoke, he refilled Mahmoud's gourd with bittersweet liquor that the boy drank greedily, needing to feel its fierce burn against the soft tissues of his throat and the explosions in his brain.

'The apostates lie fearful in their beds,' Athi was saying now. 'Yet they do not realise that paradise awaits them and that to be chosen for sacrifice is an honour. We must show them the true way, that there is nothing to be afraid of. Soon they will understand. Soon they will come willingly to me, to Athi, son of Ngai, the Divider of the Universe and Lord of Nature. And they will bow their heads and beg for the keys to paradise.'

He fixed each of his followers with the same burning stare. 'Soon Ngai will speak again,' he said. 'Soon it will be time once again.'

The four disciples looked at each other and smiled – and at that moment Mahmoud felt his spirit fill with an elation he could not begin to understand.

Later the Headhunter left the outcrop and walked alone into the wilderness that surrounded it. He knew the pathways through the treacherous swamp like the lines on his own hand. Presently he came to his meditation tree, a single gnarled baobab that somehow managed to survive in the acidic mire, and nimbly climbed to its uppermost branches. He loved to sit here, especially now as dawn was breaking across the huge Kenyan sky. From here he could view the panorama all around him. This was *his* land. He felt connected to it at a molecular level – its soil, its water were all part of him and he of them. When he breathed its thick, hot, sour air he felt re-energised, immortal. *A living god.*

It was several hours before he returned to the outcrop. The witchdoctor seemed anxious to see him, but high above a vulture was soaring effortlessly on the thermals.

'Look at it, Chipche,' he said, gesturing at the bird. 'Isn't it magnificent?'

The witchdoctor's eyes disappeared into leathery folds of skin as he watched the bird swoop close to the jagged rocks. 'They say that each vulture carries the souls of the dead in its talons, my lord,' he said.

'Surely it is the case that Ngai carries the souls of the dead in his hand?' the Headhunter snapped reprovingly.

Chipche bowed his head in deference. 'You are wise beyond mortal men, my lord.'

The Headhunter rolled his head back and forth so the bones crackled in his long neck. It was not the first time Chipche had said something that could have been construed as heresy.

'What do you want?'

'I have received a message from Ngai, my lord.'

Now the Headhunter winced, as he always did nowadays when his father sent Chipche messages. It galled him that Ngai should continue to use the witchdoctor as his conduit rather than his own son. 'What did he say?'

'It is time, my lord. The apostate has been identified.'

'Very well. Bring him to me.'

'Yes, lord.'

'And Chipche—'

For a big man the Headhunter moved with ferocious speed. In the blink of an eye he had leaped from the rock and across to where Chipche stood. His hand was a blur and in a moment the witchdoctor lay sprawled on his back, blood trickling from his mouth.

'This time I shall allow your heresy to pass, old man,' he hissed. 'But when the day comes that Ngai speaks to his son instead of through a wizened mortal, then I will not be so forgiving.'

'Of course, lord.' Chipche got slowly to his feet, wiping the blood with the back of his hand. 'I shall prepare the disciples.'

As the witchdoctor shuffled away, the Headhunter turned and, with his arms spread wide, sniffed the earthy scent of the mountains. *Oh, Ngai, you have in your wisdom blessed me. But when will you see fit to allow your own son to hear your voice?*

He climbed back on his rock and folded his long legs beneath him like an insect. To the west the golden hills were on fire.

28

Frau Maria Klinker had been pronounced dead at 3.42 a.m. that morning, and suddenly the man the rest of the homicide division had laughingly dubbed the Shanzu Smasher was a murderer. Which was why, shortly after nine a.m. and despite the crushing workload of the Headhunter case, Detective Constable David Mwangi was in the bowels of Mombasa Hospital staring into the dead woman's cloudy, unseeing eyes.

'Of course, it would be much easier if I could simply cut it off and boil it,' Christie said. 'A clean skull is a lot easier to examine.'

'I think Herr Klinker would have something to say about that,' Mwangi pointed out. 'It is his wife, after all.'

'But she's dead, dear boy! He's not going to be looking at her smiling Teutonic face across the dining table any more, is he?'

Frau Klinker, having been transported from the neurology wing to the chill, subterranean corridors of the hospital morgue, lay naked and on her back on a metal autopsy table. The bandage had been removed from her head and her hair had been shaved.

'If you please, Mr Christie.'

'Strikes me you've already been in this job too long,' Christie grumbled. 'You remind me of Jouma: bitter, twisted, treating everyone as if they were your slave. My advice is get out while you can, Constable. Make something worthwhile out of your life. Anyway – does he know you're here?'

'Why do you ask?'

'I thought it was all hands to the pump over this business with the machete madman.'

'It is,' Mwangi said. 'But unfortunately he is not the only murderer at large in Mombasa, and we only have a finite number of men.'

With a sigh the pathologist got to work. He began with a sweeping incision beneath Frau Klinker's jawline. Then he yanked back the skin of her face to expose the bone and muscle beneath. Finally, with a small circular saw, he deftly removed the top of her skull and lifted her brain on to a set of stainless-steel scales.

'What is it with you people and heads anyway?' Christie said, making a note of the weight. 'I've only just got rid of the last one Jouma brought in.'

'I take it you are referring to Justice Banda?'

'You should watch your step, young man. Jouma really is the Angel of Death. When he's on his rounds, this place is absolutely packed to the gunwales.'

'I don't think Inspector Jouma can be blamed for the Headhunter's thirst for blood.'

'Just you wait and see. You've only known him five minutes. Jouma and me go back fifteen years. Fifteen years of carnage.' Christie picked up the brain and lifted it to the light. 'I'll be making a more thorough examination, of course, but offhand I'd say that was the cause of death.' He pointed to a large purple bruise straddling the canyon running down the centre of the brain. 'There is noticeable swelling around the parietal lobe. Who did you say the consultant was?'

'Mr Vengsarkar,' said Mwangi.

'Well, he did his best – but this one was never going to make it, I'm afraid. The impact of the depressed cranium section caused far too much structural damage.'

'May I see the skull?' Mwangi said.

Christie looked at him approvingly. 'Bravo, Constable! Jouma wouldn't touch a cadaver if you paid him.'

Mwangi picked up the shallow bowl of bone from the top of Frau Klinker's head. The almost perfectly circular crater he had seen on the X-rays was now plainly visible.

'Most unusual for a blow to the head to cause this sort of damage to the skull.'

'Normally, yes.' Christie nodded. 'But I have heard of cases where the frontal or occipital fontanelle has failed to fully ossify in adulthood.'

'Pardon?' Mwangi said.

'When babies are born they have soft spots on their heads,' the pathologist explained. 'These are gaps between the skull plates which allow the head to pass through the birth canal. They are known as fontanelles. There's a small one at the back and a much larger one at the front. I understand it was once the vogue for the mothers of unwanted babies to kill them by sticking a hatpin directly into the brain through the frontal fontanelle. Ordinarily the bones knit together, closing the fontanelle, by the time the child is two years old – a process called ossification.'

Mwangi was trying not to think about hatpins and babies' soft heads. 'Frau Klinker was fifty-eight,' he pointed out.

'Indeed. And her skull should have been like reinforced concrete. But there are extremely rare instances where the ossification process doesn't work as it should. The fontanelle closes up, but the bone in that area is thin, like eggshell. Most of the time the first you know about it is when your head caves in.' He peered at the dead woman's skull. 'I'd have to send this one away for tests, but I'd wager that was the problem here.'

'Shouldn't Mr Vengsarkar have noticed this?'

'If he'd attempted a decompressive craniectomy, yes – because the skull would have shattered like an eggshell and killed her there and then. As it is, he drilled a hole in the side of the head where the bone was at its strongest.'

'So any sort of blow to that area of her skull would have been fatal?'

'Pretty much so. And not a powerful blow either. To be honest, if she had this condition I'm astonished she lasted as long as she did. She could have bashed her head on the headboard on her honeymoon night and – *auf Wiedersehen.*'

'I'm sure Herr Klinker will take great comfort in that fact,' Mwangi said.

Christie chuckled to himself.

Jouma was right, the young detective thought. He truly was a ghoul.

29

'What the hell is this, Katherine?' Larry Gazemba, news editor of the *Daily Nation*, bellowed down the phone.

In the newspaper's Mombasa bureau, which was in fact a poky office overlooking Jamhuri Park, Katherine Rapuro spun in her chair and twirled the handset cord nervously. She had heard that tone in Gazemba's voice before, and it never usually preceded hearty congratulations.

'What's the problem, boss?'

'This story you've just sent over. I'm looking at it on my screen now.'

'What about it?'

'The Church of Christ the Apostle in Kilifi is holding a candlelit vigil for an end to violence?'

'Their congregation is very frightened by the Headhunter killings.'

'There are twenty paragraphs here, Katherine.'

'OK – maybe I overwrote it.'

'By nineteen paragraphs, I would say. Is this all you've got?'

'Things are quiet at the moment, Larry.'

Three hundred miles away in Nairobi, Larry Gazemba laughed derisively. 'Katherine, there is a fucking serial killer on the loose in Mombasa – and you're telling me the best you can come up with is a vigil by a bunch of Kilifi Bible-bashers?'

'It's a good human-interest story. The effect of a killer on an ordinary community.'

'Bullshit. You can't kid a kidder, Katherine. I've been around too long.'

There was silence down the line. In the background Katherine could hear phones ringing in the newsroom.

'Katherine?'

'Still here, boss.'

'Is everything OK down there? I mean, you've been on this story nonstop. Do you need a break?'

She knew where this was leading. 'I'm fine, Larry. Absolutely.'

'Because I can always send the chief reporter down.'

'I said I'm fine. Listen, I know the Kilifi story is a bit weak.'

'A *bit* weak?'

'But I'm working on something big.'

'Big.'

'Yes, big.'

'I take it you can't tell me the nature of this earth-shattering exclusive?' Gazemba said presently.

'Not yet.'

'Well, I hope I won't have to wait too long, Katherine. The editor is breathing down my neck on this one.'

The threat was clear, and, as she hung up the phone, Katherine knew that Larry had effectively put her on the clock. That was the problem with once-in-a-generation stories – they waited for no one. Mombasa was crawling with hacks from across Africa and beyond, all of them desperate for a new angle; and it was times like this, when there was a lull in proceedings, that she feared most. If one of her competitors should come up with a Headhunter exclusive while she was filing copy about church vigils, then she would be spending the rest of her career writing wedding reports for the local weekly.

Not for the first time she thought about the Mayor's manila envelope, and there had been occasions since their meeting when her fingers had hovered over the telephone. But what would have happened if she had made the call? A front-page exclusive most probably – but at what cost? She knew damn well that a political reptile like the Mayor would not stop at a simple tit-for-tat exchange. A few lines on a plaque unveiling was in no way payback for the autopsy reports on the Headhunter's victims. No, he would want more, and he would keep on wanting more until she was little more than a cipher, rewriting his press releases for national consumption.

She looked out of the grimy window at the traffic circling the park. The relentless futility of it all seemed to sum up what she was feeling right now. But then nobody said it was going to be easy. She was a national newspaper reporter, for God's sake! Larry had given her the biggest story going, and it was about time she showed her chops instead of moping about what might have been.

She sat for a while, lost in thought, ideas whizzing around in her mind. She had promised Larry a big story, and now she had to deliver. *Shit.*

Eventually she picked up the phone. It was time to make the news happen.

30

The Sandpiper Ocean Club Hotel was only a short drive from Mombasa Hospital. Mwangi was expecting to be met at the door by Alec Standage, the manager. Instead, his car was held at a newly constructed barrier checkpoint and his details telephoned through to the hotel by a steely-eyed *askari*. When he was finally allowed to pass through into the complex, the man who waited for him in the cool atrium was short and powerful, with a bushy black moustache. He introduced himself as Mac Bowden, the hotel's head of security, and he led Mwangi to Standage's office.

Standage's already twitchy demeanour was not improved by Mwangi's news.

'*Dead*?' he croaked. 'Oh, shit.'

'The pathologist says that she had a rare condition that made her skull extremely fragile,' Mwangi said. 'Otherwise, like Mr Wuyns, she would have almost certainly survived the blow with nothing more than a headache.'

Standage looked up with bloodshot eyes. 'Things are much improved, detective,' he said, almost pleading. 'Mr Bowden here has completely restructured our perimeter security. I have employed half a dozen extra *askari* to provide twenty-four-hour beach patrols, and you will have seen the checkpoint barrier at the entrance. It is costing me a fortune.'

'Of course,' Mwangi said.

But Standage seemed desperate to elicit some sort of

approval from the young detective. 'The Sandpiper is now the safest hotel on the east coast – isn't that so, Mr Bowden?'

'It will be once all the improvements are in place,' Bowden said carefully.

Mwangi couldn't take his eyes off Standage, though. The hotel manager's hands were shaking, and there was a pulsating tic at the corner of his mouth. The Shanzu Smasher was clearly bad for business – but Standage looked as if he was about to expire.

'I'm sure that, once Frau Klinker's pre-existing medical condition is known, there will be no question of litigation against you or the hotel,' Mwangi said.

'Uh—?' Standage grunted, his mind elsewhere. 'Oh. Right. Well, thank you for coming, Detective Mwangi. Mr Bowden will show you out.'

The thirty-year-old Cortina hatchback was parked fifty yards up the road from the Sandpiper's new checkpoint barrier. Inside were the Headhunter's three seasoned disciples, two up front, one in the back. They were smoking a large pungent joint and sharing a pop bottle full of potent liquor supplied by the witchdoctor specifically for this occasion. There was a battered boombox on the dashboard, blasting out a CD of an American group called Niggaz With Attitude. They were playing the same track over and over again. It was called 'Fuck Tha Police'.

In the boot of the vehicle sat Mahmoud. He was trembling with fear and anticipation, although he was trying his best not to let the others see. They had taken to calling him Little Shit, because they reckoned he shouldn't be allowed out on such a prestigious mission, not after such a short time. All of Athi's disciples were equal in the eyes of Ngai – but some were more equal than others.

135

'Hey, Little Shit – you want a drink?'

The youth in the back seat reached over and passed him the bottle. Mahmoud drank from it, and the sensation was like swallowing fire. He coughed and they laughed at him and called him Little Shit again. Then they passed him something else. It was heavy and wrapped in an oilskin cloth.

'Are you ready for this, Little Shit?' the driver said. His name was Charles, but he called himself *Mamba*, which meant crocodile. He was the oldest of the disciples and before his initiation he had killed two men in a gunfight in a village near Lamu.

'I am ready.'

'Good.'

Mahmoud heard the roar of the Cortina's reconditioned engine and as it pulled away from the side of the road he had to grab hold of the rear wheel bulkhead to stop himself being flung against the tailgate. As the powerful car picked up speed the passenger, a heroin addict renamed *Nyigu* – the Hornet – turned the music up full blast.

Mahmoud peered over the top of the leather and through the windscreen he saw the gatehouse of the hotel approaching fast. There was a wooden barrier in the way. It was painted with red and white stripes. There was a man in a uniform holding one end. He was staring at them with wide white eyes. Now he was running away. And now the barrier was being smashed to pieces by the Cortina as if it was twigs.

And still they gained speed.

'Is Mr Standage all right?' Mwangi asked Mac Bowden as the two men made their way back to the atrium. 'He doesn't look well. Perhaps he should see a doctor.'

'He's OK,' Bowden said. 'He's just a bit jittery, that's

all. And this business with the serial killer has freaked him out as well.'

'You mean the Headhunter?'

'If that's what they're calling him, yes. I think he knew one of the victims. The judge they found the other day.'

Mwangi paused. 'He knew Justice Banda?'

'I think so.'

'I would like to ask him about that.'

'Another time, chum. One dose of bad news is quite enough for one day.'

They were in the atrium now.

'Do you think you'll catch this guy?' Bowden said.

'The Headhunter? I am in no doubt, Mr Bowden. It is only a matter of time.'

'Good luck. You familiar with the internet, Constable Mwangi?'

'Of course.'

'Then I suggest you swot up on the Yorkshire Ripper inquiry in England back in the 1970s.'

'Really? Why?'

'Because that's how *not* to catch a serial killer.'

They were almost at the door when they saw the low-slung Cortina weaving at high speed straight towards them along the tarmacked driveway leading from the gatehouse – and for a moment Mwangi and Bowden were rooted to the spot. The vehicle hit a speedbump at more than eighty miles an hour and took off momentarily, its bald tyres spinning free in the air. When it hit the ground again, it was almost up to the vast glass atrium.

Bowden leaped across and with a rugby tackle barged Mwangi out of the way just a split-second before the Cortina hit. There was a noise like an explosion and suddenly it was raining tiny shards of reinforced glass.

★

The impact of the speed bump sent Mahmoud rattling around in the back of the car like a pin-ball. In his ears he heard the engine, the music and a shrill, high-pitched yell from the front of the vehicle.

'*Yeeeeeeeeeaaaaaaaaahhhhhh!*'

He adjusted his position and braced himself for the impact, eyes wide open and mouth stretched in a silent scream – and at the moment of impact the glass atrium shattered into a million pieces and he was again bouncing around like a rag doll in the unforgiving metal and fibreglass well.

'Are you armed?' Mac Bowden was yelling into Mwangi's ear. '*Are you armed?*'

'No!' Mwangi gasped, crushed against the cool marble floor by the Englishman's weight.

Bowden rolled away. 'Then find some cover and call for help,' he said.

Mwangi looked up and saw an extraordinary scene: the Cortina had ploughed straight though the glass portico of the atrium and into the far wall, where its concertinaed bonnet had punched a large hole in the plaster. Everywhere he looked, people were running in terror and bewilderment through clouds of choking dust, steam and exhaust fumes; it reminded him of those shocking images in the aftermath of 9/11 – yet this was not New York, this was a smart tourist hotel on the Mombasa coast.

This should not be happening.

And now he saw something else: men with guns, spilling out of the Cortina, spraying the ceiling with bullets and moving purposefully through the atrium. There were three of them, and now he saw they were not men at all, but kids – swaggering kids with dreadlocks and combat fatigues.

Mwangi ferreted frantically for his cellphone and punched in 999. After what seemed like forever he was connected to an emergency operator. Speaking as slowly and clearly as he could, he gave his status and requested back-up.

It was then that he heard the unmistakable *pop-pop* of gunfire again – and the equally chilling sound of someone screaming.

31

Consultant surgeon Indira Goti peered at the four-inch vertical scar connecting Jake's breastbone to his navel and chirruped approvingly. 'I am, Mr Moore, a genius – even if I do say so myself,' she announced. 'In time, assuming you do not unduly stretch the skin by developing a pot belly, the scar will fade until it is barely noticeable.'

Jake swung his legs off the examination table. 'I'm pleased to hear it. But what about the internal damage?'

Goti, a white-haired Sri Lankan with a voice like someone shovelling gravel, looked mildly affronted. 'You doubt my surgical powers, Mr Moore? Put your shirt on and don't be so impertinent.'

Jake smiled. She might have the bedside manner of an attack dog, but Goti was right. She *was* a genius. For sixteen long hours she had fought to save his life on the operating table, when even some of her colleagues were advising her that it was a waste of time. He watched her limp arthritically across to her desk and switch on an ancient-looking Roberts transistor radio on her desk.

'Excuse me,' she said, lighting a thin cheroot. 'But I always listen to the one o'clock news on the World Service. The BBC is not what it once was, but it is the only news organisation I trust.'

As he buttoned his shirt Jake wondered if she knew Jouma's miserable pathologist friend Christie. The pair of them would get along famously.

'Does that mean I can go back to work?' he asked her.

Goti shrugged. 'Do you feel up to it?'

'As a matter of fact, I haven't felt better for years.'

It was true. His punishing daily regime had worked wonders. At least he no longer felt like puking after completing a circuit. And if pudgy Ralph Philliskirk was fit enough to handle *Yellowfin* then surely to God Jake was, even at sixty per cent capacity. Where he had once looked at Ralph on the flying bridge with resignation, now there was only bubbling resentment.

He wanted his boat back.

'My medical opinion is that you should continue to recuperate,' Goti was saying. 'At least another fortnight before you even think about any sort of robust activity. However, bearing in mind that most medical opinion is a lot of old tosh, I would suggest that, as long as you aren't pulling humpback whales out of the sea with your bare hands, and as long as you curtail your excessive drinking and smoking—'

Jake could have kissed her.

He took the stairs back down to ground level, all six flights of them. But there was a spring in his step now, brought on by the unalloyed joy of knowing that the purgatory was nearly over and that soon his life would be back to normal again. It was a state of affairs he had sometimes doubted would ever come to pass.

The stairs led to the Accident and Emergency ward. As he emerged into the bright artificial light, Jake was nearly bowled off his feet by a succession of doctors, nurses and other staff hurrying towards the main double doors, where he could now see an ambulance outside with its roof lights flashing and its rear doors wide open. There were two people inside lying on collapsible gurneys. As the gurneys were removed from the ambulance and pushed at high speed into the A&E department Jake saw blood, lots of it, covering the bodies of the two casualties. He saw their faces – they were just kids, maybe eighteen or nineteen, and he was pretty damn sure that at least one of them was already dead despite the oxygen mask over his nose and the drip in his arm. His dreadlocks were thick with clotting blood and what looked like brain matter. His eyes were wide open, but there was no life in them.

The second man was still alive, but, judging from his shallow breathing and the spray of blood emerging from the hole in his chest every time he exhaled, he would not be for much longer. He was mouthing something, but there was no sound other than an ominous gurgling as his throat filled with blood.

Another ambulance arrived and a third body was bundled out. It was another kid, this one definitely dead because half his face was blown away.

Jesus, Jake thought – it was like something straight from the streets of downtown Los Angeles. He watched, pressed against the wall as the grim procession raced past in the direction of the operating theatres, and he couldn't help thinking that on two occasions *he* had been the victim lying on the gurney with the mask on his face and blood leaking out all over the place.

He moved towards the exit, anxious to get out of the hospital before the ugly memories came back to spoil his day. But they were bringing another body out of the second ambulance now, and once again Jake could only stand and watch as the crash team raced out of the building.

What the hell had been happening? Had World War Three broken out on the streets of Mombasa?

But this time there was something terribly familiar about the bloodied body being manhandled out of the ambulance.

No – Christ, it can't be.

142

As he moved forward impulsively, a man jumped down from the ambulance. He was in shirtsleeves, but the white cotton was drenched with blood. Jake recognised him, too. He was a cop, Jouma's junior officer. What the hell was his name again?'

'Keep back, sir,' Mwangi said, pushing Jake aside as the crash team flocked around the man on the gurney.

'He's a friend of mine,' Jake shouted, and the young detective turned. He looked scared out of his wits, almost catatonic with horror. Jake pushed past him to the gurney. '*Mac!*'

Mac Bowden coughed blood into the plastic oxygen mask over his nose and mouth, but his hand reached out and grasped Jake's arm. For a moment he tried to sit up, but then he collapsed backwards on to the gurney.

'Please, stand aside!' one of the doctors was saying.

But Mac wouldn't let go of Jake's arm. He pulled his friend towards him and, with his other hand, he ripped away the oxygen mask from his mouth and, with one last supreme effort, muttered something into Jake's ear. Then his grip loosened and his arm fell away, and the gurney was pushed into the hospital, leaving Jake on his knees beside the open doors of the hospital.

He felt a hand on his shoulder and Mwangi helped him to his feet.

'What the hell *happened*?'

'Your friend,' the young detective said. 'He saved my life. He saved *all* our lives.'

32

Jake was in the hospital waiting room when Jouma arrived.

'How are you, my friend?' the little African asked, sitting next to him on the row of unforgiving plastic chairs.

'They shot Mac, Inspector,' Jake said disbelievingly. 'My old boss ... Mac Bowden ... they shot him. Kids with AK-47s, shooting up the Sandpiper Hotel.'

Jouma nodded. 'Your friend is a very brave man.'

'I was the best man at his wedding, Inspector. The godfather to his boys. Who were these bastards? What did they want?'

'Not what, Jake. *Who*. They came for the hotel manager, Mr Standage.'

Jake blinked. 'Standage? That prick? Why?'

'Because he was to have been the Headhunter's next victim.'

The pieces, when they were fitted together, told only the bald facts of what happened that day at the Sandpiper Hotel. No words could ever adequately describe the chaos and confusion, or replicate the noise of gunfire and screaming, or the smell of cordite, blood and fear. Mwangi had tried – but some synapse in his brain kept cutting out, like a safety valve, so that he relived the events as if he was watching them on TV or controlling the movements of his avatar with the controls of a sophisticated computer game.

He saw himself wandering in a daze across the shattered remains of the hotel atrium, the broken glass crackling beneath his feet. Ahead of him was the wrecked car, its doors and tailgate wide open. Through the hole in the wall he could see the pool, full of debris and scattered sunbeds.

Along the corridor towards Standage's office now. There was the sound of whooping and shouting; the occasional rasp of machine-gun fire. *Crouching!* Yes, he was crouching, heart pounding, torn between his sense of professional duty and his overwhelming human instinct to run.

Suddenly, someone grabbed his arm and dragged him into a service corridor leading towards the residents' gym and sauna complex. It was the Englishman, Bowden. The new head of security. He had a silver 9mm automatic in his hand and one finger pressed to his lips. He was waiting. The gunmen were in Standage's office, he hissed. Three of them. Perhaps it was too late and Standage was already dead.

But perhaps it wasn't.

Now there was the sound of shouting. Harsh laughter. Coming closer. Still Bowden waited and Mwangi realised then that, whoever these people were, they did not know about Standage's new bodyguard. Mac Bowden, he now understood, was the very *last* thing the three gunmen manhandling the hotel manager along the corridor expected.

Which was why, when Bowden stepped out of the alcove and into the corridor, their first reaction was to simply stand and gawp at him.

Bang. One down, a sizeable chunk of his brain blown out of a hole just above his nose.

Bang. The second was hit square in the chest, knocking him several feet backwards and on to the floor.

Bang. Three down, hit in the head again, even though he had already dropped his assault rifle and was running as fast as he could in the direction of the manager's office.

Bowden hurried across to Alec Standage, who had collapsed into a sitting position on the floor.

'You OK, boss?' Bowden said. He was reaching down to the hotel manager. There was a reassuring smile on his face. Mwangi could picture that smile clearer than anything else.

BANG!

The burly Englishman pitched forward and smacked into the corridor wall, and suddenly there was blood spattered all over Standage's face. Mwangi turned his head and there, at the other end of the corridor, was a fourth gunman. *A fourth!* In his hand was an ancient Colt revolver with black smoke pumping from its barrel.

For a moment they all stood there transfixed. But Bowden still had the automatic clutched in his fist and he fired one last time from the floor. The kid screamed as a chunk of his shoulder blew away, and the revolver fell from his fingers. He turned and ran, eluding Mwangi's grasp as the detective lunged for him.

'He must have still been in the vehicle,' Jouma said solemnly. 'Nobody knew he was there until it was too late.'

'Where is he now?'

'He got away.'

'Jesus Christ! What was your officer *playing* at?'

'Don't blame Mwangi, Jake. He is just a boy. Not much older than the gunmen.'

Jouma was right, of course. But it didn't stop the rage inside him.

The two men turned as a door opened into the waiting room. The slight figure of Indira Goti stood there in bloodstained surgical scrubs, her hair hidden beneath an oversized protective hat. The expression on her face said it all – but she told them anyway.

Mac Bowden had died on the operating table.

33

Mahmoud was many things – an addict, a pimp, and now a murderer – but he was not stupid. He knew that they would be coming after him, and he knew that his blood would lead them to him. He knew also that the hole above his right bicep was the size of a walnut, and that if he didn't do something to staunch the flow he would be long dead before they caught him.

Fuelled by adrenaline and the remaining narcotics in his dwindling bloodstream, he had fled across the hotel grounds, jumped the perimeter fence and was now hiding in the concrete shell of a half-built beach house about half a mile away. As he ran, he had ripped off his neckerchief and rammed it into the wound with his left hand, which had worked for a while; but now the material was sodden and the blood was pouring freely down his arm again.

Tears filled his eyes, but he swiped them away angrily. This was no time for crying! He was a man, not a child. He had to *deal* with the situation. He had to *act*. His T-shirt was soaked in blood and useless, so quickly he removed his jeans and, with his teeth and his one good hand, he tore them into strips. Using the same method, he was able to loop one of the strips around his shoulder and pull it tight. With the tourniquet secure the blood flow abated noticeably – but Mahmoud knew he did not have much time. He could already hear the distant whine of police sirens on the highway.

He got to his feet and began a systematic search of his

hiding place. It was a large breezeblock building with a view of the ocean that would eventually be owned by some rich white man, no doubt. But for now it was occupied by teams of poorly paid African labourers. It was Mahmoud's only slice of fortune that day that the workforce were at lunch; the house was a Marie Celeste of half-rendered walls, planks on workbenches, hardening vats of plaster and filler, copper wires and tubes. He saw what he wanted. It had been left on the wooden staircase – a handheld propane blowtorch used to weld copper tubing together.

Although he could hardly believe what he was about to do, Mahmoud sat down on the steps and removed the tourniquet. The blood began pumping out of the hole in his shoulder with almost indecent haste. *How much blood did a body contain?* he found himself wondering as he turned on the gas supply and lit the torch with a match.

Blue flame or yellow?
Yellow flame or blue?

He shook his head. He was starting to get delirious with the loss of blood.

You are dying, Mahmoud.

He jammed the bloody tourniquet in his mouth, manipulated the valve so that the flame was an evil blue arrow and aimed it directly at the wound. Pure white pain fired like lightning through his body as the ruptured flesh bubbled and seared, and he screamed into the rag because he no longer cared who heard him; in fact, he no longer cared if he died because at least death would spare him this indescribable agony. His nostrils were filled with smoke from his own body and he could barely resist the need to vomit.

Finally, when he could take no more, he dropped the canister and slumped backwards. His eyes closed and darkness swept over him, and he hoped he would never wake.

But the pain had different ideas. It yanked him from unconsciousness and brought him screaming into reality again. He could hardly bring himself to look at his shoulder – he could still hear the blistered skin bubbling gently – but when he did he saw that the wound was now a crater of charred meat and, most importantly, the bleeding had stopped.

The sirens were louder now, too. He went to one of the windows and peered out as three, four, five patrol cars went screaming past in the direction of the hotel, followed by two ambulances.

Quick! Quick!

One of the workmen had left his overalls hanging from the rungs of his aluminium ladder. Mahmoud put them on and slipped out of the rear of the house, making his way quickly across the building site of the garden and to the palm groves beyond, taking care to avoid the beach and the sunbathing tourists. After about a mile, when he was out of range of the last of the hotels on the Shanzu strip, he came to a small cove. An old man was sitting on the outrigger of his dhow, mending the nets he used to catch baitfish for the game-boat skippers. He peered myopically at Mahmoud and nodded. Mahmoud said good day to him and the man returned to his nets. Then Mahmoud returned and smashed the old man over the head with a rock. The pain shooting up his arm was agonising, but somehow he dragged the body into the undergrowth and covered it with leaves. After a few moments, when he was sure there was nobody else about, he pushed the dhow away from the shore and rolled in. Like most kids who had grown up on the coast, he knew how to sail one of these flimsy vessels, and it did not take him long to hoist the sail. Soon he was out at sea, hugging the shoreline as he slowly headed north. With luck, he would make the estuary before sundown.

But his shoulder was throbbing with a vengeance now – and when he looked down he saw that a small spot of blood had leaked on to the grubby denim overalls.

34

It was fortunate indeed, Chipche thought, as he clicked off the small longwave radio, that, when Athi, son of Ngai, was not killing people, or lecturing them about his greatness, he chose to spend much of his day in solitary meditation in his baobab tree. He did not like to imagine how the living god would react if he knew what had happened at Shanzu that morning.

Three dead disciples, the apostate still very much alive — disaster did not adequately describe what he had just heard on the lunchtime news bulletin.

And the problem, of course, was compounded by the fact that there had been four disciples in the car.

He sighed and left the hut, tapping its wooden frame as though it were an old friend. It *was* an old friend. And, despite what it was now used for, it remained a place of tranquillity for Chipche; somewhere he could step away from the madness of the Headhunter's lair.

He relished these stolen minutes, when he could shed his ridiculous pantomime garb. Soon, hopefully, when this was all over, he could be himself again. Nobody could ever appreciate the pleasures of their own life until they had endured the misery of someone else's.

In front of the hut was Chipche's plantation. He grew gourds, fat green vine fruits that always reminded him of bloated bullfrogs. Despite their ugly appearance, they were the most versatile of plants. He made ornamental bowls and drinking vessels with the husks, distilled potent *chang'aa* from the succulent flesh and sold both for enough money to supplement the meagre wages he earned from his main job.

Or rather he did when he had time. He stared at the unkempt vegetation and sighed again. How nice it would be just to spend the rest of the day tying back vines and selecting the ripest fruit.

But there was no time.

One of the reasons the plantation had been chosen for its current purpose was its inaccessibility. The other was that it provided a clear cellphone network signal for the voice of Ngai, the Divider of the Universe and Lord of Nature himself.

Chipche sat down on a wooden stump by the door and pulled a pre-paid Nokia 5310 from a wicker bag at his feet. He turned it on, scrolled down to the only number in the memory, and pressed the send button.

After one ring the call was answered.

'Well?'

'There have been problems.'

'I know. I am watching the television news at this moment. It seems the apostate had a bodyguard. Most unfortunate.'

'What shall I tell *him*?'

'We must stick to what we planned. The time has come for the living god to meet his heavenly father.'

'And the slum rat that escaped?'

'Don't worry about him.'

'What if he is captured? What if he talks?'

'Then we must hope that he is not too off his head on your loopy juice to lead the police straight to the Headhunter's lair. I would hate our friend to die unnoticed. Which reminds me – make sure you cover the body. I don't want the vultures finding him first.'

Chipche smiled grimly. 'Then it's really over?'

'We've had a good run, old friend. Better than we could have ever hoped. But yes – it's over.'

'And Standage?'

'He will be up to his ears in security for the foreseeable future – but only until he finds out the Headhunter is dead. Then we will see.'

'You're not going to—'

'I haven't decided what I'm going to do. But don't worry, Chipche, I will see that he gets what's coming to him. For the moment let's just stick to the plan. Call me again when it is done.'

As he began dismantling the phone, Chipche considered the implications of the call. He had, of course, already prepared for the inevitable. Not all his witch-doctor potions were theatrical concoctions designed to bubble, or turn green, or fill suggestible minds with powerful hallucinogens; in his wicker bag he had several lethal doses of fast-acting poison that, when ingested, would speed the living god to the afterlife before he had finished the last drop.

He stood and stretched. Despite the fact that only three of the four men were dead, he was pleased with what he had achieved. But equally he was glad it was all over. It would be a relief to quit this ludicrous pantomime. *Witchdoctor!* What a joke! What he knew about black magic could be written on the back of a postage stamp. He was no more a witchdoctor than the frauds that sold charms and spouted gobbledegook for tourists at the tribal village. He was looking forward to collecting up all his gourds, wrapping them in his ceremonial robes, and throwing the whole lot off the cliff.

He opened the door of the hut and breathed in the heavy scent of the gourds. But as he stood there he felt something sharp digging into the skin below his jaw.

'So this is where I find you, Chipche,' the Headhunter said in a low, ominous voice from off to his right. 'Ngai was right.'

'Ngai, my lord?' he said, trying to keep the rising panic out of his voice.

'Oh yes – he spoke to me. Told me where to find you.'

Ngai spoke to him? My God, Chipche thought, the madness was even more advanced than he had suspected.

He raised his hands shakily to the sky. 'Praise be to the Divider of the Universe! Let us give thanks to the Lord of Nature! He has spoken to his son, to the god who lives among us pitiful mortals. Apostates quake with fear, for Athi is at one with his father.'

He fell forward and prostrated himself in the dirt, mainly to get away from the machete blade pressed against his neck. But when there was no reaction for several moments, he raised himself to his knees again and turned his head. The Headhunter was sitting cross-legged on the ground beside one of the swollen gourds, idly picking his fingernails with the blade of his machete. He was naked, but his skin was covered in thick daubs of red, white and black paint.

'Lord?'

'It is not as I imagined,' the killer said distantly. 'His voice, I mean. He has a very *gentle* voice. Musical, almost.' He looked up, and the whites of his eyes glowed against the scarlet swoosh of paint across his face. 'But then you know how he speaks, don't you, Chipche?'

'Yes, lord!' Chipche blurted, knowing that the longer he could keep the madman talking, the more chance he had of walking away from this encounter with his head still attached to his shoulders. 'Ngai speaks with the tenderness one expects of a father to his son.'

But then the Headhunter's eyes narrowed, and at that moment Chipche knew he was a dead man.

'You fool, Chipche. As if a mere mortal could *ever* hear the voice of Ngai.'

The Headhunter unfolded his spiderish limbs and moved towards him. Chipche fell on his face again and began wailing. Then a powerful hand grabbed his robe and lifted him into the air. He opened his eyes and stared into his face, close enough to taste his hot, faecal breath.

'Please, lord . . . '

'You are an apostate, witchdoctor. You are a blasphemer. You thought you could deceive Athi.' The Headhunter shook his head sadly. '*You were wrong.*'

35

The Sabaki river springs from the foothills of Mount Kilimanjaro and winds across the Tsavo plains for more than two hundred miles before spilling into the Indian Ocean just north of Malindi. And it was here, where the river widens into the vast expanse of the Sabaki estuary, that a stolen dhow containing the corpse of a young man was found mired in a mudbank early the next morning.

An autopsy would later conclude that the boy had bled to death from a bullet wound to the upper arm that had nicked the brachial artery, despite an amateurish effort to self-cauterise the wound. Subsequent investigations would fail to establish his name, or where he was from.

It seemed he had simply arrived into the world and then left it, violently, without anybody noticing.

V

36

During the flight from Nairobi he'd steeled himself for what was to come, and as the plane began its descent into Heathrow he'd even changed into a fleece top and a pair of warm trousers. It made no difference. He'd forgotten just how bone-chillingly cold it was in London in January. The instant he stepped from the cabin he was hit by a freezing blast that knifed through a hole in the air bridge connector and stopped him in his tracks. Later, as he stood in a freight hangar and watched Mac's coffin being loaded into a waiting hearse, he could not stop his teeth chattering.

Cold and wet. It was how he remembered London and after five years away the capital did not let him down. The grey suburbs bled into the raindrops on the window of the cab and the Asian driver's choice in Bangla music was drowned out by the swash of the wipers.

Shirley lived in a nondescript semi in Poplar, within sight of the building site that was going to be the 2012 Olympic park. She hadn't changed much, he thought as she opened the door. Short and mousey, with the sort of face that looked better without make-up. She would be in her mid-forties now. It scarcely seemed credible.

'Hello, Shirley,' he said, dropping his cases on the doorstep.

Her eyes were red. 'Thanks for bringing him home, Jake,' she said.

★

The boys were at her parents' in Canning Town. It was just as well, he thought. Last time he'd seen Simon and Danny they were a pair of skinny, giggling little sprogs. Now, if the photos on the mantelpiece were to be believed, they looked like Ronnie and Reggie Kray.

'Big lads,' he said. 'I remember when I used to take them for rides on the revolving teacups at Southend fair.'

'I know,' she said wistfully. 'It's a shame the way they grow.'

She cooked some sort of nondescript pasta dish and Jake ate it more out of duty than hunger. Afterwards they sat in the living room – Jake in an armchair, Shirley on the sofa – and watched *EastEnders*.

'The woman who played Pauline Fowler,' Shirley said. 'She died. Cancer.'

'Sorry to hear that,' he said. He sipped from a warm can of out-of-date bitter that Shirley said she kept in the cupboard for visitors. There were three more at his feet. 'I forgot to ask,' he said. 'Where's the service tomorrow?'

'Lewisham Crem.'

'That's a bit of a hike.'

'It's the only place I could get Father Murtagh pinned down.'

'Oh.' Father Murtagh had been the police chaplain when Jake and Mac were on the force. Mac, who was a fatally lapsed Catholic, always liked him because he fulfilled the cliché of the priest who was enamoured of the drink a little too much. 'Who's going?'

'I thought I'd keep it small,' she said.

At that moment he knew. *She was angry with Mac because he was dead.*

'Shirley, he was doing what he thought was best for you and the kids.'

She looked at him across the neat and tidy room. 'By

162

getting himself *killed*? Why, Jake? We were doing OK, the three of us. Me and the boys. We were getting by. He didn't have to …'

Her voice trailed away, but he knew what she had been going to say. On *EastEnders* a fight had broken out in the Queen Vic. *Some things never changed*, Jake thought.

'He loved you and the boys, Shirley,' he said. 'More than anything else in the world.'

'Well, he's got a funny fucking way of showing it,' she said.

'What did he tell you about the job?' he asked.

Shirley was on to her second bottle of Lambrusco. She was smoking cheap cigarettes and her eyelids looked heavy. 'Nothing,' she said.

'Come on, Shirley. He must have said something.'

'He told me nothing. Why should he?'

Because you were his wife. Because you were the mother of his sons. 'Well, you don't just piss off to Africa without saying something.'

She dropped a half-smoked butt into the empty wine bottle and lit another. 'He said he'd met this man in a pub. Offered him work, he said.'

'What man?'

'Just a man. One of the regulars.'

'Was his name Ryeguard? Colin Ryeguard?'

'For Christ's sake, Jake, you know what Mac was like! He never told me anything, even when we were married. You knew more about him than I ever did. He never let me in.'

'OK. It's all right.'

'He came round one Saturday morning,' she said. 'It was his weekend with the boys. He said he was going to be out of town for a while, but that he would be in touch and that the monthly payments would stay the same.' She looked at him with bloodshot eyes. 'He said it was good money. Short-term contract, something to do with security. I swear he never once mentioned Africa.'

She'd made up the spare bed. It was a single cot in a room the size of a broom cupboard. It was long past midnight when he got into it, but he knew it would be a lot longer before he slept. He was thinking about a man in a pub with an offer that Mac Bowden simply couldn't refuse – an offer that would end with him getting shot in the back by some punk kid.

Shirley was in the bathroom along the hall. She was drunk. He could hear her banging around. Cleaning her teeth now. Taking a long piss. He knew she and Mac had been divorced a while, but he didn't know if she was still coming to terms with it, or if she had another man on the go. He wasn't prepared to take the chance. Quietly he slipped out of the bed and moved it so that the foot was against the bedroom door. Then he got back under the flimsy blankets and listened to the London rain slamming against the panes.

37

'We called it the Syndicate,' Alec Standage said. 'But it was just four blokes who liked to play a bit of poker on a Saturday night, that's all.'

'Four of you,' the Inspector said. They were in the dank interview room of Mombasa central police station on Makadara Road. 'You, Gordon Gould, Eric Kitonga and Nathaniel Banda.'

'That's right.'

'How did you meet?'

'We liked to play cards, I guess. We would see each other down at the Old Town occasionally, we got talking, thought it might be a nice idea if we made it a regular thing.'

'Where did you play?'

'Eric had a private room near the docks. When I say private room, it was just a room, you know? There was no monkey business. No girls or anything like that.'

'Did you play for high stakes?'

'A few hundred dollars at most. Listen, we were just friends, that's all. We'd have a few drinks, play a few hands of Texas Hold 'Em, that's all. It was relaxation.'

'It never occurred to you to contact the police when you saw that the victims of this killer were also members of your Saturday-night poker school?'

Standage shook his head. 'It just never made any sense. Why would anyone want to kill us? Why would anyone want to kill *me*?'

'But you employed a personal security guard,' Jouma pointed out.

'I got him through an agency because some mad bastard was hitting my guests over the head. He *killed* some poor woman.'

'I know. One of my detectives has been investigating the case.'

'Well, as you can see, my security was compromised. I needed to fix it pronto.'

'But you ordered him to carry a gun.'

'So what? This is a dangerous place. Listen, Inspector, I know what it looks like, but I swear to you I never thought this Headhunter would come looking for me. Don't forget, I'm the new kid on the block round here. The others had been in Mombasa for years. For all I know they were involved in all sorts of scams.'

Jouma sat back in his chair and scratched his head. 'Did Paul Yomo ever play poker with you?'

'I keep telling you,' Standage whined. 'I've never heard of Paul Yomo. In fact, when I heard that the Headhunter had cut his head off I was relieved, because then I knew that it had nothing to do with me.'

Four men who liked to play cards on a Saturday night. Three of them murdered by the Headhunter, the fourth lucky to be alive. Jouma had been looking for a connection and there it was. Yet the killer's motives were still as baffling as ever, because there was still the small matter of Paul Yomo's murder to be resolved. Standage was adamant he was not part of the Syndicate – so what the devil did *he* have to do with anything?

Except, of course, for his hopeless gambling addiction.

At the sound of the counter bell, Judith Ogalo, office manager of the Exciting Prospects Credit Agency, looked up from a stack of paperwork; when she saw Jouma it was clear from her dismayed expression that she was not pleased to see him.

'Inspector,' she said with a smile only slightly less sincere than the loan shark from the slum. 'How can I help you?'

'One of my detectives has been looking through the loan application forms you kindly supplied to us,' Jouma said, getting briskly to the point. 'There was one in particular that I found rather puzzling – not to mention irregular.'

'Irregular?'

'Yes. On May 22 of last year the Exciting Prospects Credit Agency agreed to lend Paul Yomo the sum of two thousand dollars.'

'I could not possibly comment—'

'There is no mistake, Mrs Ogalo. Detective Constable Mwangi is very thorough. He crosschecked this against Mr Yomo's bank statement and confirmed that the money was transferred on May 25. Why didn't you tell me he came to you for a loan?'

She pursed her lips defensively. 'It is against company policy to discuss personal details of employees or clients.'

'Madam, I am conducting a murder inquiry,' Jouma reminded her sharply. 'I don't *care* about company policy.'

'Yes – Paul asked for a loan,' she said presently. 'He said he needed two thousand dollars to pay for an operation for his wife.'

'And?'

'He filled in an application form like anyone else.'

'*And?*'

'I recommended his request was approved,' Mrs Ogalo said. 'I had no reason to doubt him.' Her face fell. 'But once bitten, twice shy as they say.'

'What do you mean?'

'A few weeks later, I saw his wife on Digo Road. I know her through the church social society. And when I asked her about her operation she looked at me as if I was mad. That was why, when he applied for a second loan, I turned him down.'

'A second loan?'

'He said it was for a second-hand car.'

'How much did he want?'

'Fifteen hundred dollars.'

'When was this?'

'Two months ago.'

Really? So when he was supposedly paying off one loan with the religious exactitude of a man who had quit his ruinous gambling habit, Paul Yomo was in fact applying for another. Jouma wondered whether Tabitha knew about *that*.

'Did you tell him your reasons for refusing him?'

'Yes. And he admitted that he had lied to me.'

'Did he say why he needed the money?'

'He said his father had gambling debts,' Mrs Ogalo said with distaste.

'His father?'

'He owed some Arabs from the Old Town. Paul said they had threatened to kill him if he didn't pay up.'

Oh this was rich indeed! First his wife's operation and now a father who was dead.

'I would have fired him on the spot, but he begged me not to,' Mrs Ogalo continued. 'He told me that, as soon as his father had paid off his creditors, he was going to ensure he enrolled in a self-help group for gamblers.'

'And you believed him?'

'I believe that anyone is capable of redemption, Inspector.'

38

Shirley wasn't kidding when she'd said it was going to be a small service. There were just four of them – Jake, Shirley and the boys – taking up half a pew in the chapel at Lewisham Crematorium. As the curtains opened to reveal their father's plain pine coffin, Jake glanced across at Simon and Danny standing either side of their mother, staring at the coffin and not really knowing how to react as Shirley bowed her head and wept. They were young men now, awkward around grief. Awkward around *him*. He wasn't even sure they remembered him. It was as if Uncle Jake had never existed.

Father Murtagh, face red with booze and cold, turned up with seconds to spare and reeled out the necessary platitudes. Then the taped organ music crackled through the speakers and the coffin rolled towards the furnace. Everybody was relieved.

Afterwards they went to a pub round the corner. Smoking had been banned since he'd last been in a London pub, so Jake was mildly astonished to find that it was now accepted practice to stand outside with a cigarette clamped between two frozen fingers. The pavement was thick with discarded butts. They called it progress.

When he went back into the bar, the two boys were engrossed in the quiz machine and Shirley was talking to a silver-haired man in a Crombie overcoat who was leaning across the table to her. As Jake approached, he stood and nodded a curt acknowledgement. He was a dapper man in his fifties, wearing a black tie and a crisp white shirt. A sliver of bloodied tissue paper was stuck to one ruddy cheek where he'd cut himself shaving.

'Friend of yours?' Jake asked, sitting down beside her as the man left the pub with brisk strides.

'Friend of Mac's apparently,' Shirley said. 'Name of Henderson. Said he wanted to pass on his condolences.'

Jake frowned. The man was not a copper – at least not one that he knew from the old days. But then there was nothing to say that Mac wasn't allowed to have friends outside the force.

'They told me if I go back at four I can collect his ashes,' Shirley said. She was drinking white wine from a glass the size of a brandy goblet. 'Will you come with me, Jake?'

'Of course I will,' he said, although the clock behind the bar told him it was only quarter to one.

By the time they got to the towpath at Westferry with Mac's ashes, she was so pissed he had to hold on to her to make sure she didn't fall into the river.

'He always said this is where he wanted them scattered,' she said, tottering alarmingly as the oily black water rushed by. It was dark now and the skyscrapers of Canary Wharf were like candles against the night sky. 'It's where he was born, see.' She cackled. 'It's where we used to come courting, too.'

'*Mum*,' Simon said, mortified. The boys had come with them to collect their father's ashes and now stood shivering by the river, kicking their heels with hands in their pockets, looking like they'd rather be anywhere else than here right now.

'He wasn't just your father,' Shirley snapped. 'He was my husband an' all.'

The ashes were in a cardboard box, although Jake knew that in all probability it was dust from a dozen other incinerated corpses.

'Goodbye, darling, I always loved you,' Shirley said, and tipped the ashes over the guardrail. Then she slumped down on to her knees and was violently sick.

'Fuck's sake,' Simon said, and with Jake and Danny's help they picked her up off the ground.

'I told the taxi to wait,' Jake said. He reached into his pocket for a £20 note. 'Get her home and put her to bed.'

'What about you?' Simon asked.

'There's something I've got to do. I'll see you back at the house later. Any problems, you've got my mobile number.'

For a moment the boy looked uncertain. Then his resolve stiffened and he nodded.

'Good boy.'

Jake began walking along the towpath towards the lights of the city.

'Uncle Jake!' Simon called.

He turned and for a moment his eyes met those of Mac Bowden's boys. *Christ, they looked like him*, he thought with a stab of almost exquisite sadness.

'Yes, son?'

The eldest boy shook his head. 'Nothing.'

39

Paul Yomo's father might not have existed, but the Arabs to whom Paul owed money most certainly did. Jouma knew them well.

In the warren of the Old Town there were hundreds of gambling dens, each run by a multitude of unsavoury characters, all with one thing in common – they each paid a percentage of their takings to a pair of brothers from the Yemen called Tajik and Ali ul-Mraq.

Tajik and Ali had run their Mombasa empire for years, which was a testament to their skill as well as their staying power. Of course, gambling was an evil as old as mankind and would be around until the fires of hell consumed the world – but the Arabs at least brought a modicum of *order* to the Sodom and Gomorrah over which they presided. It was why Jouma secretly liked them. The ul-Mraqs were of his generation, one that believed in a code of hard work and mutual respect.

In turn, and for the same reason, Tajik and Ali liked and respected Jouma – which was why his unannounced arrival at their typically modest headquarters on the first floor of a former colonial administration building overlooking the square was greeted with a flurry of warm handshakes, embraces and offers of sweet tea and candy. It was only when he was installed in a leather armchair in the curtained-off annexe the brothers used for private business that Jouma could tell them why he was here.

'The *Syndicate*?' Tajik said. He was the elder of the ul-Mraq brothers by a couple of years, but in their formal *dishdashahs* and *shumag* headscarves there was little to tell them apart. Both were plump, with grey-flecked goatee beards and wet, red lips. 'The name is not familiar. Ali – check the database for the names.'

Ali was sitting by a laptop computer at a functional wooden desk in a corner of the room. He began tapping unconvincingly at its keyboard with one finger.

'We felt it was time to enter the world of modern technology in order to keep a record of clients who owe us money,' Tajik explained. 'Although Ali is so slow we would be better off going back to pencil and paper.'

'You have my sympathies, Tajik.' Jouma nodded heartily.

'These men were murdered, you say, Inspector?' Ali called across, without looking away from the computer screen, one finger poised above the keyboard.

'Three of them. Their heads were cut off.'

'I hope you do not think that *we* had anything to do with it,' Tajik said pleasantly but with obvious meaning.

'Of course not,' Jouma said, and he meant it. Ostentatious decapitation was not the brothers' style. He suspected – but doubted he could ever prove – that they preferred the discretion of chain weights and the vastness of the Indian Ocean.

'I'm afraid not,' Ali called from behind his computer screen. 'The names are not here.'

Jouma nodded. 'There is another name I would like you to check.'

'I am at your service, Inspector.'

'Yomo. Paul Yomo.'

The brothers exchanged glances across the room.

'You have heard of him?' Jouma said.

'We have heard of him,' Tajik replied meaningfully.

'Yomo. Here he is,' Ali announced presently. 'Last May he defaulted on repayment of a two-thousand-dollar

173

marker at the baccarat table. We had to have strong words with him, but he paid it back in full.'

The loan for his wife's operation, Jouma thought.

'But according to our records it seems his bad luck continued.'

'Don't tell me,' Jouma said, thinking back to his conversation with Judith Ogalo and the loan for the second-hand car she had turned down two months ago. 'He owes fifteen hundred dollars.'

Ali shook his head and made tutting noises. 'Fifteen hundred dollars would be manageable, I think. But Mr Yomo is on our red list.'

'Your *red list*?'

'People who owe more than ten thousand dollars,' Tajik explained.

Jouma sat up in his chair. 'Paul Yomo owed you *ten thousand dollars*?' It was a vast sum, more than most Kenyans could hope to earn in five years.

'More than that,' Ali said. 'He had run up accumulated debts of . . . *twelve* thousand dollars.'

So the fifteen hundred was not to clear a loan – it was for a monthly repayment! Did Tabitha have any idea that her husband owed so much money at the card tables? He could not believe it. She had seemed so happy that she had paid off that last twenty-five dollars to the loan shark in the Kingorani slum, and that her dead husband was no longer in debt.

'What systems do you have in place for defaulters?' he asked.

'We do not behead them,' Tajik said pointedly.

'We like to remind them of their repayment obligations,' Ali said carefully. 'One of our financial advisers went to see Mr Yomo recently about his account.'

Jouma could imagine how that meeting must have gone. 'Recently, you say? How recently?'

174

'December 20.'

My God – what a mess! Hopelessly in debt, and with the Arabs putting the frighteners on him, Paul was desperately trying to raise money. Perhaps he thought that securing a loan of fifteen hundred dollars would keep the wolves from the door until he could win the twelve thousand back at the baccarat table. But Judith Ogalo had turned him down. And he couldn't go to Davey Cav for another loan, because Tabitha knew about his debt there and how much was owed.

'Where would a man like Paul Yomo turn if he needed money fast? If orthodox channels were blocked to him.'

The brothers exchanged glances.

'Unsecured?' Ali said. 'Unlimited interest?'

'Let's assume he was desperate.'

'Desperate enough to risk the wellbeing of his family should he fail to make a repayment?'

'Possibly.'

'There is only one person I can think of who would consider such a loan,' Tajik said, and he could not have looked more disgusted if Jouma had trailed shit into their office on his shoes.

40

According to Shirley, since he'd moved out to the bedsit just off the Commercial Road, Mac spent most of his time drinking in a pub called the Tanner's Arms. With its shit-brown walls, sticky carpets, faded banquette seats and Formica-topped tables it was a good place for a divorced ex-copper to drown his sorrows.

There were a couple of old men watching a football match on a portable telly resting on a high ledge in one corner of the bar. The barman had lank hair and stained, bitten fingers. Jake ordered a pint of London Pride and, while his drink was being pulled, he asked him a couple of questions. Then he took his pint and went and sat in an unobtrusive corner to watch the football.

Half an hour later, with the match looking for all the world like it was heading for a goalless draw, the door opened and a man walked in. Jake recognised the Crombie overcoat and the white hair. He glanced across at the barman who gave him the most blatant nod imaginable.

'It's Mr Henderson, isn't it?' Jake asked, springing from his seat to intercept the man as he reached the bar. 'Can I get you a drink?'

The man stared at him, blinking as he tried to put a name to a face. 'Do I know you?' he said.

'My name is Jake Moore. I was a friend of Mac Bowden's. I think I saw you briefly this afternoon? In the pub near the crematorium?'

Henderson remembered all right, but he remained on edge.

'I heard Mac used to drink in here,' Jake said. 'Thought I'd pop in, just for old times' sake. Adam here——' he gestured at the barman '——said you and him used to drink together.'

'He did, did he?' Henderson said, shooting an accusatory glance at the barman.

Jake raised his hands. 'Listen, I don't want to intrude on your evening. Only Africa's a long way to come for a pint of Pride and I could do with a bit of company myself after today.'

Henderson's pale eyes suddenly showed interest. 'What did you say your name was?'

'Jake. Jake Moore.'

'Then I'll have a large Scotch if you're buying.'

After pouring a couple more large Scotches down Henderson's neck, Jake knew his suspicions were right. The old man *was* the contact Mac had met about the security job in Mombasa. Twenty years ago he'd been a desk sergeant at Whitechapel nick. It seemed old coppers never died, they just became pimps for security companies. As he tipped another double down his neck, Henderson admitted as much.

'I suppose I feel a bit guilty about what happened to him,' he said, his eyes glassy now. 'Almost like it was me what got him killed. Does that make sense?'

'You can't go blaming yourself, Arthur,' Jake said, patting Henderson's hand sympathetically. 'Mac was a big boy. He knew the risks.'

'He said he was short of money, what with his ex-wife and the kids and that house over Poplar way. He never got his pension, see. Not after they kicked him off the force like that. Said he'd even applied for a job labouring at the Olympic park but that they was only taking on Eastern Europeans as they was cheaper.' He grabbed

Jake's arm and looked at him beseechingly. 'I was trying to do him a *favour*, that's all.'

''Course you were, Arthur,' Jake said, thinking that this was too easy, that he'd really wanted to take the old prick outside and kick the story out of him. But now that he had started unburdening himself, Henderson would not stop. And, strangely, Jake was starting to feel sorry for him. After all, he was only trying to help a fellow copper in need. The old man hadn't pulled the trigger.

'I told him I'd heard of this feller that had been putting the word around that he was looking to recruit men,' Henderson said. He pulled a laminated card from his wallet and waved it under Jake's nose. 'Honorary Secretary, East End Chapter of the National Association of Retired Police Officers,' he said with a wink. 'I get to hear things.'

'Was his name Ryeguard?'

'Dunno. I never heard the feller's name. All I was given was an address in Wardour Street. Above some Greek café. Mac said it was a small world, 'cos he knew which one it was.'

Jake did too. So did everyone who'd worked Flying Squad back in the day. He sipped his pint and watched the last knockings of the football match. Beside him, Henderson was having great difficulty finding his mouth with his whisky glass.

The barman called last orders. Jake went to the bar and bought another double. The match had finished and a panel of experts were analysing what little action there had been.

'You live far from here, Arthur?'

'Pedley Street. Just round the corner.'

'Come on then, old son,' Jake said. 'Sup up and I'll walk you home. The black ice is lethal out there tonight.'

41

The loan shark's name was Chow Fat and he ran a small fleet of short-haul freighters out of a warehouse next to the dhow harbour. The Korean claimed moneylending was a sideline, but it was nevertheless one that he took very seriously. If you couldn't keep up with the weekly repayments on your loan, there was no point complaining about the seventy per cent interest because Chow Fat didn't care. He had your signature on a legally binding contract and his financial advisers *would* break your arms if you didn't pay up. Then they would break your legs, take your property, threaten your family and, if all else failed, kill you. A man had to be pretty desperate to borrow money from Chow Fat. Chow Fat was where you went when there was nowhere else to go.

'Yes, he was here,' Chow Fat said. 'Just before Christmas. He wanted six thousand dollars in a hurry.'

'Did you give it to him?'

'No.'

Another refusal. 'Why?' Jouma asked. 'At seventy per cent interest you stood to make almost four thousand dollars on the loan.'

'Put yourself in my shoes, Inspector,' Chow Fat said.

Jouma glanced under the table at a pair of mouldy deck shoes and shuddered. The ul-Mraq brothers were modest about their vast wealth, but at least they presented themselves with a modicum of panache. Chow Fat, who was probably just as rich, appeared to have purchased his wardrobe from the auction of dead people's possessions held each month at Mombasa Hospital.

'I am a businessman, Inspector,' the Korean said. His fingers were like maggots. As he spoke he used them to tease a mop of tightly permed and lavishly oiled hair. 'I have to weigh profit against risk. He still owed me money from the last time.'

Jouma's heart sank. 'The last time?'

'He came to me six months ago. He needed three thousand dollars. Said he wanted to invest in property in Nyali – but I asked around. Turned out he had lost big at baccarat. Some nasty people were going to hurt him bad.'

Six months ago? Just how much money did Paul Yomo owe?

'But you lent him the money?'

Chow Fat nodded. 'At the time he seemed good for it. He had a job. An apartment in Kwakiziwi.'

'But he defaulted on the payments.'

'Just once. Nobody defaults twice. Not when they have a pretty young wife and a young stepson.'

Jouma did not doubt it. 'He has paid you back now?'

'I took his car,' the Korean said. 'That remov ed some of the outstanding debt, but it was a heap of shit. He still owes me a thousand dollars. If you see him you may care to remind him that a payment is due.'

'He is dead,' Jouma told him. 'Murdered.'

Chow Fat considered this news for a moment then shrugged. 'No matter. He has possessions. His wife has possessions.'

'You will leave his wife alone, Mr Chow,' Jouma warned him.

'He signed a contract in which he agreed to repay his loan whatever the circumstances,' the Korean reminded him. 'It remains valid even in the event of his death.'

'You are such a bloodsucker that you would impoverish a grieving widow for the sins of her dead husband?'

'Of course,' Chow Fat said. 'I am not a charity, Inspector. How else am I supposed to make a living?'

42

Spiro's Coffee Bar was one of the few businesses Jake recognised as he turned off Oxford Street and walked down Wardour Street the next morning. The rest had either changed hands or, in keeping with the times, gone bust. Indeed, it was reassuring to see that Spiro appeared untroubled by the global financial meltdown. There were a few white filaments in his moustache, but his belly was still enormous and his smile as wide as ever. But then the bottom was never likely to drop out of the coffee and baklava market the way it had from the banking sector.

'Sure I rented out the room, and it was all legal, above board,' he said.

'Who to?'

'Some little guy. Lawyer.'

'Lawyer?'

Spiro straightened and folded his arms across his bulging stomach and stared at Jake through narrowed eyes. 'I thought you said you weren't a cop no more, Jake.'

'I'm not.'

'You don't look like a cop. What's with the suntan? When you walked into my café today I thought you were a queer boy.'

The Greek roared with laughter and slammed the counter so hard with the flat of his hand that the plate glass shop front rattled.

'Do me a favour, Spiro, and just pretend I am still a policeman,' Jake sighed. 'Show me the room.'

★

In the days when Soho was a den of strip joints and porn theatres, the room above Spiro's café had been used as a shilling-a-time knocking shop by the neighbourhood hookers. These days Spiro rented it out as temporary office and storage space, but it was still accessed by a nondescript door in a seedy alleyway.

It was here that Mac Bowden had been recruited a month before he was murdered in Mombasa.

'The little guy, he paid a month's rent up front,' Spiro confirmed. 'In cash.' The corpulent Greek was still wheezing from climbing the steep flight of wooden steps up to the room. 'But he only used it two, maybe three days, I guess.'

The room consisted of a desk and two chairs. The floor was covered in grey carpet tiles. A single grimy window overlooked the street.

'I don't suppose this lawyer left a forwarding address?' Jake said hopefully.

Spiro beamed. 'Maybe he leave me a business card!'

It sounded unlikely. This lawyer, if indeed that was what he was, sounded like the type who preferred not to advertise his services.

But the Greek duly reached into his back pocket and produced an embossed business card. 'I tell him I'm thinking of buying my brother-in-law out of the business. I tell him it could get messy.'

Jake grinned. If there was one thing guaranteed to compromise a bent lawyer's discretion, it was the possibility of more filthy lucre. He reached out for the card, but Spiro snatched it away.

'Maybe now you've got a suntan you can afford to pay Spiro for his time,' he said coquettishly.

Jake sighed and reached for his wallet. His flying visit to London was starting to cost him a fortune.

Bendix, Ryeguard & Co was situated on the third floor of

an office block near Tottenham Court Road. The name suggested high-class criminal lawyers – but the words 'Compensation and Personal Injury Specialists' on the cheap enamel sign on the door indicated they were just like any other firm of ambulance-chasers.

Except they also had a lucrative little sideline in the freelance security trade.

Spiro had described the lawyer who had given him the business card as a little guy. For once the Greek had been guilty of understatement, because as far as Jake could see Colin Ryeguard was a fully-fledged dwarf. He was probably forty, and came across as immaculately presented and businesslike. But, perched on the edge of his leather-effect executive office chair, Jake couldn't help thinking he still looked like a child who had been allowed to go to work with his dad for the day.

'How can I help you, Mr Moore?' Ryeguard said.

'I'm here on behalf of a friend of mine. Name of Bowden. Mac Bowden. I understand you were able to put some work his way. Security work, to be precise. In Kenya.'

Ryeguard laced his stubby fingers on the desk. 'What makes you think that?'

'You pick up things when you keep your ear to the ground, Mr Ryeguard.'

The lawyer thought for a moment. Then he shrugged. 'We do have clients who sometimes require security operatives, that's correct. What did you say your friend's name was?'

'Mac Bowden. Ex-Flying Squad. You got him a consultancy job with a fellow named Standage at a hotel near Mombasa. Twenty grand for a month's work, I understand.'

'Well, we would never discuss our clients or our freelance operatives,' Ryeguard said. 'And we would certainly never discuss our fees. So I really don't see how I can help you.'

184

'Mac's dead. Killed in the line of duty, you might say.'

Ryeguard blinked with surprise, but Jake knew fine well that the lawyer knew all about Mac's death. Even if he hadn't been an employee, his murder had been all over the news channels and the papers. 'I'm sorry to hear that, Mr Moore.'

'Yeah. I was pretty cut up about it, too. And so were his ex-wife and his two boys. You see, Mac had earmarked most of that twenty grand for them.'

'Really.'

'Yes. And you know something? The last words he said to me – the last words he said to *anyone* as a matter of fact – were these: he said, "Make sure Shirley and the boys are all right, Jake." So the reason I'm here, Mr Ryeguard – apart from bringing my mate's body back to England – is just to confirm that you will be honouring his contract and that the twenty thousand will be transferred into his bank account.'

At this, Ryeguard shifted slightly in his seat. 'Like I say, Mr Moore, I am not at liberty to—'

'No, I appreciate you're not,' Jake interrupted. His gaze was steely. 'But you will also appreciate my position.'

'Your position?'

'I'm godfather to Mac's boys. It's my duty to see they don't go short of anything. I'm also an ex-copper myself, which is how I know that shyster operations like yours have a habit of ripping off their operatives. So I would be very angry if I thought that my old pal Mac wasn't getting what he was due. In fact, if that money isn't in his account within the next seven days, then I might even consider mentioning your little operation to my friends in the Fraud Squad.'

'Are you threatening me, Mr Moore?'

Jake smiled. 'Yes,' he said. 'As a matter of fact I am.'

★

'Do you have to go back so soon, Jake?' Shirley said. She was standing in the doorway of the spare room watching him pack.

'There's nothing for me in London any more, Shirl,' he said without turning. 'And I've got a business to run.'

'Of course. Well – thanks for everything.'

Now he looked at her. 'Mac saved my life,' he said. 'You and him, you were like family to me.' He picked up a shirt and started to fold it. 'Will you be all right?'

She nodded glumly. 'I've still got the boys,' she said.

'They're good kids.' He nodded. 'They'll look after you.'

'I know.' Her eyes were beginning to fill with tears. 'Oh, Jake – I don't half miss him.'

He held her. 'Me too, Shirley. Me too.'

Two hours later, a taxi dropped Jake off at Terminal Five check-in at Heathrow. Three hours after that British Airways flight 382 to Nairobi took off. Jake sat by the window and watched London briefly stretched out like a cobweb beneath him. Then they hit low grey cloud and the city was obliterated.

After a while, a stewardess came round and asked him if he wanted a drink. Jake took a whisky and drank it neat while he watched the computerised icon of the plane inch its way south on the TV screen in the seat-back in front of him. Soon they were over southern Europe and the British Isles were no longer visible.

He had done what he had come to do. Mac's money was secure, and so were his ex-wife and kids.

But the job was only half finished. Because back in Africa there was a man who had promised to pay his friend twenty grand to protect his life. Mac had kept his side of the bargain – now Jake was going to make sure Alec Standage kept his.

186

VI

43

Sometime around four a.m., a fishing dhow operating three miles off the coast, south-east of Mombasa near Funzi Island, had snagged something unusual in its lines. It was heavy, about five feet long, and wrapped in plastic sheeting secured with blue plastic cord. The five men on the boat, villagers from the south shore near Mwachema Bay, thought at first it might be a drugs shipment. If so, this was excellent news. They were honest men and they knew that the Mombasa coastguard paid handsome rewards for anyone who happened to find such shipments and hand them in. And, while they knew little about drugs, they realised that a haul this large would surely be worth a small fortune.

They were disappointed, therefore, to open the package to find it contained a headless human corpse.

For the best part of an hour, as they bobbed in the ocean, the men argued about what to do. When they had finished, two were in favour of throwing the body overboard, and two wanted to take it to Mombasa to see if the coastguard would be interested in paying them a reward. That meant the casting vote was left with the skipper. He had watched proceedings with amused interest, because he was much older than his four teenage crew and therefore knew many things that they did not. He knew, for example, that it was not uncommon to hook human body parts from the ocean. Close to the fishing ground where they were currently positioned there was a vast submarine shelf, where the

189

continent of Africa abruptly dropped away into the Indian Ocean basin five miles below. Consequently, it was a popular spot to dump murder victims. But, unless you were an experienced fisherman like the dhow skipper, you would not know about the strong east-to-west current that had a habit of snatching debris dropped from the surface and sweeping it back from the precipice and into shallower waters.

The skipper had been fishing here for more than twenty years, and in that time he had recovered at least seven dead bodies in various forms of mutilation. Each time he had dutifully returned them to Mombasa, where they had come from, and each time he had received a written commendation from the chief of police and a bounty of sixty thousand shillings from the public purse.

So it was that shortly before dawn the dhow and its cargo berthed at the Old Town docks. The police were called, and thirty minutes later an experienced detective sergeant from Mombasa CID arrived to examine the remains.

They had been placed respectfully in a pallet of fish ice in the shade of the loading shed, and a uniformed officer was standing guard. The DS told the officer to disperse the crowd of fascinated stevedores who had gathered at the scene and, when they were gone, bent over the catch to examine it more closely.

The wrapping appeared to be standard heavy-duty plastic sheeting, the sort that would be found on building sites. It was secured with two metre-long lengths of spiralled, blue polyurethane tubing. The lengths had been wrapped around the sheeting and then tied together in a knot.

The corpse was African in origin, although the dark skin had lightened and buckled slightly with decomposition and exposure to salt water. Its head had been removed cleanly, though its limbs were still attached. The male genitals were also still intact, although shrivelled. There was what appeared to be a mark – a dimple perhaps – just above the left nipple.

'I take it you called an ambulance?' the DS said to the uniformed officer.

'Of course, sir.'

The detective, who was wearing a pair of the new standard-issue white rubber gloves, carefully picked up the lengths of plastic cord, which had now compressed to a third of their size and coiled into manageable spirals, and carefully eased them into an evidence bag. Then, with the scene secured to his satisfaction, he returned to the squad room at Mama Ngina Drive where he wrote up a report on one of the squad room's two computers. He read it through diligently, and amended the mistakes highlighted by spell checker. Then he saved the document, called up the relevant folder and dropped in the report.

His job done, the detective finished his coffee and then idled away the rest of the morning completing the crossword in the newspaper before going for his lunch.

44

Like his father before him, Brigadier Charles Wako Chatme had been appointed commander of Mtongwe base, the primary naval dockyard situated south of Mombasa island – but this great honour was merely the crowning glory of a career that had begun thirty years earlier as an officer cadet at the Royal Naval College in Dartmouth, England. During that time he had served with great distinction both at sea and on land and, later this year, when he finally stood down, he would do so as the recipient of the Kenyatta Commemorative Medal, the Presidential Installation Medal and the Ten Great Years of Nyayo Era Medal, as well as being awarded the Order of the Golden Heart and Chief of the Order of the Burning Spear.

The Brigadier's life outside the navy had been equally starry. He had always struck a dashing figure. The gossip columns told of a string of glamorous women on his arm, and it was almost inevitable that one of them should be the beautiful Ellen Riordan, only daughter of one of Nairobi's wealthiest ex-pat landowners. It was testament to the esteem in which Charles Wako Chatme was held on all sides of the racial divide that, when they married in 1974, the union of a black man to a white woman should have attracted so little negative comment.

Their meeting was set for two o'clock sharp, and Jouma knew that it would not do to be late. He was met at the guard post and escorted by a uniformed rating to

192

a well-appointed office on the first floor of a block overlooking the dockyard and the wharves. The spacious office benefited from a view over the bay towards the airport. A small, grey-painted naval ship was moored to the wharf outside. Its top-heavy superstructure bristled with antennae and the barrel of a large gun jutted from a domed turret in front of the bridge section. The name on the bow was *KNS Shupavu*.

The Brigadier sat at a polished oak desk in a stiff-backed leather chair. He was wearing a crisp white shirt with epaulettes. He was talking to another officer, a tall, sandy-haired white man in his thirties. He waved Jouma in and pointed to a chair on the other side of the room. Jouma sat obediently while the two naval men continued their conversation.

'I'm aiming to complete first hull inspection this afternoon, sir,' the younger man said. 'The men are just running through a few last-minute equipment checks.'

'Very good, very good. And your deep-water training?'

'Very successful, sir.'

He glanced at Jouma, at which point the Brigadier grudgingly saw fit to introduce him as Colonel Robert Sutherland, officer in charge of the navy's Clearance Diving Unit.

'And this is Jouma. Mombasa CID.' The contempt dripped from his voice.

Sutherland's handshake was firm but cursory.

Their business concluded, the Brigadier ushered Sutherland to the door. 'We're having a few people round for drinks this evening, Robert,' he said. 'Ellen wanted to know if you and Clara were free to join us.'

'Be delighted, sir.'

'Good – seven o'clock it is.' He lowered his voice conspiratorially. 'I shall apologise in advance for the grief you'll get from Ellen. She's got it in her head that your lives will not be complete without the patter of little footsteps.'

'Suits me, sir.' Sutherland smiled. 'It's Clara who's the career girl.'

The Brigadier grunted. 'In the Mayor's office? I don't call working for that perfumed fool a career.'

While this exchange was going on, Jouma was gazing around the office. The walls were covered in citations and certificates, memorabilia and mementos. On the far wall was a large oil painting of the Brigadier as a much younger man and, in a small glass cabinet next to the chair where he now sat, a small ornamental pistol in an open presentation box.

'It was presented to me by Rear Admiral Kimichi of the Japanese Maritime Self-Defence Force during a visit to Mombasa of the JDS *Kashima* in 1995,' the Brigadier said, returning to his desk. 'Do you know anything about firearms, Inspector?'

'Nothing at all.'

'The Kolibri Car Pistol. Patented in 1910 by an Austrian watchmaker named Franz Pfannl. It fires only specially made 2mm bullets. Magnificent workmanship, but next to useless as a weapon. It was used mainly for self-defence. They haven't been in production since 1938.'

The Brigadier stared at it wistfully, then snapped back to attention. 'You wanted to see me? I must warn you I have a meeting of the junior officers in twenty minutes – and it will take me ten to walk to the mess.'

'Thank you for your time. I did not realise that Mtongwe was such a big place.'

'Because it is small most Kenyans don't realise their country has a functioning navy,' the Brigadier said sharply. 'I find these people have no appreciation of the perilous nature of their own existence. In the past I have been tempted to cease all inshore patrols, just to see how many freighters would be kidnapped by Somali pirates before they realised the importance of our work.'

'I sincerely hope you never do.'

'So. Have you caught Paul's murderer?'

'Not yet, sir.'

'Are you any *closer* to catching Paul's murderer?'

'Our investigations are ongoing.'

'Pah! And in the meantime people are dropping like flies.'

'Did you know Paul was nearly twenty thousand dollars in debt to Old Town gambling syndicates, Brigadier?'

It was a long time before the Brigadier spoke. 'What are you talking about?'

'Cards mainly. Poker, baccarat – any table he could raise the stake to get a game. Your daughter knew he had a problem, but he convinced her he had seen the error of his ways. In reality, he was getting further and further into debt. Eventually, just before Christmas, he found himself in the position where not even Mombasa's most pernicious loanshark would bail him out. I wonder, Brigadier – did he ask *you* for money?'

Beneath their heavy brows, the Brigadier's eyes seemed ready to pop out of their sockets. 'I don't know what you are trying to insinuate, Jouma—'

'I am simply asking a straightforward question: did Paul ask you for money?'

'No!'

'Did you know about his gambling addiction?'

'No, I did not! And what has this got to do with his murder?'

Jouma shrugged. 'Possibly nothing. Possibly everything. I am just trying to piece together Paul's last movements, what was going through his mind in those last hours. He was a desperate man, and desperate men can sometimes do things that can get them killed. If you weren't his last hope, Brigadier, then I need to find out who was.'

The Brigadier raised himself imperiously from behind his desk. 'Well, you won't find your answers here, damn it. And I think you should get the hell off my base before I have you marched off.'

As he drove away from the base, the Brigadier's indignation still ringing in his ears, it struck Jouma that the old man was right: there was no way Paul would have gone to his in-laws for money. On the contrary, a man who had survived for so long by living an elaborate lie would do everything he possibly could to maintain the charade. Normality was the façade behind which every addict hid.

No, Paul was desperate – but even if Chow Fat had turned him down there was always *someone* with money to lend. You just had to know where to look.

The question was, *where*?

The more he thought about it, the more he was convinced Alec Standage was lying. Even if Paul was not a member of the Syndicate, the fact that he was an Old Town gambler who had ended up decapitated was simply too much of a coincidence.

Had he gone to *them* for money?

The bank accounts of Gould, Kitonga, Banda and Standage showed no evidence of unexplained wealth. But that did not mean they didn't have their loot stashed somewhere else. After all, even their own wives had no idea that their husbands knew each other. The Syndicate, it seemed, was a secret all four men kept close to their chests.

Money. That was the key to this mystery. Money won, money lost, money owed. Somewhere along the line things had gone catastrophically wrong and it had cost four men their lives.

All of which made Jouma suspect that there was more to the Headhunter than met the eye. Suddenly there was a logic to the murders, and it was rooted not in the mind of a crazed serial killer but in something far more mundane.

The answer was almost close enough to touch — and yet it was still agonisingly out of reach.

As he pulled on to Mama Ngina Drive and indicated to turn into the police compound, Jouma saw a familiar figure loitering at the main gate. When he wound down his window Davey Cav, the Kingorani loan shark, beamed at him from beneath the peak of his baseball cap.

'Inspector Jouma!' he said, his tone slightly reproving. 'I lost your card, so I thought I would come and see you in person.'

'It's nice to see you, Mr Cav. But another time, perhaps. I am rather busy at the moment.'

'Time is money, Inspector,' Cav said. 'I too have been busy on your behalf, like you asked me to.'

'Really?'

'Really. Billy Kapchanga? Remember?'

It took Jouma a moment to register what Cav was talking about. Billy Kapchanga — the father of Jonas Yomo.

'You have found him?'

'Have I found him! You're talking to Davey Cav, Inspector Jouma. I live to serve.'

'I'm sure your many debtors would say otherwise. Where is he?'

Cav grinned, slipping smoothly round to the passenger door. 'I'll even take you there, Inspector,' he said.

45

After the storm, dead calm. It was less than a week since the attempted abduction of Alec Standage had reignited the Headhunter story, but already Katherine Rapuro could recognise the signs of impending doldrums ahead. Soon Larry Gazemba would be on her back again, and this time he wouldn't put up with stories about candlelit vigils. Last time she had weaselled her way out of trouble by writing a feature on famous Kenyan serial killers of the past fifty years. This time her news editor was unlikely to be so accommodating. That morning, as she stared in despair at her empty notebook, she found herself starting to think about the Mayor's manila envelope again – which was always a bad sign.

So it was that, later that day, Katherine found herself manoeuvring her company Datsun along a pot-holed road towards a godforsaken boatyard next to a mosquito-laden creek in the middle of fucking nowhere. The man she hoped to interview was called Jake Moore. He was a thirty-five-year-old Englishman who co-owned a boat business named Britannia Fishing Trips Ltd, and who coincidentally happened to be the best friend of the hero bodyguard from the Sandpiper Hotel. If he was prepared to talk it would make a great human-interest piece – especially as she understood he had just got back from returning Mac Bowden's body to his wife and kids in London.

If not – well, it was back to the drawing board and the lash of Larry Gazemba's tongue.

She came round a bend and was confronted by an unprepossessing building overlooking a shallow inlet with a wooden jetty. She parked up and went in through an open door into a dark, cool workshop that stank of diesel oil. In the far corner was an office. There was a man in the office, thin and tall and with a beaky nose jutting from under the bill of a baseball cap. He was slumped at a desk with his feet up. His eyes were closed and he was snoring gently.

'Excuse me.'

Harry opened one glassy eye. 'Yes?'

'I'm looking for Jake Moore.'

'He ain't here.'

'Where is he?'

'Who wants to know?'

Katherine introduced herself and flashed her laminated press card. Harry seemed unimpressed.

'You're wasting your time, my dear,' he said.

'And you are?'

'You're wasting your time there as well.'

He shut his eye and pulled the peak of the cap down over his face.

Katherine cursed under her breath and went back outside. *Bloody fishermen!* They were all the same. Sour-faced, suspicious, booze-fuelled misanthropes the lot of them. She stomped across to her car. Well, if that was how they were going to play it, then she was going to get more than a little creative with her reporting. See how Britannia Fishing Trips Ltd liked having their boatyard described as a festering eyesore. See how many potential customers *that* put off.

She started the engine, but as she did so she saw a boat making its way upriver towards the inlet. It was a thirty-footer, and its white paint gleamed in the sunlight. She watched it swing round towards a mooring post, and one of the two men on board expertly loop a length of rope around it. He was thick-set and powerful-looking, with short-cropped hair and a craggy face that had clearly been exposed to the sun and the sea.

And, although she had never seen Jake Moore, Katherine knew instinctively that she had found her man.

Terrified. Five years Jake had skippered *Yellowfin*, and yet the prospect of taking his boat out again had absolutely terrified him. And the worst part of it was that he didn't know why. Was it because the last time he'd been out on the open water someone had tried to kill him? No – he refused to believe any of that post-traumatic stress disorder shit that Indira Goti had spun him. Nor did he hold much truck with Harry's typically sanguine theory that he had been ashore so long he had forgotten how the hell to pilot a thirty-footer.

No, when it came to crises of confidence, Jake's world was firmly sketched in black and white. You just got back in the saddle, pretended nothing had happened, and made sure nobody suspected a thing.

Even so, he hadn't reckoned on taking her out so soon. No, he'd flown back into Mombasa intent on confronting Alec Standage about the money he owed Mac. But the hotel manager was still being questioned by the police and was therefore out of bounds. So it was that Jake's rehabilitation as a fishing-boat skipper began the day after his return from London, hands shaking as he gripped *Yellowfin*'s throttles and guided her out of Flamingo Creek into the vastness of the Indian Ocean.

Below him in the cockpit was Ralph Philliskirk, occupying himself with the rigger booms and with not getting in Jake's way. Sammy the bait boy, overjoyed to see his boss back, was down by the stern rail, gutting baitfish like they were going out of fashion, even though they weren't going anywhere except out there, beyond the horizon, where he could put his boat through her paces and get to know her again.

And, two hours later, when they came back into the mouth of creek, Jake was exhausted but exhilarated; and his hands were steady as a rock as he piloted the thirty-footer through the navigation channel and back to the boatyard.

'Looks like you won't be needing me any more, Jake, old man,' Harry's brother said as they chugged upriver towards the yard. He brought a cold Tusker to his lips and guzzled it gratefully.

'Listen – you're welcome to stay for a while,' Jake told him – which was something he never thought he'd hear himself say. 'Harry and I really owe you one.'

Ralph smiled. 'You know something? I couldn't think of anything better. You've got it good here, Jake. And, although I'd never say it to his face, I'm proud of what you and Harry have achieved. And bloody envious. But this is your show. I'd soon be like a spare prick at a wedding – and, to be honest with you, I'd be sorely tempted to push you under a bus just so I could get behind the wheel again.'

'What will you do?'

'I've got business that needs my attention back in England. But I shall return to the dank, drizzly shores of Blighty with a song in my heart – and hopefully more of a suntan than when I left.'

'Well, take it from me, Ralphie – Blighty's dank and drizzly all right. And fucking cold, so wrap up warm.'

They slowed to let Sammy dive for Jalawi village, then idled the remaining half-mile to the boatyard, enjoying the late-afternoon sunshine and the raucous screeching of the birds and monkeys in the trees.

'Tell you what, Ralph,' Jake said. 'Why don't you bring her in? Just for old times' sake?'

Ralph beamed at him. 'It would be an honour, skipper.'

It was only when they were back on dry land that Jake discovered he had a visitor.

46

Billy Kapchanga played bongos with a cabaret band called Los Cinco Julios at a roadhouse forty miles west of Mombasa on the road to Nairobi. He was a handsome Tanzanian in his late thirties with a bald head, a well-groomed goatee beard and an earring made from a polished shark's tooth.

'Tabs? Sure I remember Tabs,' he said, sipping at an iced tea in the gloomy bar. 'How is she?'

'She's been better,' Jouma said.

'Yeah – I read that shit about what happened to her husband. That was bad. They say it was that serial killer who got him. Can you imagine that?'

'How did you meet?'

'I had a residency at a club in the Old Town. The Kitty-Kat – you heard of it? Long gone now, man. Anyway, Tabs used to come down some nights to watch us play. One night we got talking after a show, and, well, she was a cute kid. We got along fine.'

'You got her pregnant, Mr Kapchanga.'

Kapchanga shrugged. 'We all make mistakes. But hey – it wasn't a one-night stand. We'd been together for a couple of months. We were an *item*. Billy and Tabs. You ask anyone. We were in love, man.'

'Tabitha says she hasn't seen you since Jonas was born.'

'These things happen.'

'I thought you said you were in love. *Billy and Tabs*. What happened? Being a father was too much responsibility for a nightclub musician?'

'It wasn't like that.'

'It doesn't bother you that you haven't seen your son in nine years?'

'That's just the way it is. The way it *had* to be.'

'Or maybe it does bother you, Mr Kapchanga,' Jouma said. 'Perhaps you don't like the idea of your Tabs being with anyone else, your son calling someone else "Dad".'

Kapchanga's studiously laid-back demeanour stiffened. 'Listen, man – I'm not stupid. The only reason you're here is because you think I killed this guy. Her husband.'

'Well, did you?'

'No. It wasn't like that with me and Tabs.'

'Then how was it?'

'When I heard she was getting married I was pleased for her, man. Like I say, she's a nice girl. I didn't like the thought of her bringing up Jonas on her own.'

There was a whoop from the other side of the empty, smoke-reeking bar as Davey Cav hit the jackpot on one of the slot machines. The coins spat into the trough and he scooped them into the pocket of his jeans.

'One thing puzzles me, Mr Kapchanga.'

'Fire away.'

'If you thought so much of Tabitha, why did you leave her in the first place?'

He smiled sadly. 'You might say I didn't see eye-to-eye with her old man. Seems he didn't like the idea of their only daughter shacked up with a bongo player.'

'He banned you from seeing her?'

'In a manner of speaking. The Brigadier made it very clear that he didn't want me around no more.'

Kapchanga placed his glass on the bar and, swivelling slightly in his seat, lifted his shirt to expose his back. Jouma gasped when he saw a row of ugly-looking welts.

'One night I was coming out of the club. Next thing

I know there's a bag on my head and I'm in the trunk of a car. Then they tied me to a post and whipped the shit out of me.'

'The Brigadier did that?' Jouma gasped.

'Like I said, I had a bag on my head, so I didn't see anyone. I don't know if he was doing the whipping, but I heard what they whispered in my ear when they were done.'

'What did they say?'

'They said, "*The Brigadier says if you go near his daughter again he will kill you.*"'

47

Jake did not like reporters. Never had. Certainly not investigative reporters like Katherine Rapuro, because too many of his police friends had lost their jobs thanks to unwelcome media prying – usually when the real culprits were high-ranking senior officers. Friends like Mac Bowden, hung out to dry thanks to a couple of hacks from the *Sunday Times* and a whistle-blower from the Flying Squad who didn't like the way the old guard did things.

So when Katherine turned up at the boatyard asking if he wanted to say a few words in tribute to Mac, his instinctive reaction was to tell her to fuck off. But almost as quickly he relented, because he knew enough about newspaper reporters to know that she would write the bloody story anyway, whether he commented or not. Then it struck him that, yes, he *did* want to say a few words about Mac, and maybe a few more about the money he was owed – and so, to Harry's astonishment, he took the young *Daily Nation* hack to Suki Lo's bar, got her drunk and told her exactly what he thought of his best friend.

'Will that do?' he said, two hours and six beers later.

Katherine's eyes were glassy. 'That's just brilliant,' she said. 'Thank you ever so much.'

'Just one more thing.'

She prepared her pen.

'If you do a hatchet job on him, I'll fucking kill you – understand?'

She nodded, and Jake immediately felt bad about what he'd said.

'I'm sorry. But he was a good friend.'

'From what you've said that's quite clear,' she said, feeling equally bad about what she'd been planning to write about Jake's business. He was a dour sort, without a doubt. But somewhere inside him she could detect a sliver of a heart – and she could tell that Bowden's death had put a knife through it.

You're drunk, Katherine. She glanced at Jake and wondered why, when he'd had just as many bottles of Tusker as she had, he didn't seem to be affected by the alcohol in the slightest.

'So you're covering the Headhunter case,' Jake said. 'What's the latest? I've been out of town for a while.'

Trying her best not to slur, Katherine explained how the case appeared to have stalled. Then she giggled.

'What's so funny?'

'I was about to say that I'm desperate for a story – but that isn't very complimentary about you.'

'Don't worry about it. I was a cop for ten years. I know all about stalled cases.'

'I hope you don't mind, but I looked you up on our cuttings service,' she said. 'It strikes me that you haven't exactly given up being a cop.'

'What do you mean?'

'You and the detective in charge of the Headhunter investigation – Inspector Jouma – have a bit of history. Something to do with a sex-trafficking case a while back?'

That was only the half of it, Jake thought, suppressing a wry smile as he thought of the way he and Jouma seemed to attract trouble like flies to elephant shit.

'Jouma and I run into each other occasionally,' he said. 'Normally all hell breaks loose when we do, so we try to keep out of each other's way as much as possible.'

'Only I'd be very keen to do an interview with him,' Katherine said. 'I wondered if you might be able to put a word in for me—?'

This time Jake laughed out loud. 'Jouma doesn't do interviews.'

'Tell me about it,' she said grumpily. 'Every time I put in a request I get blanked by the police press office.'

'This is a tough case. Jouma takes his job very seriously.'

Katherine took another swig of beer. 'What if I had some information that might be of help to the investigation?' she said. 'You think he would talk to me then?'

Jake looked at her knowingly. 'I know what you lot are like. If you had anything worth printing, it would be on the front page of the *Daily Nation* by now.'

'No – it's nothing that can stand up as a story.'

'Then what?'

She shook her head. 'It's probably nothing.'

'Tell me.'

Katherine finished her drink and took a deep breath. 'What if this wasn't the first time the Headhunter had gone on a killing spree? What if he had struck before?'

48

Shortly after midday, there had been an attempted robbery at the Akamba Handicraft Cooperative on the other side of the Makupa causeway. The manager had been locking up the showroom for lunch when a masked man brandishing a chisel had jumped out from behind the metal sheds where the wood carvers spent their days creating traditional-style tribal masks, giraffes, bead necklaces and other tourist gifts. The robber had demanded the takings – but the manager, a man named Rafique, had hit him over the head with a newly carved *rungu* club, retailing for eighty shillings, and killed him instantly.

Mwangi, diligently but fruitlessly sifting through missing-persons reports in an attempt to identify the teenage boy found dead in the dhow, also happened to be the most junior homicide detective in the building when the call came in. Without Jouma to protect him, he stood little chance against the senior officers, who still regarded him as teacher Simba's pet and were therefore anxious to make his life as difficult as possible.

He reached the scene shortly after one. The dead man, it transpired, was one of the wood carvers – but he was also a man whose dextrous skills were in almost total contrast to his mental acuity. Thirty minutes before his attempted robbery, a Securicor van had arrived at the showroom to transfer the contents of the safe to the bank.

Rafique was still adamant that he had done nothing

wrong – and certainly nothing that warranted arrest on suspicion of murder.

'It was self-defence, Detective,' he explained from behind folded arms. 'He came at me with a chisel.'

'Where is the body?' Mwangi asked one of the attending officers from Chamgamwe station. As he expected, it had been moved from the scene of the crime and deposited in the shade of a wood shed on the other side of the compound. He went across and lifted the banana leaf that had been considerately placed across its face. A pair of wide sightless eyes stared back at him, and it was obvious that the single blow to the man's forehead had killed him instantaneously.

Mwangi peered at the purplish indentation where the skull had been caved in.

'Is everything all right, sir?' asked the uniformed officer.

'Get the manager. Bring him here immediately.'

Rafique sauntered across a few moments later and glanced down at the dead man. 'His name was Terence,' he said indifferently. 'Not a bad carver, as carvers go, but—'

Mwangi cut him off impatiently. 'What did you say you hit him with?'

'A *rungu*.' The manager chuckled to himself. 'Probably one that Terence himself carved. Now there is an irony, Detective.'

'Where is the club now?'

The uniformed officer stepped forward and cleared his throat. 'I took the liberty of placing the murder weapon in the glove compartment of my car for safe-keeping, sir.'

'Then go and get it.'

'And it's not a *murder* weapon,' Rafique protested as the officer hurried to his patrol car. 'I tell you I struck this dog in self-defence.'

The *rungu* was a fearsome object, carved from a single foot–long piece of ebony. The business end of it was the size and shape of a baseball. Mwangi slipped on a pair of rubber gloves and carefully placed the ball against the dent in the centre of the dead man's forehead. The fit was snug.

'They are quite a weapon,' Rafique said proudly. 'I have seen Masai kill wildebeest with just one blow.'

In that case it would not take much of a blow to kill a human, Mwangi thought. Especially if the victim's skull was already as brittle as an eggshell.

49

Driving drunk in the Mombasa rush hour was not to be recommended – but Jake was an old hand at it, and forty minutes after leaving Suki Lo's he and Katherine were in the tiny *Daily Nation* bureau office overlooking Jamhuri Park, bolting down strong coffee in an attempt to get sober.

It was not how Jake had envisaged a newspaper office. He imagined it as a sprawling, open-plan hive full of ringing telephones and burly, chain-smoking men wearing visors shouting at each other. Katherine had laughed and assured him that the *Daily Nation* newsroom in Nairobi was open-plan, but that reporters now conducted their business to the soft rattle of computer keyboards and the tinkle of incoming emails. Smoking, she said, had been banned long ago.

'And if my news editor knew that I was drunk I'd be sacked on the spot.' She giggled.

'I thought journalists were supposed to be hard-bitten boozers?'

'Not any more.'

Jake flopped into a chair. 'OK. So tell me why you've dragged me all the way into Mombasa. What's this story you were talking about?'

'It was a quiet day and the newsdesk were on my back,' Katherine said. 'So I decided to do a cuts job on Kenyan serial killers.'

'A cuts job?'

'A cuts job is what you do when you have nothing

new to report,' she said. 'Basically, you trawl the archives for anything similar and write a piece around whatever you can find.'

Katherine explained that, in the days before stories could be archived digitally, the most important people in any newspaper office were the librarians. Not only were these unsung heroes responsible for painstakingly cutting out every individual story from every edition, pasting them to a sheet of paper and filing them in the relevant subject folder, they were the only ones who understood their own complex filing system.

The *Daily Nation*, in common with most national newspapers, once had a large team of librarians. Now there was only one left. He was a sixty-year-old man called Kenneth, although he was known by the younger generation of reporters as Google. It was said, with only a hint of irony, that if Google ever fell under a bus then fifty years of history dating back to the paper's inception would be lost forever.

'And this guy Google—'

'Spent an afternoon in the editorial library digging out every serial killer story he could find from the last fifty years.' She went to her desk and raised a sheaf of photocopied sheets. 'There were two hundred and forty-seven.'

Jake whistled. 'That's a hell of a lot.'

'Well, it depends what you classify as a serial killer,' Katherine said ruefully. 'Kenya is very different to your country. People are murdered all the time, but most mass murders tend to be internecine. Have you heard of the Naivasha Monster?' She flipped through the pages until she found the one she wanted. 'Jonah Muhu – killed his father, his wife and his two sons in the Rift Valley.'

'Jesus.'

'Yes. But his first murder was in 1938, and his last was

fifty years later. He was in his eighties when they finally caught him. That's pretty typical. Somebody like the Headhunter, who kills prolifically and in such a short period of time, is highly unusual.'

Jake shook his head. 'You say he's been active before now?'

Katherine glanced sheepishly at papers on her desk. 'I also said it was probably crazy.'

She handed him a sheet, a cutting dated June 1989.

Machete Boy, 12, Slaughters Family

A 12-year-old boy was due to appear in court today accused of the murder of eight members of his own family at a house near Loki, Turkana District.

Isiah Oulu is said to have decapitated his grandmother, father, mother, uncle, two brothers, a sister and a cousin during a frenzied machete attack on the night of June 11.

He is then alleged to have hung the heads from baobab trees on the outskirts of the border town, claiming that they were 'unbelievers' and 'apostates' who needed to be freed of their mortal sins.

Loki police refused to comment on the case yesterday. However, a neighbour, Mr A T Kungo, described the boy as being 'strange'.

Mr Kungo, 52, said: 'He was a very tall boy, 6ft before he was 10 years old. He used to go around cutting the heads off stray dogs, leaving them in public places such as public lavatories and on one occasion on the altar of the Church of the Christ's Salvation on Lodwar Road.'

'His poor mother used to despair, and said he was possessed by a demon,' Mr Kongo added.

'Sounds familiar,' Jake said.

'Loki's a hick town in the far north-west of the country, right on the Sudanese border,' Katherine told him. 'The sort of place where people go crazy with machetes all the time and it'll make a couple of paragraphs in the provincial editions. But this was comparatively big news at the time, because the kid killed his own family.'

'So what happened to him?'

'That's the thing. There was no trial, and the provincial authorities have no record of what happened to him. It seems he just disappeared off the face of the earth.'

'Disappeared? A kid who murdered eight members of his own family?'

'A kid from a remote backwater, hundreds of miles from the nearest civilisation,' Katherine reminded him. 'You have to remember that places like this are still in the Middle Ages when it comes to superstition and witchcraft. You read the article – even his own mother thought he was possessed by a demon.'

'So where did he go? They burn him at the stake?'

'That's not such a far-fetched notion. Like I said – I did some digging. Spoke to an old guy up there who used to work as a stringer for the paper back in the eighties. He said that, as soon as Isiah was found, he was taken into protective police custody. They locked him in a cell in Loki while the lynch mob was outside baying for his blood. Except later that night some important-looking people showed up with an armed guard and whisked the kid away in the back of a car. He was never heard of again.'

'"Important-looking people"?' Jake said. 'Sounds like an episode of *The X Files*.'

'The stringer was only telling me what the local police chief told him. But the odd thing was, when he filed the story the next day, the newsdesk spiked it.'

'Why?'

215

'They never said. Mind you, they wouldn't – the guy was just a lowly freelance hack out in the sticks.'

'Can't you find out? It's your paper.'

'The only person who worked on the newsdesk back then and is still alive is living in a retirement home in Nairobi. When I called him he said the order came from on high, and when that happened nobody asked questions. We still don't.'

Jake went across to the window and leaned against the sill. He needed a moment to think, to switch his mind into that rapidly fading detective mode. There were obvious similarities between Isiah Oulu and the killer known as the Headhunter: the decapitations, the flagrant display of the heads. And if he was twelve back in 1989 he would still only be in his early thirties now.

But if it *was* him, why wait twenty years to strike again? And where had he been all this time?

'I don't know, Katherine,' he said, shaking his head. 'It strikes me as a whole bunch of coincidence.'

Her face fell. 'I know. It's stupid. I shouldn't have even bothered mentioning it.'

'Having said that, when I was a cop I never paid much heed to coincidence. And I know Jouma thinks the same way. I think he'd be interested.'

She looked surprised. 'You do?'

'Oh, he'll probably tell you to stop wasting police time. But if Isiah is out there, then who knows? Maybe you've just stumbled on the biggest story of your career.'

50

'Did you hear what I said, Daniel?' asked Winifred Jouma.

Jouma realised he had been staring blankly at the kitchen wall, lost in his thoughts.

'*Uh?*'

His wife gave him a reproving look over the top of her bowl of stew. 'Why is it that, whenever I mention my sister in Lake Turkana, you go off into a world of your own?'

'I'm sorry, dear.'

'You know she is very fond of you, Daniel. She is forever asking why we never come to visit.'

'I have said on many occasions that you should arrange it,' Jouma said.

But Winifred merely tutted. 'What? And put up with you sitting there like a tree, staring at the walls?'

'What about her? Your sister – what were you saying?'

'All I was saying is that her doctor says she may require a small operation on the cyst on her back. I was thinking I may go and see her.'

'Really.'

'I have been putting aside my housekeeping money. I have two hundred dollars in the box in the bathroom medicine cabinet. I thought I might catch the train.'

'You should,' Jouma said, but his interest in Winifred's sister could be measured in fractions of a second.

The same could be said of his supper. Winifred was perhaps the best cook in Mombasa, yet the Inspector

217

was not hungry. He was thinking how things were never simple, how whenever a case looked to be heading for resolution something else came along to change everything.

He was thinking about the ugly scars on Billy Kapchanga's back.

About a death threat hissed in the musician's ear.

He was now seriously considering the possibility that Brigadier Wako Chatme had killed Paul Yomo.

It seemed fantastic, yet this was a family that was mired in lies and dark secrets – Paul's debts, Tabitha's relationship with Billy Kapchanga, and now the revelation that the Brigadier had whipped Billy to within an inch of his life and threatened to kill him. Who was to say that buried somewhere beneath the deceit there wasn't a brutal murder, one made to appear the work of a serial killer?

But speculation was one thing. What he needed was proof.

He stood and pulled on his jacket. 'I have to go.'

'Go? But you've only just come home.'

'I know, but—'

But what? Jouma was almost out of the door and he didn't even know where he was going. All he knew was that he had to do something. It was no good brooding, he had to make something *happen*.

He stooped to kiss his wife and she took his hand. 'You work too hard, Daniel,' she said tenderly. 'You are no longer a young man.'

Jouma pulled away. 'Don't wait up, Winifred,' he said.

His car was in the minuscule parking area that was one of the few perks for residents of his apartment block. Wearily he started the engine and backed out – but he did not see the equally lived-in Land Rover that had suddenly swung round behind him from the main road. There was a bang, a sharp jolt and the sound of a rear bumper clattering on to the concrete.

The two drivers leaped out and squared up to each other.

'What do you think you are doing?'

'Don't you ever look in your mirrors?'

'Look what you've done to my car!'

'Look what you've done to *mine*!'

Jouma leaned forward and sniffed suspiciously. 'Have you been drinking?'

'Yes,' Jake said.

'Then you'd better come inside and have some tea.'

'Have you got three cups?'

51

'Don't tell me,' Christie the pathologist said, as Mwangi entered his basement office at Mombasa Hospital. 'Jouma's found another one.'

'Thankfully not,' Mwangi said.

In his hand was the *rungu* club he had taken from Akamba Handicrafts. He gave it to Christie, who slapped the vicious-looking bolus into the palm of his hand appreciatively.

'A club similar to this was used earlier today to kill a robber in Chamgamwe. I expect you will see the body tomorrow.'

'Lucky me,' said Christie. 'You know, I've heard that just one blow with one of these things can kill a wildebeest stone dead.'

'I was rather more interested in its effect on a human head,' Mwangi said.

'Somehow I thought you might be. Come on, then. You're in luck, she's not due to be shipped back to *Deutschland* until tomorrow.'

Mwangi waited in the white-tiled autopsy room. After a few minutes the doors banged open and Christie came in, wheeling Frau Klinker's body on a gurney. He snapped on a pair of gloves and Mwangi watched impassively as the pathologist selected a scalpel and carefully nipped the sutures holding the dead woman's face together.

'It's always much easier the second time,' Christie remarked, grabbing the skin in his fingers and pulling it smoothly from the bones of the face like he was unpeeling a banana. The top of the cranium had been reaffixed to the skull with some sort of gum, but it did not take him long to rive the two sections apart.

'Where is the brain?' Mwangi asked.

'It's in a jar waiting to be sliced. Do you want to see it?'

'No – no, thank you.'

'Don't be shocked,' Christie said. 'Half of this job is smoke and mirrors. As long as the cadaver *looks* presentable to the next of kin, it doesn't matter what's missing. Or added, for that matter. I could tell you stories about the things I've chucked in that would make your hair stand on end.'

'I'm sure you could, Mr Christie. But the skull will do for now.'

Christie removed the top of the skull from its covering of skin and held it up to the light. The circular dent that had ultimately killed Frau Klinker was plain to see. 'Now, Mwangi – hand me the weapon.'

The pathologist delicately nuzzled the ball of the *rungu* against the cratered bone. Then he chuckled to himself.

'What do you think?' Mwangi asked.

'Well, it's not a perfect fit, but then I suppose every *rungu* is different. However, if you want to find your killer, then I'd say you'd do well to keep your eyes open for a Masai warrior dragging a dead wildebeest behind him.'

52

Winfred poured three cups of English breakfast tea and left her husband with his guests.

'Thank you, Mrs Jouma,' Jake said after her.

She turned at the living-room door and smiled primly, but only because she was a firm believer that manners cost nothing. In reality she was not at all pleased to see the English fishing-boat skipper. It seemed that every time he and her husband got together it ended with either one or the other of them getting into trouble. The last time, Daniel had come back with stitches in his face and his smart suit in ribbons. And, despite his protestations, her husband was *not* a young man any more. He should not be gallivanting around like a man half his age.

No – she didn't like Jake Moore one little bit, and it worried her that he was here in her house once again. As for the girl – well, she was presentable at least; but she was also a newspaper reporter, a profession that in Winifred's humble opinion was only slightly better than that of a fishing-boat skipper.

'You're welcome,' she said, and shut the door behind her. A moment later came the sound of her favourite radio programme.

Jouma read the newspaper cutting, then placed it on the kitchen table in front of him.

'Do you remember the case?' Jake asked him.

The Inspector shook his head. 'Only very vaguely. It was a long time ago.'

'Is there any way of finding out what happened to Isiah?' Katherine said.

Jouma glanced at her, still not sure whether he should even be speaking to the *Daily Nation* reporter – or indeed what her ulterior motives really were.

'Who have you spoken to?'

She told him about her phone calls to the provincial administration and to the newspaper stringer.

'Did he mention the name of the police chief at Loki?'

'Captain Bakhrani.'

Jouma thought for a moment. 'Wait here.'

He went through to the living room and made a telephone call. When he returned several minutes later, his expression was resigned.

'I have just spoken to an old colleague of mine who works at Rift Valley Province headquarters. Captain Bakhrani died seven years ago.'

'Shit,' Jake said, then looked guiltily at Winifred Jouma's bedroom door. 'Does your friend have *any* idea what might have happened to Isiah? Or who these mysterious people were?'

Jouma sat down and began idly stirring a spoon in his tea. 'The fact that there are no official records, either in the provincial archives or the police files, suggests to him – and to me – that some sort of government agency might have been involved. In which case, we have no chance of ever finding out the truth.'

'So that's it?' Katherine said. 'The trail ends here?'

'Most likely, yes,' Jouma said testily. 'But assuming they did not have Isiah disposed of, it would seem logical to me that they must have taken him *somewhere*.'

'They would have to make sure he couldn't kill again,' Jake said. 'A max-security prison?'

'Unlikely. The safety of the other inmates would be at risk.'

'Maybe they just drove him a hundred miles over the border into Sudan or Ethiopia and dumped him there,' Katherine suggested.

'Possible — but again, there is always the risk that he might come back.'

Jake shrugged. 'Then they must have killed him. It's the only viable option.'

'Not necessarily,' Jouma said. 'Have you heard of the Kalami Secure Mental Hospital near Malindi?'

Their blank looks confirmed they hadn't. Jouma told them about his visits to Dr Lutta regarding the Headhunter case, and his earlier association with Lutta's boss, Dr Klerk.

'Dr Klerk has been a pre-eminent figure in the field of criminal psychology here in Kenya for more than fifteen years. Indeed, many people credit him with having dragged the profession out of the Dark Ages. He often spoke to me about the frankly barbaric conditions and treatment patients were subjected to until very recently. They were, in his words, little more than lab experiments to be abused and discarded.'

Jake leaned forward. 'Discarded?'

'If you were to look back through your newspaper's archives to the early 1990s, Miss Rapuro, you would come across a story which created quite a scandal at the time. It seems it was common practice among certain state-run mental institutions to release back into the community patients they judged to be *cured*. These included several who could be classified as criminally insane.'

'But surely to God you can't cure someone who is criminally insane?' Jake said.

'Perhaps not. But you can *neutralise* them. A common factor among those who had been released was many had been lobotomised.'

Katherine looked aghast. 'You're saying the doctors deliberately operated on their brains and then kicked them out?'

'There were some who thought it was a convenient way of reducing overcrowding. But Dr Klerk believes that most were genuinely attempting to use brain surgery to influence behavioural patterns. Unfortunately, their techniques were extremely rudimentary.'

'What if Isiah was one of their guinea pigs?' Jake said. 'A twelve-year-old kid who's just murdered eight people would make a damn good experiment. It would explain why the brass were so keen to get hold of him.'

'What if they thought their experiment had worked?' Jouma murmured. 'That Isiah was somehow cured? *What if they let him out?*'

'We have to speak to Klerk,' Katherine cried. 'He's bound to have access to the records.'

Jouma looked at the clock on the kitchen wall. 'It's too late now. I will arrange to meet him at Kalami tomorrow.'

'Great! What time?'

'*You* will not be coming, Miss Rapuro.'

'No way, Inspector. This is my story and if you're going to Kalami then I'm coming with you.'

'Out of the question.'

For a moment Jake felt like the referee in a heavy-weight bout as the two boxers squared up to each other. In the background, Winifred Jouma's radio was playing an utterly incongruous melody by Mantovani.

'Would it help if I came along too?' he suggested. 'In a purely diplomatic capacity, of course. Then, if you have a punch-up, I can drive the loser to hospital.'

Katherine laughed, and even Jouma smiled reluctantly.

'I will be leaving at seven o'clock sharp,' the Inspector

said. 'And remember – this is a police investigation first, a newspaper story second.'

Jouma remained deep in thought long after Jake and Katherine had gone. Presently Winifred came out of the bedroom in a cotton nightshift.

'What is it, Daniel?'

'Nothing, my dear. Go back to bed – I will be in shortly.'

'I don't like it when you are with that English fellow. I worry about what will happen next.'

He smiled. How he loved his wife. 'This time, I assure you I am perfectly safe.'

'So you always say,' she said, then pecked him on the top of the head. 'Goodnight, my love.'

'Goodnight, Winifred.'

But it would be several hours before Jouma went to bed that night. Even then he found it difficult to sleep. His mind was buzzing with thoughts and theories, speculation and dread. And at the middle of the maelstrom was a twelve-year-old boy holding a bloodied machete in one hand, and Jouma's severed head in the other.

VII

53

Nicholas Lutta stared into the blank face on the other side of the table. It belonged to a man who, sixteen years ago, had been convicted of the rape, murder and subsequent cannibalisation of a rent collector in Kwale district. He claimed he had done it because that was what the rent collector had, metaphorically, been doing to him for the last five years. The victim, he later said, tasted of gold.

Lutta took a square of tissue paper from his jeans pocket, twisted it into a point, and jabbed the end into the dilated pupil of the man's left eye to test his blink reflex. Next he carefully inserted a pin under the nail of the man's right index finger to assess his pain threshold.

There was no reaction – but then sixteen years was a long time to be incarcerated in the Kenyan mental health system. The man's arms were still peppered with needle marks where strong behaviour-altering drugs had been pumped into his bloodstream, and on his temples were the shadows of electrodes that had fired 20,000 volts into his brain in order to scramble his synapses.

Lutta sighed and made a note on a yellow legal pad.

'Take him back to his cell,' he said to the bored-looking orderly standing by the door.

When he had gone, Lutta turned to the second man sitting at the table in the examination room – Dr Cyrus Klerk, head of the clinical team at Kalami Hospital.

'So there you are,' Lutta said.

Klerk nodded sadly. He was a balding Zimbabwean émigré who had more than forty years' experience in criminal psychology. 'Such a pity,' he said. 'When he first came here I thought we had a real chance of bringing him back – but the conscious regression has been almost exponential.'

'He has become almost vegetative,' Lutta observed.

'Yet his cognitive signs remain normal. He obeys commands. He *walks*, for goodness sake.' He tapped his dome. 'But it's like there is a black hole in there, growing, sucking at his mind.'

'I would like to keep him under observation, Dr Klerk.'

'By all means, Nicholas. If nothing else, you will get another paper out of it.'

The two men walked through the cell block and back towards the clinical annexe where their respective offices were housed. As they climbed the stairs they were met by a flustered-looking secretary coming the other way.

'Thank goodness,' she said. 'Dr Klerk, Inspector Jouma from Mombasa is here. He wishes to speak to you urgently.'

They continued upstairs to Klerk's office. It was a lot more spacious and tidy than Lutta's, but even so the three people waiting inside made it seem almost claustrophobic.

'Dr Klerk,' Jouma said, stepping forward. 'It is good to see you again. And you, Dr Lutta.' He introduced Jake and Katherine as associates, but was careful not to go into specifics of who they were or why they were there.

'A rare pleasure to see you these days, Inspector,' Klerk said amiably, sitting down at his desk. 'I was beginning to feel envious of the time you were spending with young Nicholas here – even though it was my idea.'

Jouma smiled. 'Dr Lutta's insight into the Headhunter case has been invaluable. But it is you I have come to see.'

'Then I'll leave you to it,' Lutta said, sauntering towards the door.

'No – please stay, Dr Lutta,' Jouma said. 'You may be interested in what I have to say.'

For a moment Lutta looked slightly nonplussed and his small, dark eyes switched between the people in the room. But then he shrugged and perched on the arm of a chair by the window.

Klerk also appeared tentative all of a sudden. 'This all sounds very intriguing, Inspector. How can I help?'

'I was telling my friends here about the somewhat rudimentary nature of mental health care in Kenya in the old days,' Jouma said. 'How your predecessors tended to regard their patients as experimental specimens.'

Klerk still looked uneasy. 'Well, thankfully we have come a long way since then – although we are still trying to undo the damage they did. In fact, when you arrived Nicholas and I were in the assessment suite with a patient who arrived here five months ago after nearly sixteen years in a state-run institute in Nairobi. Unfortunately, it would seem that we are too late to help him.'

'Help him?' Jake said.

'There's a school of thought that there may be a less brutal way of treating these people than frying their brains and drilling holes in their skulls,' Lutta said.

'Nicholas is being modest,' Klerk said. 'His own techniques have proved remarkably successful.'

'Gentlemen,' Jouma interrupted. 'I am here because there is a possibility that the Headhunter may be a former psychiatric patient who was treated, then

231

released back into the community in the mistaken belief that he was no longer a threat to society.'

'A patient at this hospital?' Klerk asked, his eyes wide.

'His crimes were committed in Rift Valley Province twenty years ago, when he was a twelve-year-old boy. I assume he would have been incarcerated in a secure mental unit in that area of the country, but I can't be sure. I was hoping, Dr Klerk, that you may have access to patient records – or at least know where I can find them.'

Klerk rubbed his bald scalp thoughtfully. 'Records from that time are patchy. Their reliability depends very much on the diligence of the medical staff, and whether they were kept at all. A lot of data was deliberately destroyed during the investigations of the mid-1990s.' He looked up. 'But yes – I am sure I can make some enquiries on your behalf, Inspector. What was this patient's name?'

'Oulu,' Katherine said. 'Isiah Oulu.'

Klerk and Lutta immediately looked at each other, and their expressions of amused astonishment were identical.

'Isiah was a patient here up until a couple of months ago,' Klerk said – and at that moment it was the turn of the other three in the room to look at each other in amazement.

'Where is he now?' Jouma demanded.

'Oh, he's still here,' Klerk said matter-of-factly. 'In fact, if you would care to follow me, I'll take you to him.'

54

In the office of Britannia Fishing Trips Ltd, Harry Philliskirk sat at his desk and grew cold with fury.

His problem was his elder brother. Harry's problem was *always* his elder bloody brother.

In every sector of his life, Ralph Philliskirk had always been unreliable – as the three wives, numerous sackings and two years in HM Prison Ford for tax evasion bore witness. But despite that he was still blood, which was why Harry had, against all his better judgement, been prepared to offer him one last chance to prove himself.

Well, Ralphie had proved something all right in the short time he had been in Kenya.

He had proved that a leopard couldn't change its spots.

And that Harry was a bloody fool.

Harry was a connoisseur of most of life's vices, but gambling had never been one of them. To Harry the very word was redolent of spiv turf accountants, seedy casino owners, exploitation and misery.

He was also aware that it had been the ruin of his own family.

By the end of the nineteenth century, thanks to shares in the East India Company, the Philliskirks had accumulated substantial wealth and property in the south of England. By 1920, however, Harry's grandfather, the Right Honourable Lucien Philliskirk MP, had quite spectacularly squandered almost all of it at the gaming tables of Mayfair, Knightsbridge and Fitzrovia. In the post-war years what little was left was single-mindedly frittered away at Ascot, Newmarket and Cheltenham by his son, Lorton Philliskirk, a criminal barrister who would drink himself into an early grave at the age of forty. And despite the penury into which gambling had taken the family, the gene passed without obstruction to Lorton's eldest son Ralph.

As far as Ralph was concerned, he was answerable only to Lady Luck, and if she smiled on you all was well, and if she didn't – well, there was always tomorrow. He really was the last of a dying breed, a happy-go-lucky roué who somehow survived because he was always able to reach into the back pocket of a pair of trousers and come up with one last fiver for the roulette wheel or the poker table.

But his was a breed that was dying for a reason – and that reason was the number of London gambling clubs now run by Eastern European hard men who didn't give a shit for the nod-and-a-wink traditions of gaming credit practised for centuries by the likes of Ralph Philliskirk. Their philosophy was simple: if you owed money, you paid up on time and with interest. If you didn't, they took what you owned. And if you owned nothing then they either maimed you or killed you to send a message to others.

It seemed to Harry that, when the call finally came, he had been waiting for it all his life.

'H, old man – sorry to bother you and all that, but I think I may be in something of a jam.'

Ralphie was in a jam all right. He owed fifty thousand pounds to a gang from Uzbekistan, and he'd just got back to his flat in South London to find they'd left the skinned carcass of his Yorkshire terrier hanging from the light fitting in the sitting room.

Three hours later, he had boarded a flight for Kenya, hand luggage only, ticket bought by his little brother.

Harry stared at the clock on the wall, watching each minute pass until midday came and went. Then he heard the sound of *Yellowfin*'s engines, and when he went to the window and looked out at the creek he saw the thirty-footer turning into the inlet. Ralphie shinned down from the flying bridge and looped the mooring rope around the buoy.

Oh, he was getting good at that.

A few moments later the launch nudged against the jetty and Ralphie hopped ashore.

'Harry? Harry – are you in, old chap? I'm back from the repair yard. Missy Meredith says there might be a slight problem with the rudder housing, but nothing fatal. She says to bring it in next time you're passing and she'll take a look at it. Harry?'

Harry, staring out of the window, did not move. 'In here.'

There was the sound of footsteps on the concrete floor of the workshop and a muffled exclamation of pain as Ralph bumped into something sharp in the shadows. And then the office door opened.

'You all right, H?'

'Where is it, Ralph?'

'Eh? Where's what? Did you hear what I said about the rudder housing?'

Harry turned. 'Where is it?'

Ralph, who had flung himself into a canvas-backed chair by the door and was wrestling with the top of a bottle of Tusker, looked at his brother with bemusement.

'What *are* you on about?'

'The money you took from the floor safe.'

He pointed at the open hatch sticking up from the concrete floor of the office.

'I honestly don't know what you're talking about, H.'

'Thirty-five grand, Ralphie. All the fucking money we've got. It's gone. Now where is it?'

Ralph blinked then, and Harry, who knew every last trick in his miserable brother's repertoire, and had seen and heard the same pathetic routine one too many times now, walked calmly across the office and punched his elder brother squarely on the jaw.

'Christ, Harry – I'm sorry,' Ralph wailed, as he sprawled on the floor with beer spilling all over his shorts. 'I'm going to pay you back, I swear, all of it with interest. But these fucking Uzbekis! They're going to have my guts for garters the second I step off the plane at Heathrow. I needed the cash for the game. It was high stakes. And I was so bloody *close!*'

Harry stared at him. 'How much did you lose?'

'It's not as bad as you think, old man.'

'*How much?*'

Ralph's face dropped. 'Pretty much all of it. But listen – there's another big game next week. We're talking thousands in the pot.'

Harry stared down at his brother and for a moment all that was in his mind was the desire to kick him, to hurt him so badly that he would fully appreciate the extent of what he had done.

Instead, he turned away.

'You bloody fool, Ralphie,' he said. 'You've killed us.'

55

The unmarked grave was one of several dozen arranged in no particular order in a field two hundred yards from the perimeter wall of the secure hospital. Like the others it had been crudely dug and the earth covered with large rocks to keep the wild animals from digging up the body.

'He passed away in November,' Dr Klerk said. 'Cholera. Not uncommon here, I'm afraid. We do our best to keep patients' hygiene standards as high as possible – but there is only so much we can do with an erratic water supply.'

There were five of them standing around the grave. They looked, Jake thought, like mourners. *More than at Mac Bowden's funeral*. He looked across at Jouma, who was staring at the grave with a resigned expression that summed up everyone's mood.

'If it's any consolation, I can understand why you might have thought it was him,' Klerk said. 'His age and the nature of his crimes did indeed earmark him for radical correctional treatment; he spent most of his life being moved from institution to institution, undergoing all manner of experimental techniques. It's a miracle he lasted as long as he did, in my opinion.'

'When was he transferred here?' Katherine asked.

'Eighteen months ago. He'd been at a state institute in Nairobi for several years, and they had pretty much given up on him. I saw his notes and thought he would be an ideal patient for Dr Lutta.'

'Why?'

Lutta snapped out of a reverie. 'Because his mind was largely still intact. Normally he would have been subjected to the usual invasive treatments – electroshock, chemical, ultimately lobotomy – but because he was so young his doctors shied away from the traditional techniques. They were more interested in observing the way his brain developed. They'd never seen a psychopath grow up before.'

'And what were you interested in, doctor?' Jake said.

'What made him a psychopath in the first place. I have always believed that if it were possible to identify the subconscious root from which psychopathic delusion ultimately flourishes, then it might be possible to suppress it.'

Katherine held up the newspaper cutting. 'It says here that, when he was arrested twenty years ago, Isiah said something about his parents being *apostates* and *unbelievers.*'

Lutta nodded. 'He believed he was a living god. The son of Ngai.'

'Ngai?'

'The Divider of the Universe and Lord of Nature. Ngai is worshipped as a supreme god by a number of Kenyan tribes. According to their beliefs, he lives on Mount Kenya.'

'And Isiah thought he was Ngai's son?' Jake said.

Lutta nodded. 'It is a common delusion. In western societies it is known as the Messiah Complex. The subject believes they are born of the Supreme Deity and act accordingly. Most are harmless, the sort you might see shouting on a street corner. But occasionally the delusion leads the subject to acts of violence against those they believe to be unbelievers or apostates.'

Jake laughed hollowly. 'Like cutting off their heads.'

'In Isiah's case, yes.'

'Then he sounds like a 24-carat nut job, to me. And now he's dead, so good riddance to bad rubbish.' He went over to Jouma and put his hand on the detective's thin shoulder. 'Sorry, Inspector. This is my fault. I thought it was worth a punt, but it looks like my policeman's hunch has lost its magic.'

Jouma nodded but said nothing.

Slowly, the party began to move away from the grave and back towards the looming hulk of the hospital. In the far corner of the ramshackle cemetery, two scrawny Africans were busy digging a fresh hole. As he watched them methodically churning the dry dirt, Jake felt sorry for Jouma. In fact, he felt guilty about it. The little detective looked dejected as he trudged back to the hospital – and Jake had seen the look before, on good coppers who just couldn't get a break and who started to take it personally. After a while, it started to gnaw at you, keep you awake at night. You felt the ghosts of the victims leering over you, pointing accusatory fingers, telling you how fucking useless you were because you couldn't catch their killer. And eventually it just consumed you until you could no longer function, and you too had become a victim.

'*Wait!*' Jouma suddenly exclaimed, and they all stopped stock still in the middle of the cemetery as if they were playing a macabre game of statues. 'Dr Klerk, when a patient contracts cholera, where is he taken?'

'There is an isolation ward on the far side of the compound.'

'And, when they die, what happens then?'

Klerk looked mystified. 'They are brought here and buried.'

'By who?'

'The orderlies.'

'And are the bodies put in a coffin before they are buried?'

'Inspector Jouma! This is a hospital, not a charnel house. I can assure you that all necessary hygienic procedures are—'

There was a glint in Jouma's eye now, and Jake wondered just what the hell he was getting at.

'In the newspaper cutting Isiah Oulu is described by a neighbour as being unnaturally tall for a boy of his age,' he said.

'He was.' Klerk nodded. 'He must have been six feet eight or nine.'

'I believe he was of Masai stock,' Lutta said.

'Yes,' Jouma said. 'Then perhaps you could explain something to me.'

He marched back to Isiah Oulu's grave and, mystified, the others followed him.

'If Isiah was nearly seven feet tall,' he said, pointing at the rock-covered mound of soil, 'then how do you explain that?'

Suddenly Jake understood.

The grave in which Isiah Oulu was buried was less than six feet long.

56

According to the rota for November 20, the day Isiah Oulu died of cholera, there was one orderly on duty in the isolation ward. He was a forty-two-year-old man named Chipche Molonga, who had finished his shift that day and not been seen since.

'It happens quite a lot,' Klerk said. 'Turnover of ancillary staff is quite high.'

'What do you know about him?'

'He seemed to be a diligent chap.'

'How long had he worked here?'

Klerk blushed, and Jouma knew then that the head of the clinical team wouldn't have recognised Chipche Molonga if he'd passed him in the corridor.

'What you have to appreciate, Inspector, is that a lot of people are scared by this establishment. Mothers in Malindi tell their children that, if they don't behave, then the evil monsters from Kalami will come for them in the night. It is difficult to get staff to work here as it is without having to subject them to rigorous vetting procedures that might put them off. I know it is not ideal, but it is the best that we can do.'

They had returned to Klerk's office, still stunned by what had been unearthed in Isiah Oulu's grave.

Or rather, what *hadn't*.

The grave was empty. In fact, it wasn't even a grave, but a shallow hole no more than six inches deep, filled in with earth and covered with stones. Whoever had dug it – and everything so far pointed to the missing orderly Chipche

Molonga – had made a convincing job of it, except for the single glaring error of making it almost eighteen inches smaller than the length of the corpse that was supposed to be buried in it.

'I knew Chipche,' Lutta said dully. 'He used to look after Isiah – bring his food, clean his cell and so on.'

'Is it possible that Isiah was able to somehow control him?' Jouma asked.

'Isiah was an immensely charismatic personality. Most people with the Messiah Complex are. And Chipche was intellectually weak. It would not have been difficult, I suppose, over a period of several months, for Isiah to influence him.'

'OK,' Jake said. 'I'll buy the fact that he must have had an accomplice on the inside. But I thought Isiah had been struck down with cholera. Don't you have doctors in this place? I mean certified, vetted *medical* doctors?'

Klerk shifted awkwardly in his chair again. 'A doctor from Malindi Hospital comes once a week to check on the patients. But the isolation ward—'

'Don't tell me – he throws some antibiotics through the door and lets them fight over them.'

'So Isiah could have easily faked his illness?' Katherine said.

Klerk nodded slowly. 'The symptoms of cholera are diarrhoea, vomiting and severe stomach cramps.'

'Which he could have got by drinking a couple of pints of seawater,' Jake said. 'Bravo!'

'That's enough, Jake,' Jouma warned.

Jake bit his tongue – but he couldn't help thinking that if it wasn't for Klerk and his Third World concept of high security then Mac Bowden might well be alive right now.

'This condition of Isiah's,' Jouma said to Lutta. 'This Messiah Complex . . .'

'A misleading term in my opinion,' Lutta said. 'Isiah claimed to be a god, but in my view it was only because the world scared him. In reality, he kills out of a deep-rooted fear.'

Jake shook his head, unable to hold his silence. 'But the people he killed – they were all part of the same *card* school, for Christ's sake! Now that doesn't make any sense at all.'

Silence fell over the room. It seemed that, when it came to the Headhunter's choice of victims, even the experts were stumped.

'We should go and find the orderly,' Jake said to Jouma. 'If he's still alive, he will know where this bastard is hiding.' He went across to a framed map of Coast Province on the wall. The hospital was ringed in marker pen. Eight miles east of it was Malindi, west was the exposed bush of the Tsavo East National Park and to the south the main coastal settlements. The area was vast. The Headhunter could be anywhere.

'You say that Isiah is *scared* of people, Dr Lutta?'

The psychologist nodded. 'If we are being simplistic about his condition, then yes.'

'Then it stands to reason that he would want to hide somewhere as remote as possible.'

'I suppose so.'

Jouma tapped his finger on the map. 'The body of the fourth gunman was found in a dhow here, a mile up the Sabaki estuary.'

'Yes – but there was a search of the area at the time and nothing was found,' Katherine pointed out. 'I should know, I wasted a day covering it.'

'Because there are *people* there, Miss Rapuro. Look – villages on both sides of the river, a main road. If you are right, Dr Lutta, then this is the *last* place Isiah would choose to hide. What if the boy in the boat was trying to get somewhere else but died before he could complete his journey?'

Jake went across to the map. 'You mean further upriver? But there's nothing there.'

'Precisely,' Jouma said.

'*The plantation*,' Lutta murmured. Everyone in the room looked at him. 'Chipche had a gourd plantation on the Sabaki river. He grew them in order to make ornaments, bowls, drinking vessels, pots. He used to sell them in the tourist market in Malindi.'

'Whereabouts on the Sabaki?'

Lutta went across to the map. 'He was always very secretive about its location,' he said. 'He thought, if they knew, the other gourd traders would sabotage his crop. I always thought he was paranoid, but he said there was good money to be made from top-quality produce.'

'*Where*, Dr Lutta?' Jouma said.

'Somewhere round here.' Lutta's finger had come to rest on a small highlighted area on the south bank of the river, about ten miles inland.

'The Chakama Reserve?'

'I think so.'

'What is the Chakama Reserve?' Katherine asked.

Jouma stared at the map. 'Not so much a reserve as three square miles of swampland, Miss Rapuro. It used to be a hideout for pirates and smugglers. Later the Mau Mau used it as a location to store arms. They say there is an impressive array of birdlife there – although you are more likely to be eaten by a crocodile.'

'You think Isiah is there?'

Jouma nodded slowly. 'If Chipche Molonga knows the terrain, and he is indeed a disciple of the living god, then I can't think of anywhere else the Headhunter *could* be.'

57

Alec Standage had been in what amounted to protective police custody in his house north of Shanzu for the best part of a week. But, having weighed up the risk of being murdered by the Headhunter or going stir-crazy within his own four walls, he had opted for the latter.

And, even though the hotel was still closed for business while repairs were carried out, Standage was taking no chances. When Mwangi arrived he found the hotel grounds crawling with burly-looking men trying to look inconspicuous in wraparound sunglasses and bulges under their jackets. Standage, supervising building work in the wrecked atrium, had two bodyguards shadowing his every move and was clearly paying a fortune for private security.

When he saw the young detective, his eyes lit up. 'Have you caught him, Detective?'

'Not yet, sir,' Mwangi said. 'But there is a development in the other matter.'

Standage looked at him uncomprehendingly. 'The other matter?'

'Frau Klinker?' Mwangi reminded him. 'Mr Wuyns?'

'Of course!' He laughed nervously. 'You know, with everything that's been happening lately I had forgotten all about that.'

They went through to the manager's office. The two security goons wanted to search Mwangi, but Standage told them to wait outside.

'They're very keen. But they're on five hundred

dollars a day, so they should be. Clyde used to work in Iraq.'

'Mr Standage,' Mwangi said, interrupting the flow of nervy chat. 'Do you know what this is?'

Standage examined the *rungu* that the detective had brought with him in his briefcase. 'Yeah. A few of the hotel *askari* used to wear them hanging from their belts like six-shooters – until I told them in no uncertain terms that it was not the sort of image I was trying to promote for the hotel. Why?'

'I believe the assailant used a club similar to this one to attack your guests.'

'Jesus. One of my own fucking *askari* did this?'

'Possibly.'

'Why?'

'I don't know. Would any of them have any reason to hold a grudge against you, Mr Standage?'

Standage shrugged. 'No. They were the best-paid *askari* on the strip – ask anyone. *Askari* from other hotels aspire to work here, detective.'

'You haven't had cause to sack anyone? Over the carrying of a *rungu* perhaps?'

'No – they were fine about it. As well they might be on their wages. Listen, I've only had to let one *askari* go in the time that I've been here, and that was because he was about a hundred and forty years old and was starting to lose his marbles.'

Mwangi flipped open his notebook. 'What was his name, Mr Standage?'

58

'Are you sure about this, Daniel?' said Superintendent Simba. She was looking at a large-scale map of the Sabaki river that Jouma had spread across her desk.

'It makes perfect sense, ma'am. According to Dr Lutta, at the heart of Isiah Oulu's Messiah Complex is a pathological fear of society. The Chakama Reserve is one of the few places where you are virtually guaranteed not to find other people. And of course Chipche Molonga, Isiah's disciple, knows the area like the back of his hand.'

'Kenya is a big place,' Simba pointed out. 'What about the plains, or the mountains? He could be hiding there for all you know.'

'The Reserve is situated on the river, and is therefore within easy reach of the areas where his victims live. The Sabaki is also a busy waterway. Remember, Isiah requires his victims to be brought to him, and nobody would look twice at a boat. Also remember that the dead youth in the dhow was found in the Sabaki estuary. He was obviously trying to get upriver.'

Simba looked at the map. 'The Reserve is a big place, Daniel. We will require men, dogs, helicopters.'

'I agree.'

'You do realise we will have to go cap in hand to the Mayor for this, don't you?'

Jouma nodded. Securing the necessary manpower and resources for such a large-scale air, sea and land operation would require more authority and a bigger budget than Simba, or even the Provincial Police Chief himself, could call upon at such short notice.

'It's the chance he has been waiting for,' Simba groaned.

'Yes, ma'am,' Jouma said.

Last year the Mayor had been responsible for the appointment of the inept Detective Inspector Oliver Mugo to oversee the Lol Quarrie investigation – a disastrous decision that both Jouma and Simba had taken great pleasure in exposing. The resulting scandal had nearly cost the Mayor his job. Indeed, had he not only recently filled the post after the previous incumbent was indicted on corruption charges, his position would have been untenable. But he had survived – and ever since he had been looking for an opportunity to get his own back.

He had already been vocal in his criticism of the way the Headhunter case had been handled, and both Jouma and Simba knew full well that the price of co-operation would be their heads.

But, as Simba put her head in her hands, the Inspector permitted himself a knowing smile.

'I wouldn't worry too much about the Mayor, ma'am.'

She looked up. 'Why not?'

'I just have a feeling that he will be more than happy to oblige your request,' he said.

The Mayor's smile could not have been broader.

'Miss Rapuro – *do* come in,' he said, moving easily from behind his large oak desk and gesturing towards a pair of leather sofas facing each other on a plush circular rug by the fireplace.

'Thank you for seeing me at such short notice,' Katherine said. She sat down and placed her leather satchel primly on her knees.

The Mayor slid on to the sofa opposite. 'How can I help you?' he said expectantly.

'I was thinking about what you said the other night. About a *quid pro quo* arrangement.'

'*Ye-es.*'

'Well, in hindsight I think I may have been a little bit hasty.'

'Hindsight is a wonderful thing,' he said with aching sincerity. 'I think you reacted with admirable restraint. It is refreshing to meet a journalist with such high moral and ethical scruples. Would you care for a drink? I have some chilled white wine in the cabinet over there.'

She shook her head. 'No, thank you, sir. I would rather get down to business.'

'Of course, of course.'

Katherine reached into her bag and handed him a sheet of paper. On one side, beneath her name, were five hundred words of tightly wrought prose. The Mayor read it, and his supercilious smile melted away.

'What the devil is this?' he demanded, all pretence gone now.

'Exactly what it looks like. A front-page story about how the Mayor of Mombasa attempted to bribe a *Daily Nation* reporter with classified and potentially damaging information about an ongoing murder investigation in return for favourable publicity.'

The Mayor's eyes bulged. 'This is preposterous! I will deny everything. And do you think your newspaper really wants to enter into costly litigation with the second most powerful man in Coast Province?'

'Deny it all you like, sir,' Katherine said coolly. She reached into her bag again and removed a small, credit-card-sized Dictaphone. 'But when the second most powerful man in Coast Province breaks into my house, my instinctive reaction is to record everything he says.'

For a long time the Mayor was speechless.

'You mentioned a *quid pro quo*, Miss Rapuro,' he said presently. 'What is it you want?'

There was also a packet of Marlboro in her bag, an emergency supply to be used only in times of extreme stress. But when she emerged from his office five minutes later, Katherine's hands were shaking so much she could barely bring the cigarette to her lips.

Outside, on the steps of the State House, she paused to suck the harsh smoke deep into her lungs. Only when she felt that her legs would not give way did she continue out to the road where the battered Land Rover was waiting for her.

'How did it go?' Jake asked her as she climbed into the back seat.

'I think you can tell your Superintendent that she can make the call, Inspector,' Katherine said. 'But if he'd asked to listen to my recorded conversation it might have been a different matter.'

In the front passenger seat, Jouma smiled. 'Thank you, Miss Rapuro. I think you have earned your exclusive.'

The vehicle pulled out into the traffic and headed for Nyali Bridge, where the main highway led north towards the Sabaki river.

59

The *askari* who had been laid off from the Sandpiper
Hotel was called Stanley Kikwete, a sixty-one-year-old
resident of the Kongowea slum known locally as
Sergeant Major Stan on account of his military background and the fact that he was never seen without his
smartly pressed uniform. And according to his nearest
neighbour – a fat woman with no teeth who ground her
gums together with an unnerving squeaking noise – he
had not been seen for over a week.

'He is a rather stern gentleman,' the neighbour told
Mwangi. 'But never less than civil – even if he is a little soft
in the head these days, due to his advanced years.' The
woman seemed almost contemptuous of Kikwete's age,
although she herself didn't look a day under eighty. 'You
know that he had worked at the Sandpiper Hotel for twenty
years? Oh, that job was his life! You'd have thought they
could have given him *something* to do instead of getting rid
of him like that. Polishing boots or clearing up coconuts.'

They were sitting in two wooden chairs outside her
shack in the sprawling, corrugated-iron hinterland of
the slum.

'By "soft in the head" do you mean senile?' Mwangi
asked.

'*Confused*, I think. Forgetting what day it is, or what
people's names are. The way old people get.' She leaned
forward and gestured with a cane at a house on the
other side of the narrow street. 'If you ask me, when
they gave him the push it made him worse.'

'In what way?'

She laughed wheezily, exposing the blackened gums. 'I would sit here and watch him go out in the morning, dressed in his uniform. He said he was going to work his shift – but everybody knew the silly old fool was just walking up and down the beach, shouting at the boys selling trinkets.'

'Did he carry a club with him when he went out?'

She cackled again. 'Ah – that *rungu*! Carved by his own father from *mbambakofi* wood! It was his pride and joy.'

'Did you ever see him use it on anyone?'

'Who – Stanley? No! He always said that in twenty years he had never used it once. He was very proud of that fact. He said that it was "a deterrent".'

'You say you have not seen him for a week, madam?'

For the first time a flicker of concern crossed the old woman's gnarled face. 'Is he dead?'

'Not to my knowledge.'

'On second thoughts, perhaps I should have reported it to the police. He did not seem his normal self lately.'

'In what way?'

'He seemed, I don't know – down in the dumps.' She sighed. 'And when I said to you that he never used his *rungu* on anyone, that is not strictly true. A couple of weeks ago a couple of tearaways from the other side of the slum were calling him names and, well—'

'Go on, madam.'

'He hit one of them over the head. Not hard. A tap, really. But it did the trick. They never called him names again.'

'Do you have any idea where he might be, madam?' Mwangi said. 'Did he have any family?'

'A sister – she lives over in Kilifi, I believe. She used to visit, but it made him angry so she stopped coming.'

Mwangi left the old woman and walked back through the slum to his car. What she had told him pretty much tallied with the information he had gleaned from Alec Standage. Stanley Kikwete had been a first-class *askari* at the Sandpiper ever since he had left the Army, but his deteriorating mental health – memory loss, confusion – had given the newly arrived manager little choice but to let him go.

But it seemed that Sergeant Major Stan had reacted badly to redundancy – to the extent that he had taken to attacking the very guests he had dedicated his life to protecting. Was it vengeance? Mwangi doubted it. If the old man had really wanted to get his own back on Alec Standage, he would have administered more than a tap on the head with his *rungu*. No, it was far more likely that he was trying to send a message to the hotel manager that without the Sergeant Major the safety of the guests could not be guaranteed.

The logic of the plan could not be faulted, Mwangi conceded. And Standage had indeed beefed up his security. It was just a pity that Frau Klinker's skull had been paper-thin.

He got into the car and opened his roadmap. Kilifi was just a few miles north along the highway.

It was at that moment that the police radio on his dashboard crackled to life and, to Mwangi's surprise, he heard the despatch operator calling his own name.

Mwangi acknowledged the call and made a note of the instructions. Jouma, it seemed, wanted him to report to the police station at Malindi immediately. He looked at the map again and saw that Kilifi was on the way.

Hannah O'o'nga lived in a single-storey clapboard house on the south bank of Kilifi creek. She was a rubicund woman of fifty, who kept pigs and chickens in a small corral beside the house and a deadbeat drunk of a husband in an even smaller hut on the other side of the yard.

'Welcome, Detective Mwangi,' she said. 'Would you like some papaya juice?'

'If you don't mind, madam, I am rather pressed for time,' Mwangi said.

Hannah's face fell. She did not get many visitors. 'Follow me,' she said. 'He is this way.' She led him around the house and along a dirt track through a coconut grove. 'He arrived here yesterday. I think he must have walked. His clothes were filthy and the soles of his shoes were hanging off – but whenever I try to speak to him he just . . . well, you will see.' She looked up at him sadly. 'Is it true? What he did?'

'I believe so, madam.'

'What will happen to him?'

'We will let the doctors decide that.'

Presently they arrived at the riverbank.

'There he is,' Hannah said, pointing at a figure sitting forlornly on a fallen log, staring up at the vast concrete roadbridge that carried the Mombasa highway over the creek. 'That is all he does. He just sits and stares in his filthy uniform.'

'I see.'

She cupped her hands to her mouth. 'Stanley! There is a gentleman here from Mombasa to see you.'

The old *askari* turned slowly. 'Mombasa?'

'Yes.'

Stanley Kikwete deliberately screwed his oversized beret on to his head. Then, with his chest puffed out officiously, he strode across to where his sister and Mwangi stood.

'Good morning, Mr Kikwete,' said Mwangi. 'I was wondering if I might have a word.'

Stanley frowned. 'Are you a resident? You know this is a private beach? Do you have your wristbands?'

'No, sir,' Mwangi said softly. 'I don't.'

Quick as a flash Stanley removed the *rungu* club hanging from his belt and twirled it sharply into the palm of his other hand. 'Then I think you should move on now, sir,' he said.

Mwangi smiled at him. '*Mbambakofi* wood, isn't it?' he said, nodding at the cudgel.

Stanley seemed taken aback. 'Yes.'

'I understand it is the very best kind.'

His weatherbeaten face twitched with a sudden burst of memory and he smiled. 'Yes. My father made it for me.'

'I would like you to tell me about your *rungu*, Stanley,' Mwangi said, putting his hand on the *askari*'s thin shoulder and leading him along the bank. 'I hear that in the right hands you can kill a wildebeest with just one blow.'

VIII

60

A beetle was crawling across Isiah's bare stomach. He watched it for a few moments, then skewered it with his fingernail and popped it into his mouth.

Its blood had a pleasing bitterness.

He was sitting cross-legged on a rock, high on the granite outcrop that protruded from the swamp like a fist emerging from water. The outcrop was surrounded as far as the eye could see by thick tangles of briar, wind-blasted mangroves, impenetrable reed beds and vast, stinking expanses of glutinous black sludge. High above vultures circled, the only visible sign of life; feral creatures, creatures of the night, scuttled invisibly in the dank undergrowth.

Dawn was breaking. Isiah watched the sun nudge the horizon, filling the sky with the colours of crimson and gold. To the west he saw the purple thunderheads that had formed above the plains.

A storm was coming.

Isiah smiled. *They were coming.*

It was as Ngai had prophesied. His work here was almost done.

At that moment Jouma and Mwangi were being helped out of a rubber dinghy and on to a Port Authority river patrol vessel idling at the mouth of the Sabaki river estuary. At the wheelhouse they were greeted with visible scepticism by Sergeant Odenga of the General Service Unit, Kenya Police's elite stormtroopers. Odenga, a bull of a man who seemed about to burst out of his combat fatigues, had travelled overnight from Nairobi with the rest of his twenty-strong platoon and was in no mood to be ordered about by a puny plainclothes detective from Mombasa. But he had his orders, and so did his men, who were sitting on deck, making last-minute checks of their assault rifles.

'Good morning, Sergeant,' Jouma said. 'Are you and your men ready?'

'Of course,' Odenga growled.

Jouma smiled wanly. He knew of the GSU's hard-nosed reputation. They called themselves police, but they were to all intents and purposes a paramilitary outfit called upon to bash skulls in the slum hotspots of Nairobi and the Rift Valley. Many of them, like Odenga, had served as special forces troops in the Army.

'Good. Then we should get going.'

'I understand you want this maniac taken alive,' the Sergeant said.

Jouma nodded. 'If possible, yes.'

'Well, I'm just warning you that it may *not* be possible. If at any time I decide my men are at risk, then I will have no hesitation in ordering them to shoot to kill. Is that clear?'

Jouma glanced at Mwangi, who seemed to be transfixed with terror. 'Perfectly,' he said.

'And another thing. Who is *that*?'

He pointed at a thirty-foot game-fishing boat moored a hundred yards off the patrol vessel's stern.

Jouma felt his throat go dry. 'That, Sergeant Odenga, is a support vessel.'

'A *what*? Nobody said anything about support vessels.'

'It has orders to keep at a safe distance,' Jouma said lamely, wondering what Odenga would say if he knew who was on board the fishing boat.

'Well, do me a favour, *Inspector*,' Odenga scowled. 'Fucking keep it well away from me and my men.'

★

A coastguard helicopter was approaching from the south. From his position on *Yellowfin*'s flying bridge, Jake watched with schoolboyish wonder as it roared low over the estuary and thumped upriver, its rotors slicing the sultry morning air.

A hundred men with dogs, a platoon of GSU thugs *and* helicopter support. It was, he had to admit, an impressive assembly at such short notice. If the Headhunter was indeed hiding out in the Chakama Reserve, then he was going to be in for a rude awakening this morning.

And, all being well, he would be there to see the bastard brought down. The prospect of staring into the eyes of the man responsible for Mac Bowden's death outweighed any consideration of his own safety – or indeed that of his passengers.

'The Mayor's done you proud,' he said to Katherine, who was sitting beside him on the bridge. The reporter was chainsmoking Marlboros and had been ever since they had left Flamingo Creek at five that morning. 'The power of the press, eh?'

She grunted something indecipherable and Jake chuckled. 'You're not nervous, are you?'

'Just impatient,' she said. 'How long do we have to wait here?'

He pointed at the patrol vessel powering upriver. 'As soon as they're out of sight.'

'The Inspector promised me an exclusive.'

'And you'll get it.'

'Christ, it'll be all over before we get there.'

'I bloody well hope it is,' Jake said with feeling. 'The guys in those boats have got guns. All I've got is a couple of filleting knives and a harpoon.'

Below them the cabin door opened and a young

white man with a camera round his neck tottered out into the cockpit. Katherine's photographer had spent most of the journey north from Flamingo Creek being violently and loudly seasick in the latrine.

'You all right down there, Barry?' Jake called cheerfully.

'Fine, fine,' the snapper muttered unconvincingly as he slumped into the fighting chair bolted to the deck next to the stern rail.

Up ahead, all that could be seen of the patrol vessel was its boiling wake as it disappeared round the bend in the river. Jake fired up *Yellowfin's* twin diesels and the thirty-footer began to move slowly upriver.

The first couple of miles passed uneventfully. They saw villages and waving children, fishing smacks and dhows. With the sun shining and the water glittering it was almost idyllic. Standing in the cramped, enclosed wheel-house of the patrol boat, staring over the coastguard skipper's shoulder at the river ahead, Mwangi found himself reflecting that, were it not for the fact that lurking somewhere up there was a maniac with a machete, it might even have been enjoyable.

'If he knows we are coming, won't he just escape?' he asked. It still seemed slightly surreal to him that he was here, on a boat full of armed GSU troopers, heading up the Sabaki river towards the killer's lair. It was exciting, but at the same time there was a part of him that wished he was back in his office on Mama Ngina Drive, with a pile of paperwork and a hot cup of coffee.

'Escape where?' Jouma said. 'There are men and dogs positioned at all points around the perimeter of the Reserve. Trust me, Mwangi – he has nowhere to go.'

Mwangi nodded, but he was not convinced. There was a big difference between catching a murderer from behind a desk and physically hunting him down. And, as

262

far as he could see, the Sabaki river was a huge place where a single man could easily make himself invisible.

Jouma looked at the tension on the young detective's face and smiled grimly. Less than twelve hours ago, due to his exemplary policework, Mwangi had cracked his first case. And Jouma, while he would never admit as much in words, was inordinately proud of him. But that was then and this was now – and Isiah Oulu was a completely different proposition to a sad, senile old *askari*. There would be time for back-slapping once the Headhunter was behind bars once again.

The river began to narrow alarmingly. And suddenly the reassuring signs of civilisation dwindled away to the occasional hut, or the exposed bones of an abandoned boat trapped in the mud. Even the hoots of the birds and animals in the jungle seemed to have fallen silent, Jouma thought. Or was he just letting his imagination run away with him?

Half a mile downriver *Yellowfin's* speed was little more than a crawl as Jake peered intently at the river ahead of them, gauging depths and weaving a course through the encroaching mud banks. In parts the river was so narrow that overhanging branches scraped the tarpaulin sun screen over the flying bridge, and there was the ominous scrape of *Yellowfin's* hull against some submerged obstacle.

Barry the photographer clambered up the ladder from the cockpit. 'I don't mean to spoil the party,' he said. 'But I'm not sure how much further we can go.'

Jake raised his finger to the sky, where two huge vultures were circling lazily and patiently above the forest canopy, studiously ignoring the coastguard chopper zigzagging like a huge dragonfly in the distance.

'I get the feeling we're nearly there,' he said.

The spotter in the helicopter had seen the hut and relayed its location to the patrol vessel. Chipche Molonga had chosen well, Jouma thought. The gourd plantation was the first sign of life they had seen for over a mile – apart from the vultures wheeling directly over it. If anybody had it in mind to steal the orderly's precious crop, they would need a qualification in junglecraft to find it first.

Sergeant Odenga came into the wheelhouse. 'This is it?' he barked.

'I believe so.'

'Very well.' He ordered the skipper to bring the boat as close to the bank as he dared. Then he slapped his meaty paw on the vessel's high-powered ship-to-shore radio. 'You have this thing tuned to the comms frequency?'

'Everything is ready, Sergeant.'

Odenga nodded grimly. 'Good. Then we'll go.'

He went back on deck, where his men were assembled in readiness to go ashore. There was a barked order and Jouma watched as the platoon jumped down into the thigh-deep water and began wading ashore, their weapons held above their heads.

'Turn her around so she's facing downriver,' he told the skipper. 'If we have to leave in a hurry I want to be ready.'

Odenga's men moved swiftly towards the hut, weaving through the low, unkempt vines and their engorged fruit. Some had burst open and oozed thick, sweet, rotting flesh. As they neared the ramshackle wooden building, a vulture the size of a dog watched them disdainfully from the open door. Then it turned and began tugging violently at something inside. When it raised its head again, a scrap of flesh was hanging from its powerful beak.

The single gunshot rang out with shocking suddenness, and the previously turgid river exploded with the shrieks and whoops of bird and animals.

'What the hell was that?' Katherine said.

Jake brought *Yellowfin* to a standstill, mid-river. Two hundred yards ahead, facing them now, was the patrol vessel. He could make out figures moving behind the glass window of the wheelhouse. *Jouma?*

He glanced at the ship-to-shore, and thought about hailing the other boat. But by now they would have switched to a comms channel enabling the various components of the manhunt to keep in contact with each other.

No – he would keep out of it. That was the deal, and he would stick to it for now.

'I heard a shot fired, Sergeant?' Jouma said into the comms handset, trying to keep his voice calm. 'What is your status?'

Odenga's voice crackled through the speakers. 'Vulture,' he said.

Jouma almost laughed with relief. 'Understood.'

'But we've found something. A body. African male, middle-aged I would say – although it's hard to tell because his head has been removed.'

The two detectives looked at each other.

Chipche.

The headless body of the orderly was bloated in the heat, the torn remnants of his robes crusted with dried blood. The vulture had made short work of tearing

265

into the succulent muscle of the exposed neck, but it was not the only creature to have dined on the remains.

Odenga stepped over the body and went inside the hut. The air was humid and stank of rotting vegetation and sweet human decay. Several dozen gourds had been stacked against one wall and in front of him was a metal shelf and wooden chair. In the light from the open door he saw that the chair was splashed with a dark substance that had also formed a larger stain on the baked-earth floor. And, now that his eyes were adjusting to the gloom, he saw more looping spatters on the fibrous walls and even on the roof.

The Sergeant knelt and tentatively dabbed the stain with his finger. It was dry, but when he held his hand up to the light he saw that the sandy residue that clung to his skin was a heavy purple colour, like the sediment from an expensive bottle of red wine.

'Blood, Inspector,' he said into his radio. 'Lots of blood. This must be where he killed them.'

'Secure the area, Sergeant,' Jouma said. 'And keep your men out of there – it is now a crime scene.'

Odenga clicked off his radio and shook his head. *Fucking pen-pusher.*

'Sir!'

One of his men was hunkered down by the door, where he had spotted something lying on the hard-packed earth.

'A *cell*phone?' Jouma said.

'It is a . . . Nokia 5310,' Odenga reported.

Mwangi nodded. 'Ask him to turn it on.'

A few moment later the sergeant reported that the battery was dead.

'Detective Mwangi wants you to retrieve the SIM card,' Jouma said.

'What the fuck does that mean?'

'Just put the phone in your pocket and bring it back to the boat.'

'Roger that,' Odenga said. 'But we won't be back for a while. There's a trail next to the hut that leads to the swamp. We're heading there now. Eagle One, do you copy?'

There was a sudden blast of static and the distorted voice of a helicopter spotter said, 'Copy. On our way.'

In the cabin of the patrol boat, Jouma heard the *thwok-thwok* of rotors and the flimsy vessel shuddered as the chopper rose suddenly from behind the tree line and flashed overhead in the direction of the Reserve.

The Headhunter moved swiftly and silently through the swamp, its labyrinthine tracks second nature to him. He watched, invisible, as the mortals splashed and cursed their way across the treacherous quagmire, tearing their skin on the clawlike thorns. How *ungainly* they were, he thought. How *pathetic*. They had the audacity to claim that they ruled the earth and were masters of nature, and yet once they were out of their comfortable towns and villages they were helpless. He would be doing them a favour by killing them. He would be setting them free.

The two-man chopper hung a thousand feet above the badlands of the Chakama Reserve, and in the glass bulb of the cockpit the coastguard spotter, trained to pick out tiny, flickering signs of life in the vastness of the Indian Ocean, peered down at the ragged line of antlike figures struggling across the thick mud and dense undergrowth.

It was like a sea, he thought. A black sea of roiling mud and shit, and in the middle of it a small island of jagged rock. Never had he felt so glad to be up here,

267

above it all. To be one of the GSU men currently heaving their way across the swamp would be his idea of hell.

'Eagle One, a path would be helpful,' Odenga bellowed in his headphones. Then he heard the Sergeant curse freely.

The spotter shook his head. 'Negative from our present position. We'll swing round to the north and see if we can see anything.'

He tapped the pilot's elbow and felt a lurch in his stomach as the chopper swooped down towards the outcrop. It was then that his highly sensitive eyes detected movement among the rocks at the base of the cliffs. Again he signalled to the pilot, who expertly brought the chopper into position barely a hundred feet above the crags. And now he could see that something *was* moving down there.

It was a pair of vultures. The birds were standing in what appeared to be a circular pit dug from the peaty earth, heads bobbing as they feasted on what from five hundred feet looked like a pile of mouldy sticks but, on closer inspection through a pair of high-resolution binoculars, were in fact human limbs in an advanced state of decomposition.

Jesus Christ.

The spotter exhaled – and the noise that came from his mouth was akin to a sob.

'Eagle One – what the hell are you doing?' Odenga demanded over the comms channel. 'We're getting bogged down in this shit!'

'Report that we have found a grave,' he said unsteadily. He gave the map coordinates. 'There appear to be human remains.'

Back on the patrol boat Jouma felt his stomach tighten. *They had reached the dark heart of the killer's lair.*

'Be advised, Sergeant, you are very close now,' he said into the handset. 'Please exercise extreme caution.'

But no sooner were the words out of his mouth than the radio speakers erupted with an unearthly noise that filled the cabin. Indeed, the noise was so unspeakable it took Jouma a moment to realise it was the sound of men screaming in terror.

The speed of the attack was bewildering. Three of his men were already dead before Odenga realised what was happening. Even then he could not be sure, because he could not see the enemy. All he could see were men running in confusion. His ears were filled with the sound of gunfire and screams.

He felt something running down his face. It was fresh, warm blood. *His own?* He turned to his second-in-command, Corporal Tambo – but, even as he did so, it was as if Tambo had been sucked backwards into the impenetrable undergrowth, the expression on his face one of bemusement. A moment later something was spat from the bushes and Tambo's head landed at his feet with a moist splash, its expression unchanged.

'Eagle One, what is going on?' Jouma shouted into the handset.

He heard the noise of the rotors and the sound of screaming and machine-gun fire. Then the spotter's voice cut through the racket.

'They are ... *under attack.*'

'Explain, Eagle One! Under attack from who?'

'I – I can't see. I can't *see!*'

'You must be able to see *something*, dammit!'

The spotter fell silent.

'Come in, Eagle One!' Jouma said.

'I can see bodies,' the spotter said, his voice so quiet it

was barely audible over the noise of the chopper. *'Bodies and heads.'*

When the gunfire finally stopped, it seemed to Jake that the silence was even more profound than before. Even the breeze that had tickled the overhanging branches of the trees had stilled. The only sound was the muffled throb of the helicopter, so faint as to be almost indistinguishable from the ever-present hum of the insects.

'This is creepy, man,' Barry the photographer said.

Too fucking right it was. Jake snatched the ship-to-shore handset from its clip. 'Inspector? What's happening? What was all that shooting?'

But the response was static. The patrol vessel's radio was still tuned to the comms channel.

'Maybe they've got him,' Katherine said.

Maybe they had. Maybe they were on their way back now, with the Headhunter's body bound by his wrists and ankles to a pole like he was a big game trophy. But Jake couldn't shake the feeling that, somewhere out there in the wasteland of the Chakama Reserve, something had gone terribly wrong.

From two hundred yards away the figures in the wheelhouse of the patrol vessel were little more than indistinct shadows. They didn't *seem* to be in any sort of panic – but then at this distance it was impossible to tell.

Fuck this. Jake jabbed the starter button and *Yellowfin's* diesels coughed to life.

'What are you doing?' Katherine asked.

'Something's not right. I'm going over there.'

But even as he spoke the thirty-footer's engines were making a noise like fingernails being drawn down a blackboard – and when he looked over his shoulder Jake saw jets of white smoke hissing from the stern.

270

'Goddammit!' he exclaimed.

'What is it?'

'The props have fouled. We're too far upriver; the water is thick with weeds and vines. They must have snagged when I started the engines, or maybe the intakes are clogged. I'll have to clear them.'

'Great,' Barry said. 'How long will that take?'

Jake fixed him with a venomous look. 'Maybe you can roll your trousers up and give me a hand,' he said.

He smacked his fist angrily on the wheel. Clearing the obstruction could take the best part of an hour, and would involve repeated dives under the surface of the murky water. He would need a facemask and cutting equipment from the cabin.

He would also need help.

'Downstairs now,' he ordered. 'We've got work to do.'

As Jake followed Katherine and Barry down the ladder to the cockpit, he noticed that upriver the patrol vessel seemed eerily quiet, like some miniature Marie Celeste. Maybe Jouma and Mwangi were on deck – from this angle all he could see was the boat's wide bows and the superstructure of the wheelhouse.

Just then he saw the dark, bulky form of another vulture drop from one of the overhanging trees and land lightly on the wheelhouse roof of Jouma's boat. He shivered, because he fucking hated vultures. As far as Jake was concerned, the flesh-eating birds were proof of the theory of evolution – because no God in His right mind could have ever dreamed up such a nightmarish creation.

But as he stared with grim fascination across the expanse of water the bird seemed to mutate before his very eyes, like a pool of black ink spreading upwards and outwards. And it was then that he realised that it wasn't a vulture on the roof at all. It was a man, the naked limbs unfolding as he stood from his crouched landing position to his full enormous height.

And in the man's left hand was something silver and sharp, its foot-long blade still dripping blood.

The time before his rebirth had no linear structure; rather it was constructed of incomplete moments, like shards of glass from a broken mirror. He remembered his time among the mortals, how their existence consisted of shouting and fighting like animals for space, food, light, *attention*; and how the very idea that these pitiful creatures were somehow his own flesh and blood had disgusted him so much he had excised it from his mind almost as soon as he developed conscious thought. He remembered how killing them had filled him with a rapture so astonishing that it was almost too much to bear.

And he remembered the darkness that followed – voices and faces burned indistinctly on to his memory, trying to make him renounce Ngai, his own father, with words and insinuation at first, and then torture and poison.

He knew now that it had been a test, just as his whole life among the mortals had been a test. To understand the apostates, those who denied Ngai, he had to live among them. He had to experience for himself the temptations of a mortal existence and reject them. Only then would he be worthy to join his father.

Only then could the living god become truly immortal.

The day Ngai spoke to him was the day he knew he had succeeded – and when at last he understood that his time here in the wilderness was at an end.

The apostates had come for him in their legions, as he knew they would. But their guns were no match for the power that flowed through him. He had moved among them like the wind – and their blood now coated the gleaming steel of his machete.

The prophecies had been fulfilled. And now that he had reached the boat one last step remained before he was free.

'Eagle One – what is your status?'

'Still in position.'

'And Sergeant Odenga?'

'I don't see him. I see five men running back towards the river.'

'Is that all?'

'Yes.'

Five men left out of twenty who had gone into the Reserve? My God – what sort of a monster were they up against?

Jouma felt the blood draining from his face.

'How long do you have left in the air, Eagle One?'

'Fifteen minutes maximum.'

'Stay there as long as you can and look for survivors. When the rest of the men get here we will head back to the estuary.'

'Roger that.'

Jouma clicked off the transmission and turned to Mwangi. 'Get *Yellowfin* on the radio and tell Jake he's got to get out of here,' he said. 'Where did the skipper go?'

'He said he was worried about the engines getting fouled with weeds. I think he is out back.'

Jouma hurried out of the wheelhouse. The deck was littered with surplus equipment the GSU had left behind – empty magazines, water bottles, webbing, utility belts – and Jouma suddenly wished Odenga's men had left a couple of assault rifles.

The skipper was at the rear of the boat, on his knees

with his back to the wheelhouse, leaning over the stern rail as if he was being sick.

'Captain – the GSU men are on their way back. We may need medical equipment ready.'

The skipper did not move.

'*Captain!*' He went across and grabbed him by the shoulder. 'Did you hear what I—'

The skipper toppled sideways along the rail and landed with a soft thud against the rear scuppers – and even though Jouma saw it with his own eyes his brain seemed unwilling, or unable, to register the fact that his head had been cleanly removed from his neck.

'Is this what you are looking for, mortal?'

Jouma turned in the direction of Isiah Oulu's resonant voice, and his legs buckled underneath him.

The Headhunter was squatting on the roof of the wheelhouse like some grotesque gargoyle. The skipper's head was between his feet, the eyes thankfully closed and the face seemingly at peace.

'Why, Isiah?' Jouma whispered. '*Why?*'

For a moment the killer seemed surprised. 'Isiah is a name I have not heard for a long time,' he said. 'Do I know you, mortal?'

'No – but I know you.'

'Then you will know that I am Athi, son of Ngai, Divider of the Universe and Lord—'

'*Shut up!* Shut up, you sick murdering bastard!'

Jouma was trembling now, a heady concoction of fear and absolute fury fizzing in his veins.

Then the wheelhouse door opened and Mwangi came sauntering out. He stared quizzically at Jouma sitting on the deck and was about to speak when the machete swooped down from above, so fast that Jouma had no time to shout a warning.

The young detective stood there, motionless, for

what seemed like an eternity. Then his mouth opened and a gout of bright-red arterial blood spewed out; and in that same moment his head wobbled and fell backwards and his body pitched forward on to the deck.

The Headhunter just smiled. '*I am Athi. Son of Ngai. Divider of the Universe. Lord of Nature.*'

Jake moved through the brackish water in what seemed to him like slow motion, his lungs and limbs burning with every painful stroke. He'd thought he was fit, some kind of superman who could brush off the effects of being stabbed in the guts with just a couple of weeks' running. The truth was he was still as weak as a kitten, his traumatised body still months away from recovery and certainly in no state to swim two hundred yards against the current.

But he pushed himself on towards the boat, every inch a fresh agony but every second vital if he was to have any chance of saving the lives of the men on board. Up ahead he could see the killer now on the wheelhouse roof. The Headhunter had his back to him, which was the single tiny advantage he had. But even that would cease to exist if Katherine or her dopey photographer should happen to shout out; he had slipped into the water without them noticing, but the nearer he got to the patrol vessel the more it seemed impossible that they would not see him.

Fifty yards, twenty, ten. He reached out a hand and felt the tough fibreglass of the prow. He had made it.

But what horror would he find now that he was here?

The Headhunter leaped nimbly down from the roof, and landed catlike on the balls of his feet in front of Jouma.

'Is this all there is, Isiah?' the Inspector said. 'Killing people? How many must die before you are satisfied?'

The Headhunter stared with fascination at the rivulets of blood on the blade of his weapon. 'This is a world of non-believers. Apostates, like you, who take the word of Ngai in vain. You deserve to suffer eternal torment – yet my father is merciful. He embraces you in his kingdom. And now the time has come for me to join him.'

Jouma laughed. Somehow it seemed the appropriate response to a madman who very soon was going to kill him.

'Something amuses you, apostate?'

'I was wondering how you plan to join your father in the afterlife, Isiah. By cutting your own head off?'

'No,' said the Headhunter. '*You* will take me to him.'

Using the mooring rope and what dwindling reserves of strength he had left, Jake hauled himself up on to the snub-nosed bow of the patrol boat. He could hear voices from the other side of the wheelhouse – one of them unmistakably Jouma's, the other deep and powerful.

For Christ's sake, keep him talking . . .

Jake frantically scanned the bow area for something he could use as a weapon – but all he could see were coils of rope. Anything vaguely resembling a blunt instrument was bolted to the deck.

There was no time. He would have to improvise. There were narrow walkways on either side of the boat's superstructure leading to the main assembly deck. Silently he moved along the port rail, his back pressed to the metal bulkhead.

'You will take me in this boat to the far horizon,' the Headhunter was saying, 'where the sun rises from the darkness and sheds its light on the world of mortal man. There I shall join with Ngai and together we shall ...'

He was, Jouma concluded, utterly insane. But the Inspector kept nodding frantically, playing along with the ceaseless torrent of gibberish, because now he had seen Jake moving slowly round the side of the wheelhouse. Slowly, agonisingly slowly, the Englishman crept forward, on to the deck now, closer ... *closer* ...

With a noise like the end of the world, Eagle One came tearing over the trees on its way downriver. The Headhunter turned to look – and as he did he saw Jake no more than five feet behind him. He raised his machete, and in that instant Jake hit him with everything he had left. The shoulder charge was only glancing, but the deck was slippy with Mwangi's blood and the killer lost his balance momentarily. It was enough for the tiny Inspector to scramble to his feet and wrap his arms around the Headhunter's waist, his momentum bringing the seven-foot Masai crashing to the ground like a felled pine. Skittering through the blood on his hands and knees, Jake fell on him, jamming his right forearm into the Headhunter's throat as he writhed and roared and using his left hand to pin the killer's wrist – and his machete – to the deck.

'*I can't hold him,*' Jake gasped through gritted teeth.

Jouma grabbed the nearest thing to hand – a GSU utility vest. He found something metallic and heavy in one of the pockets and he began smashing it into the Headhunter's face.

'*Jesus Christ, no, Inspector!*' Jake screamed, staring in horror at the cylinder in Jouma's hand. '*It's a fucking stun grenade!*'

He knew that the device, although designed not to explode into shards of shrapnel like a normal grenade, would unleash a massive bang and a retina-scorching burst of light.

Jouma looked down and only then did he see the pin mechanism at the top of the cylinder. He did not know what a stun grenade was – and nor did he care.

'I am Athi, son of Ngai,' the Headhunter was bellowing. 'Divider of the Universe, Lord—'

Jouma pulled the pin and shoved the grenade as far into the killer's open mouth as it would go. The two men rolled away from the Headhunter a split-second before the device detonated, unleashing a blinding flash of magnesium and ammonium perchlorate and a percussive bang of more than 170 decibels, loud enough at such close quarters to blow out his eyeballs and his small, sharpened teeth, and turn every artery and blood vessel in his brain to mush in an instant.

Jake had no idea how long he lay there. All he knew was the piercing ringing sound in his ears. He called for Jouma but he couldn't hear his own voice. After a while he pushed himself up on trembling arms.

'Inspector?'

Jouma was sitting upright against one of the deck bulkheads, staring at the wheelhouse with blank eyes. There were trickles of blood coming from his ears and his nose, and for a moment Jake thought he was dead.

But then suddenly the Inspector's eyes filled with tears.

IX

61

Dr Nicholas Lutta was deep in thought. He was sitting at his desk in the clinical block of Kalami Secure Mental Hospital, studying the records of the patient who had raped, killed and eaten his rent collector. But the words were not registering. He had other things on his mind. Things that nagged and irritated him. Loose ends. Unanswered questions.

A page was missing from the records. Lutta absently got up from his chair and went to an untidy stack of papers hanging perilously from a shelf on the other side of the office. He found it. He knew all too well that there were those among the clinical staff – Dr Klerk mainly – who wondered openly how on earth he could ever find anything in this mess. But Klerk of all people should understand that the human mind was not designed to be tidy or compartmentalised; even a cursory glance at the chaotic ribbons of the brain should be an indication that it was a purely organic structure rather than one that had suffered human impositions on its design.

Lutta knew exactly where everything was in his office. He did not require artificial filing systems, because his own was flawless. It was precisely when people started meddling with the natural development of the mind that problems arose. And, sadly, that meddling usually began at birth.

He left his office and locked the door behind him. He crossed the cell block and went into the assessment suite. His patient was waiting for him. Staring, immobile, vegetative.

Lutta pulled up a chair.

'So then, Thomas,' he said with a smile. 'Where were we?'

The killer of the rent collector did not react. But then his brain was in a stasis. It was, as Lutta himself had described it in one of his papers, like a car engine turning over but refusing to fire. Just to make sure, Lutta dabbed the killer's eye with the tissue-paper spear and jammed a pin deep beneath his fingernail.

'You are progressing well, Thomas,' Lutta said, scribbling a note in his pad.

And Thomas *was* coming on well. Of that there could be no doubt. Six months ago it had been an effort to shut him up. He couldn't help but tell anyone who was prepared to listen just what he had done to that rent collector and why. He really couldn't understand what he was doing in a mental hospital. As far as he was concerned, he had done the world a service.

After just two weeks under Lutta's supervision, however, Thomas was talking less. After two months, he was struggling to remember where he was. A month later, what he had done was becoming a distant memory. Four months into his treatment, he had begun to lose the power of speech. Five, and Thomas's cognitive functions had decayed to the extent that when Lutta brought a mouse into the room the psychologist was able to convince him that they were blood relatives. A week ago, Thomas had regressed into a vegetative state. He no longer spoke or thought. He had no exterior sensation. All he did was eat and shit and breathe and listen and obey.

It was, Lutta thought, becoming too easy.

He looked up from his notepad. Thomas stared at the

wall. A tear was running down his cheek, but only because he had temporarily lost control of his blink reflex. That could be easily remedied.

Lutta stared at him and for a moment was at a loss. In front of him was a blank canvas upon which he could paint anything. A masterpiece, or a childish rendering of a house with four windows and a chimney with curly smoke. This was his achievement. How perverse it was that after so much struggle it should now be almost second nature to him.

Ah, Thomas – what shall I do with you? Shall I create an artist? Or another monster?

Now was not the time to decide. Lutta had far more important things to preoccupy him at the moment. He smiled at the orderly, who was waiting by the door.

'I think that's enough for one day, Michael,' he said. 'You can take him away now.'

62

'My brother has a disorder,' Harry Philliskirk said. 'It makes him think and act irrationally. Unfortunately, this manifests itself through gambling.'

Tajik ul-Mraq stared at him dispassionately from his chair, switched his gaze to Ralph, then switched it back again. A cool breeze blew through the open window of the Arabs' office in Mombasa Old Town.

'That is most unfortunate,' he said.

'It has come to my attention that my brother recently, and ill-advisedly, became involved in a poker game.'

'I know,' Tajik said. He gestured at his own brother, who was perched, hawklike, at his laptop computer. 'Ali and I arranged the game.'

'I say ill-advisedly,' Harry continued, 'because not only is my brother a rotten poker player, but he also did not have the financial wherewithal to cover his stake.'

'Oh, but he did, Mr Philliskirk. He had enough for a seat in the game, and enough to lose thirty-thousand dollars during it.'

'And there's the rub, Mr ul-Mraq. That money did not belong to him.'

The Arab shrugged. 'Who it belonged to is irrelevant.'

Harry sighed. He knew it would end up like this. Had he seriously believed that he could get his money back by appealing to the better nature of the ul-Mraq brothers? He glanced across at Ralphie, at the blooming bruise on his brother's jaw, and he wished to God he'd hit the stupid bastard harder. It was one thing to gamble nearly forty grand on a game of poker – but against a professional like Tajik ul-Mraq?

Harry looked into those coal-black eyes and the Arab might have just strangled his own mother for all the clues they gave out.

'I cannot stress how important that money is to my livelihood and that of my partner,' he said, 'and how neither he nor I sanctioned my brother to use it as collateral in a card game.'

'What do you expect us to do?' Ali said. 'We are honourable men, but we won the money fair and square. Had your brother won, would you expect us to come to your place of work to beg you to return the money? I think not.'

Harry smiled. 'Of course not.'

'Then I repeat: what do you expect us to do?'

Ralph stepped forward. 'Listen, this is all my fault. And I will do anything to rectify it. *Anything*, Mr ul-Mraq.'

The ul-Mraq brothers exchanged glances and Harry wondered why it should be that he and his own brother were so hopelessly inadequate compared to the Arabs.

'There is only one thing you can do,' Tajik said presently.

'Name it,' Ralph said.

'Win it back,' Ali said.

63

Detective Constable David Mwangi was buried in a small plot in the corner of his parents' estate on the outskirts of Nairobi. The ceremony was simple and heartfelt and attended by just a few close friends and family. Jouma and Simba both attended, but both kept their distance – and when it was over they did not stay for the wake.

As they made their way to the taxi waiting to take them to the airport, Mwangi's father intercepted them. He was tall and handsome, like his son, a former government minister who had also served as an ambassador in Europe.

'Inspector Jouma?'

'Mr Mwangi.'

'Thank you for coming today. Thank you both.'

Simba nodded – but she could see that it was Jouma he wanted to talk to. 'I'll wait for you in the taxi, Daniel.'

The two men walked across a well-kept lawn with views to the hills in the distance.

'I wanted to say that David spoke very warmly of you, Inspector,' Mr Mwangi said. 'I know you weren't together very long, but it is clear that he respected you a great deal.'

'Your son was a fine young man and a credit to you, sir. I have no doubt he would have made it to the very top of his profession.'

'I heard what happened that day at the Sabaki river. It sounded like carnage.'

'A lot of good men lost their lives, including David.'

'And you? Are you recovered?'

'I still have slight difficulty hearing out of one ear – but perhaps that is a result of old age,' Jouma said.

Mr Mwangi laughed awkwardly. Then he stopped and grasped Jouma by the arm. 'It was what he always wanted, Inspector. Ever since he was a young boy he dreamed of being a detective. If there is any comfort to be taken from this, at least David died having fulfilled his dream.'

Jouma opened his mouth to speak, but the words would not come.

They walked back to the taxi. This time Jouma stopped.

'You know that he solved a murder case, don't you, Mr Mwangi? Not only that, but he did it himself. The first I knew about it was when he turned up with the guilty man handcuffed in the back of his car.'

The old man's eyes twinkled. 'No. I did not know.'

Jouma glanced at the taxi. Simba could wait. 'If you have a few minutes, sir, I would very much like to tell you about an old, retired hotel *askari* by the name of Sergeant Major Stan.'

On the shuttle flight back to Mombasa, Simba ordered herself a large Scotch and water.

'Would you like something, Daniel? Tea, perhaps? Mineral water?'

Jouma looked at the drinks cart. 'If it's all very well with you, ma'am, I think I will have the same as you.'

The drinks arrived and Jouma, who had allowed alcohol to pass his lips on perhaps two occasions in his life, savoured the taste of the liquor.

'It's not like you,' Simba observed.

Jouma shrugged. 'What is the greater crime? Breaking the habit of a lifetime, or allowing life to pass you by?'

Simba smiled. 'You thought a great deal of the boy, didn't you?'

'Yes, ma'am. I did.'

The Kenya Airways 737 sped on through the night, and far below the great plains were shrouded in black.

'I appreciate this is not the time to be talking shop,' Simba said, 'but I thought you should know – there is to be an official inquiry into what happened at the Chakama Reserve.'

'Twelve GSU officers were killed. There has to be an inquiry, ma'am.'

'You will be required to give evidence.'

'Of course.'

'I read your case report. There is one thing that remains unanswered.'

Jouma nodded. 'Why the victims were targeted. Unfortunately it would seem the answer died with Isiah Oulu.'

'I was thinking specifically of Paul Yomo, Daniel. You aren't convinced that he was a Headhunter victim at all, are you?'

'There are certain aspects of the case that still bother me, yes.'

'You know that Brigadier Wako Chatme has complained to Provincial Police Officer Iraki about what happened at Mtongwe the other day.'

'I did hear something. Do you want me to drop the case, ma'am?'

She looked at him reprovingly. 'No. Not if you think there may be something in it. But tread lightly. I want the evidence to be one hundred per cent watertight before we act.'

At Mombasa Airport, they went their separate ways, Simba to her apartment in Nyali, Jouma to the police hostel where Mwangi had lived. There he collected the young detective's remaining belongings, placed them neatly in cardboard boxes and put them in the boot of his car. Tomorrow he would arrange to have them returned to his family. It was, he thought, the least he could do.

It was after ten by the time he was ready to leave, but the traffic in central Mombasa was as bad as ever and the main road to Makupa was solid. Instead, he took a short cut, past the Old Town and round the northern shoulder of the island through Kwakiziwi district. The road took him past Tabitha Yomo's apartment block and he pulled over. There was an estate agency sign in the garden and the curtains were closed.

It seemed the final link with Paul had been broken.

He was about to drive away when the front door of the apartment building opened and Ellen Wako Chatme came out. She was wearing riding jodhpurs and a low-cut blouse, and her hair was worn in a casual ponytail. A moment later a second person emerged from the building, and Jouma recognised him as Colonel Robert Sutherland, the diving instructor from Mtongwe base. He was casually dressed in a denim shirt and jeans and, as the door closed behind him, he lit two cigarettes and handed one to Ellen.

Jouma ducked down in his seat, feeling uncomfortably like a voyeur as the couple walked along the garden path towards the street. At the gate they stopped and kissed – and Jouma, who would never in a million years describe himself as an expert on such matters, could tell that this was no friendly embrace between two close friends. It was much more than that and, judging by the way Ellen's fingers slid into the waistband of Sutherland's jeans, it was the culmination of whatever had been going on in Tabitha's apartment.

The couple finished, and exchanged words. Sutherland laughed, then took her head gently in his hands and kissed the top of it. Then they went their separate ways and Jouma ducked down even further as the Colonel strode purposefully past his car. A few moments later there was an unearthly roar and he raced back along the street on the back of a powerful Harley motorcycle.

When he had gone, Jouma waited for several minutes before leaving. As he swung back on to the main road he was immediately stuck in traffic again.

Who were all these people? Where were they going?

Jouma shook his head, because it was pointless to ask. People were unknowable, their motives a mystery. After thirty years as a policeman he thought he'd understood that by now – but every day he discovered that in fact he didn't have a clue. He just bumbled along making assumptions until the truth came up and smacked him in the face.

Ellen and Robert Sutherland were having an affair. The Brigadier's wife and the Brigadier's golden boy.

And who on earth would have ever thought *that*?

64

The mood at the corner table in Suki Lo's bar was ugly, if not downright murderous. Even garrulous Suki had retreated to the other side of the bar so as not to intrude upon the three sombre-faced men sitting there.

'So what did Tajik say?' Jake asked.

'He said we have to win it back,' Harry said.

'Not you. I'm talking to this prick.'

His finger jabbed across the table until it was an inch from Ralph Philliskirk's nose. Harry's brother was ashen. His face looked as if it had collapsed.

'He said we have to win it back,' he said.

'And how do you propose to do that?'

'There's a big game tomorrow night, down at the Old Town. Five grand a chair.'

'And is there five grand left from the money you stole?'

Ralph shook his head miserably.

Jake turned to his partner. 'Get him out of my sight, Harry, before I kill him.'

As Harry hurriedly shepherded his brother out of the door, Jake took a swill of Pusser's rum. It was not a tipple he particularly favoured – it reminded him too much of his old man and those afternoons he'd stagger in from the Low Lights Tavern after drinking there since four in the morning. But the savage burn on the back of his throat seemed entirely appropriate considering the news he'd just been given. *Thirty-five grand!* Not only stolen but pissed against the wall in some Old Town gambling den. Just when the business was finally starting to show some signs of solvency, when they could pay their bills and still look forward to some profit at the end of the month.

Now they were back to square one. No money, creditors to pay and the biggest ever financial meltdown sending businesses like theirs to the wall every day. Last time they'd hit rock bottom they'd been bailed out.

This time there was no fairy godmother – they were well and truly fucked.

He poured himself another stiff measure. Harry came back and sat down. Jake poured him a drink.

'I'm really sorry, old man,' Harry said presently. 'It's my fault. I knew what he was like.'

'He's your brother, Harry.'

'That doesn't stop him from being a first-class arsehole.'

'Agreed. So what are we going to do?'

Harry shrugged. 'There's nothing we can do. Ralphie's got nothing. Any assets he might have had back in England will have been appropriated by the Uzbeki thugs he owes money to. And the family silver – well, that went years ago.'

'You're one hell of a family.'

'Tell me about it. So we're screwed.'

'Well and truly.'

The Pusser's bottle got another hammering.

'Of course, it's all irrelevant anyway,' Harry said. 'Even if we had five grand to play in this poker game, who the hell do you trust to win our money back? Ralph? I think I've got more idea about poker than he does, and I've never played the game in my life.'

'Me neither,' Jake said glumly, then he laughed and tinked his partner's glass. 'But it's been a hell of a ride, hasn't it?'

Harry nodded. 'Wouldn't have swapped it for

anything, old man. After all, friendship is the most important thing in the world, isn't it?'

But Jake was suddenly thinking about another dear friend, and about something he'd said over a beer at a hotel in Shanzu shortly before he'd been gunned down in cold blood trying to protect his client. And, although the idea that was forming in his mind made him recoil, he couldn't help thinking that if Mac Bowden was in his position he would do exactly the same thing.

65

Another day, another funeral. This time Jouma watched impassively as the cheap wooden coffin was manhandled into an eight-foot-long hole in the ground by a two-man burial detail at Kalami Hospital cemetery. Jouma watched as the powdery earth was shovelled over it and waited until the last stone had been placed on top of the unmarked grave.

'In a strange way I feel sad, Inspector,' Dr Klerk said as the two men walked back towards the hospital. 'I wish there had been something we could have done for him.'

'You did your best, Dr Klerk. But some people are beyond help.'

'I suppose you are right. Still, I can't help feeling a twinge of regret. Isiah was a deeply disturbed man, I agree, but did we fail him? I think of the time Dr Lutta spent with him. I know that at one stage he was very hopeful that his methods might result in a breakthrough.'

'Where is Dr Lutta? I thought he would have been here.'

'He is in Berlin, presenting a paper on the uses of hetero-suggestion in the treatment of the psychopathic subconscious.'

'You have lost me.'

'It is a technique he himself devised. In layman's terms, it involves using highly controlled and specific hypnotic suggestion to address the deep-rooted psycho-pathic tendencies of murderers. By delving deep into the subconscious, Dr Lutta hopes to identify the causes and correct them. Of course, it flies in the face of the opinions of the psychological community. And I have to confess I have my doubts about its effectiveness. But I am a firm believer in letting youth have its head – and Nicholas is a most brilliant young man.'

'Well, I'm afraid I can only nod sagely and pretend I understand what you are talking about,' Jouma said.

They walked on, and suddenly Klerk chuckled.

'You know it's ironic, Inspector. The primary case study in Dr Lutta's paper is Isiah Oulu. To think we have just buried him – and yet, thanks to him, Dr Lutta is enjoying an all-expenses-paid trip to Europe.'

'It is indeed a strange world, Dr Klerk,' Jouma said.

Two hours later Jouma was back in his office at Mama Ngina Drive. Without Mwangi it suddenly seemed terribly large and empty, and he realised he had come to enjoy the young detective's presence there.

There was a note on his desk requesting he call Christie at once.

'This body I've just examined,' the pathologist said down the phone. 'It *is* one of yours, isn't it?'

Jouma frowned. 'Which body?'

'The one picked up by that fishing boat last week. Been on ice here ever since. I've just this minute had a chance to look at it.'

'I honestly don't know what you are talking about, Mr Christie.'

Christie groaned impatiently. 'Headless body. African male. Single gunshot wound to the chest. Come on, Jouma – I know you've been preoccupied lately, but this is your case, isn't it?'

'I'll be right there.'

★

By the time Jouma arrived at the white-tiled chamber of horrors, the body had been opened and then stitched together again with thick black twine.

'Ring any bells?' Christie said.

The pathologist drew his attention to the stump of neck and in particular to the crisply sliced spinal column.

'I knew nothing about this body,' Jouma said, his anger still boiling. 'It seems it was processed by a detective who somehow managed to lose the report on the computer system.'

'That's computers for you, old fellow. Me, I prefer the old ways. You'll be pleased to know I have sent its fingerprints off to be analysed, but just in case you were anxious to know the identity of our fishy friend here . . .'

Christie reached for what looked like a cardboard hat box. Inside, nestling in polystyrene chips, was a gleaming white skull.

'Paul Yomo, I take it,' Jouma said as the pathologist lifted the skull from the box.

'The boiled-down version. Makes life much easier.' He carefully positioned the skull so that the remaining nub of connected vertebrae made contact with the exposed spine of the headless body. '*Et voila*, Inspector!' he announced triumphantly. 'A perfect fit.'

Yes it was, Jouma thought. Just like a jigsaw piece.

'You mentioned a gunshot wound?'

'The degrading effects of immersion have played merry hell with the skin,' he said, pointing at the odd indentation in the middle of the chest. 'But it's a wound nevertheless. In fact, there is still some evidence of charring and residue around the edges, suggesting the weapon was fired at pretty much point-blank range. Mind you, in order to bisect the aorta with a calibre this size, you'd need to hold it close.'

'What do you mean?'

Christie went across to his metal surgical table and returned with a small, clear plastic jar. In it was a twisted piece of copper-coloured metal. 'I retrieved this from under our friend's right scapula. Do you know much about bullets, Jouma?'

'Only that they kill people.'

'Well take a look. This, my friend, is a 2mm.'

'A 2mm?'

Christie looked at him pityingly. 'Jouma, this bullet is an antique. In fact, it was extremely rare even when it was in production, because it was specially designed for one make of pistol. And they don't come much smaller.'

'The Kolibri Car Pistol,' Jouma said. 'Patented in 1910 by Franz Pfannl, discontinued in 1938.'

Christie attempted unsuccessfully to mask his astonishment. 'You know why I like you, Jouma?' he said. 'We have known each other for fifteen years and yet you never cease to amaze me.'

66

One hour later, a Mombasa Police squad car, its siren wailing, raced through the checkpoint at Mtongwe naval base and squealed to a halt outside the administration block. Jouma and two uniformed officers jumped out and hurried upstairs to the office of Brigadier Charles Wako Chatme.

The Brigadier was playing golf, but that did not matter. The presentation box containing the Kolibri Car Pistol was removed from the glass display case, carefully bagged and driven to the offices of Evidence International, an independent forensic-science consultancy situated on the top floor of a modern air-conditioned building on Kenyatta Avenue. There it was taken to a laboratory belonging to Dr Alfgerd Fridgaard, the company's senior investigator. Her services would cost Coast Province CID five hundred dollars an hour, because Evidence International was normally employed by the defence counsels of rich white landowners and government ministers. But if Jouma was about to arrest one of Mombasa's most powerful and well-connected men for murder; if he was going to accuse him of using the antique 2mm pistol to kill Paul Yomo; and if he was going to allege that he cut off his son-in-law's head to make it appear to be the work of the serial killer known as the Headhunter, then he could not afford to be wrong. It was the biggest call of his career, and he was not prepared to risk everything on Kenya Police's beleaguered forensic department.

He had to be absolutely sure. And he had to act quickly.

Dr Fridgaard got to work in the sealed surroundings of the laboratory. She worked alone and she worked fastidiously. The pistol was scanned for fingerprints and residue, the stubby barrel swabbed minutely for evidence that the weapon had been fired. Samples were taken, chemical analysis carried out and ballistic comparisons made between the bullet retrieved from Paul Yomo's body and bullets from the gun.

'My God, Daniel, if you are wrong this will be the end of us both,' Simba said, staring at the sea from her office window.

'The end of *me*, ma'am,' Jouma corrected her. 'I was acting independently and did not consult you, either in the matter of obtaining the search warrant for the Brigadier's office or for hiring Dr Fridgaard to carry out the forensic tests. I am just sorry it could prove an expensive mistake.'

She returned to her desk. 'Where is the Brigadier now?'

'He had a tee booked at Mombasa golf course at one o'clock.'

'Then wait until the forensic report is in.'

'And then, ma'am?'

She stared at him. 'Be discreet, Daniel.'

The Brigadier was lining up a putt on the tenth green when the report arrived on Jouma's desk. By the time the Inspector arrived at the clubhouse to arrest him, he was preparing to tee off on the eighteenth.

Simba had told him to be discreet, and Jouma had no intention of disobeying his orders. He had come in his own car without uniformed officers in support. He intended to arrest the Brigadier on suspicion of murder, but if the suspect wanted a post-round gin and tonic then that was fine. There was no hurry.

As he waited in the car park, Jouma looked again at the forensic report. Dr Fridgaard had been thorough and her conclusions were indisputable: the bullet found in the body of Paul Yomo was fired from the same antique Kolibri Car Pistol that had been taken from Brigadier Wako Chatme's office earlier that day. Residual evidence proved that the gun had been fired recently. The fingerprints lifted from the handle of the pistol were the Brigadier's.

The mechanics of how Paul was decapitated and the body later dumped at sea were less clear. But Jouma knew there was more than enough solid evidence to charge the Brigadier with murder. Motive was certainly not an issue: when it came to Tabitha's boyfriends, the old man had form – and Exhibit A was Billy Kapchanga's back. Billy's crime was to be a lowly Old Town bongo player; imagine the red mist when Paul came cap in hand for twenty thousand dollars to pay off his gambling debts.

Simba had said she wanted watertight evidence, and it didn't come much more conclusive than this.

And yet as he sat in his car, watching the Brigadier marching down the eighteenth fairway towards the clubhouse, Jouma did not see a cold-blooded killer like Isiah Oulu. He saw instead a respectable, highly regarded pillar of the community.

More than that, he saw a father who clearly thought the world of his daughter. He had recognised that unspoken, unconditional love that very first day in the apartment at Kwakiziwi when he'd seen the Brigadier stroking Tabitha's head and wiping away her tears. Was that *really* a man capable of murdering his daughter's husband, decapitating him and leaving the head on the doorstep on Christmas morning?

It was an act of such unspeakable cruelty it almost defied belief.

And the more he thought back to that day the more Jouma thought about the last time he'd been in Kwakiziwi, just last night in fact, and what he had seen by the weak sodium glow of the streetlights outside Tabitha and Paul's apartment.

He watched the Brigadier putting out on the eighteenth green and shaking hands with his three playing partners. Then he watched him walk into the clubhouse.

No. This was not right. There was something here that he had overlooked.

And as he drove back to police headquarters he was pretty sure he knew what it was.

67

Mrs Jubumbwe, who ran the evidence locker at Mama Ngina Drive, was a fearsome woman who put the fear of God into even the most senior detectives. In order to release evidence she required notification in triplicate, signed by a superior officer. If you did not have the necessary paperwork, then it was a case of whether Mrs Jubumbwe knew you well enough to trust you. But even Jouma, who had known her for more than twenty years and was probably the most trustworthy detective in the Coast Province force, still had to rely on her being in a good mood – or as near to what counted as a good mood in Mrs Jubumbwe's case.

'What did you say?'

'The sheeting, Mrs Jubumbwe. The plastic sheeting that was used to wrap the body found off Funzi Island.'

'Why would you want that?'

'As I said, I don't want the sheeting. I want the cords used to tie it.'

Mrs Jubumbwe peered suspiciously at him through narrowed eyes, as if he had just asked for access to her underwear drawer.

'You do not have the necessary paperwork,' she noted.

'No. I do not have time.'

'This is most irregular.'

He smiled at her. 'Please, Mrs Jubumbwe?'

'Only because I know you, Inspector,' she said. 'And because I know who your superior officer is.'

'You are a most wise and wonderful woman.'

She grunted, then waddled off into the aisles. A few moments later she returned with a large paper sack. 'You are not to leave the room with this,' she said.

'Of course not,' Jouma said.

Slowly she pushed the bag through the mesh grille separating her indexed empire from the rest of the world.

'Thank you,' Jouma said – then snatched the sack and ran from the evidence locker like a schoolboy stealing from a sweet shop.

At her house in Nyali, Ellen Wako Chatme checked herself in the full-length wardrobe mirror and, satisfied, went downstairs. She moved through the sprawling house to the kitchen and filled the kettle. Normally the day staff would be in attendance to do such things, but she had given them the afternoon off. It was not that she doubted their loyalty, but nor did she trust them either. The jackals from the society magazines were desperate for any sort of insight into what was happening inside the Wako Chatmes' house, and they had the money to loosen tongues.

'Well?' a voice said from the kitchen table.

She turned to find Colonel Robert Sutherland looking at her expectantly. 'Well what?'

'The phone rang. You went upstairs to answer it. Was it him?'

Ellen laughed softly. 'It was my personal trainer asking if she could rearrange our Wednesday-afternoon session. You should learn to relax, Robert. Today is Charles's golf day. When he's finished golf he goes to the Naval Club where he proceeds to get drunk enough to bore all his friends with the same old war stories. He won't be back till two or three in the morning.'

303

Sutherland shook his head. 'I don't understand why you put up with him.'

'Oh, you know Charles,' she said breezily, as she plucked a bag of redbush tea from a box in the cupboard and dropped it into a mug. 'He is a very independent soul.'

'Stupid old goat,' Sutherland said.

Ellen came round the table and kissed him on the top of his head. 'Are you jealous, Robert?' she said coquettishly.

He grabbed her and pressed his head into her breasts. 'Yes, I bloody well am,' he said.

The doorbell sounded, and Sutherland stiffened. 'Who's that?'

Ellen frowned. If this was a member of the press then she would be instructing her solicitors to file a trespass suit against them. She had *specifically* told them that the family had no further comment to make about that horrible serial killer, and that any intrusion into their privacy would be regarded as harassment.

Angrily she stormed to the front door.

It was Jouma. He was accompanied by two uniformed officers. And standing behind them, his face like thunder and still wearing his golfing attire, was the Brigadier.

'Inspector Jouma!' Ellen exclaimed. 'Darling!' Her expression immediately changed to one of concern. 'What is it? What's happened? Is it Tabitha?'

'Is he here?' the Brigadier said, pushing past her into the house. '*Is he here?*'

'Good afternoon, madam,' Jouma said, shuffling his feet on the doorstep. 'May I come in?'

She stepped aside to let him pass. Jouma caught a waft of expensive perfume.

In the kitchen he found the Brigadier standing in the doorway with his fists on his hips, and Sutherland sitting ashen-faced at the kitchen table.

'Robert . . .' he said. 'How *could* you?'

'Charles – I can explain.' His eyes flipped up hopefully as Ellen entered the room. 'Ellen – tell Charles that this is all a misunderstanding.'

'Oh, shut up, Robert,' she snapped. 'Can't you see it's all over?'

'Over?'

'Inspector Jouma has worked out that it wasn't that ghastly serial killer who murdered Paul, haven't you, Inspector?'

'Yes, madam. I have.'

'I always thought you would. You always struck me as such a *clever* man.'

'*Ellen!*'

She stared at Sutherland with contempt. 'You have no concept of breeding, have you, Robert? Of self-respect. Do you really think I'm going to get on my knees and plead my innocence like some common, lying, snivelling Mombasa wallet thief? What would people *think*?'

'You're fucking insane, woman!'

'And you're pathetic.' She turned and smiled at Jouma, transformed once again into the perfect society hostess. 'Would you like a cup of tea, Inspector?' she said. 'Charles – I expect you will have something stronger?'

'I confess the connection should have been made much sooner than now,' Jouma said. 'Regretfully an administrative error led to the original report about the discovery of Mr Yomo's body off Funzi Island being mislaid; and then, due to my own enthusiasm, I neglected to fully digest the finer points of the report.'

They were sitting around the kitchen table. To anyone witnessing the scene, it would have looked for all the world like four old friends gathering for afternoon tea – except there were two uniformed officers at the door, and the topic of discussion was the murder of Paul Yomo.

Jouma reached into the paper evidence bag and placed one of the plastic cords on the desk.

'These were used to secure the plastic sheeting around the body. Brigadier, you have already seen them – but I wonder if you would be so kind as to explain what they are.'

'It's hose wrap.'

'And what is hose wrap used for?'

'The plastic is fitted around the scuba hose to protect it and also colour–identify the diver.'

'Look closely at the end of the wrap,' Jouma said. 'You see the stamped letters?'

'*K.N.C.D.U.*'

'It means something to you, Brigadier?'

'It stands for Kenya Navy Clearance Diving Unit,' he said, glaring across the table at Sutherland.

'According to the vessel logs we have received from Mtongwe dockyard, Colonel Sutherland's unit was practising deep–water manoeuvres off Funzi Island the day Paul Yomo disappeared.'

Sutherland shook his head. 'Charles, I don't know what this man has been telling you—'

'Shut up, Robert,' the Brigadier growled.

'Would it be correct to suggest, Colonel Sutherland, that you and Mrs Wako Chatme used the Brigadier's antique pistol to kill Paul Yomo, initially as a means of incriminating the Brigadier, and that you subsequently decapitated the body to make it appear the work of the serial killer known as the Headhunter?'

'Absolute tosh,' Sutherland spluttered. He turned to the Brigadier. 'This is pure fantasy, Charles.'

Ellen Wako Chatme lit a menthol cigarette. Nobody,

Jouma concluded, could smoke a cigarette with such insouciance when they had been accused of conspiring to murder their son-in-law.

'Have you ever been humiliated, Inspector?' she asked him. 'I mean really, devastatingly humiliated?'

'*Ellen.*' This time it was the Brigadier. 'You don't have to—'

'I have,' she continued. 'Not once, but twice. You see, my husband is a coward.' She waved her cigarette dismissively. 'Oh, don't believe all that Alpha Male, king of the pride swagger. It's all show. When it comes down to getting things done, he would rather bury his head in the sand. Especially if it involves his darling Tabitha.'

'Please, Ellen.'

Jouma cleared his throat. 'From what I understand, madam, your husband was most forceful when it came to seeing off men he regarded as unsuitable.'

She laughed softly. 'You mean that deadbeat musician? That *bongo drummer*? What did he tell you? That Charles had him whipped to within an inch of his life so that he would stay away? You really shouldn't believe everything you hear. It was *me* who arranged it. I had to. Can you imagine what people would have said behind my back? "Don't look now, but that's the Brigadier's wife. Her daughter is shacked up with a deadbeat bongo drummer." My life would have been insufferable.'

The Brigadier looked as if he had just been slapped in the face.

'The Brigadier didn't know?'

'My husband doesn't know anything. He can command the entire Kenyan Navy about, but he'd rather turn the other way than make a decision that involved his own family.'

Jouma looked at her with astonishment. 'You care so much about what people think of you?'

307

'You have no idea of the circles I move in, Inspector. There are people who will scrutinise every scintilla of your life looking for faults if you give them half a chance. But there was nothing I could do about that bastard child of hers. When he was born I didn't dare show my face in public for over a year. Let me tell you, it hurt, Inspector Jouma. It hurt like hell.'

'You mean Jonas?' the Brigadier said. 'Your own *grandson*?'

'Believe me, Charles, if I could have forced her to get rid of it, I would have done. But she had her darling daddy to run to. And you were always putty in her hands.'

Jouma was finding it hard to reconcile the serene matriarch he was used to with this bitter, self-absorbed vixen sitting across the table from him now. They were two different people.

'I tried so hard with her, Inspector, believe me I did. You would not believe the number of dashing young officers from Mtongwe I introduced her to. But she was never interested. She preferred deadbeats.'

'Tell me about Paul.'

'Paul?' Ellen snorted derisively. 'What is there to say? He worked for a loan company. And if he'd worked there for another hundred years he would have still been shuffling applications. I told Charles that he was utterly unsuitable for her – but because Tabitha said she loved him, that made him good enough in my husband's eyes. It was *pathetic*.'

'Why didn't you just make him go away, like Billy Kapchanga?'

She crushed her cigarette into a marble ashtray. 'Because Charles saw how much Tabitha loved him, that's why. If Paul had suddenly disappeared like the bongo drummer, I think even he would have managed

308

to put two and two together. And even though he is a coward he is still a powerful man. He would have ruined me, wouldn't you, darling?'

The Brigadier was staring blankly at the last wisps of smoke curling from his wife's cigarette end.

'But Paul knew about your affair with Colonel Sutherland,' Jouma said.

'It was ironic.' She smiled. 'Robert was one of the eligible young men I had in mind for Tabitha. But when she wasn't interested, I realised that *I* was. We used to rent a room at the Hyatt in Nairobi, didn't we, Robert? Oh, we were very discreet. But one of Paul's polytechnic friends was waiting tables. He recognised us and was unable to keep his mouth shut.'

'So when Paul came to you for money to pay his gambling debts—?'

'You might say he had leverage.'

'You had no idea he was in such trouble?'

'Like most chronic gamblers he had perfected the art of plausibility. I never suspected a thing, until he came to see me.'

'And that is when you decided to kill him?'

She looked at him with vivid violet eyes. 'I really had no choice, Inspector,' she said. 'I have a reputation to uphold.'

'So you lured Paul to a dry dock at the naval yard,' Jouma said. 'Told him that you wanted to see him, Brigadier. And why should he suspect anything? He regarded you as a father. Colonel Sutherland shot him through the heart with the Kolibri Car Pistol from your office. They planned to leave him there to be found the next morning.'

'But why did they want to incriminate *me*?'

The Brigadier looked like a small child who has just been told Santa Claus does not exist.

309

'Because it would kill two birds with one stone,' Jouma said. 'Get both you and Paul out of the way at the same time. He would be dead, you would be behind bars. Your wife and Colonel Sutherland would be free to carry on their affair.'

He looked at her with bewilderment. 'You hate me that much?'

'Oh, don't be so wet, Charles,' Ellen snorted.

'But you cut off Paul's head! You left it on the doorstep for your own daughter to find. For *Jonas* to find. Why, Ellen? In the name of God, *why*?'

'Because she changed her mind, for Christ's sake,' Sutherland said wearily.

Ellen chuckled softly to herself. 'Well well, Robert. And there was I thinking you were going to plead innocence.'

'There's no fucking point now, is there?' he snapped.

'Why did she change her mind, Colonel Sutherland?' Jouma pressed.

'She said that incriminating Charles was too risky, that he had powerful friends who would get him off. She was frightened that it would all come out in the wash about me and her. Of course, I told her she was being paranoid, but she wouldn't have it. She was terrified of what people might think. She always was.'

'So you cut off his head to make it look like the work of the Headhunter,' Jouma said.

'Well, the newspapers were full of it. It wasn't exactly rocket science, Inspector.'

'How did you do it?'

'With a machete – just like him. We wanted it to look genuine.'

'Except you didn't know that the Headhunter's victims were always decapitated with a single left-to-right cut.

310

Sutherland shrugged. 'Hey – nobody's perfect.'

'And I suppose it was your idea to dispose of the body at sea.'

He nodded. 'I was due to lead the unit on a training dive at Funzi; I stowed the body in the amphibious craft. All I needed to do was get out to the shelf and drop it over the side. Nobody gave it a second thought. We get rid of a lot of junk that way. Old tanks, worn diving skins, that sort of thing.'

'What about your men? They weren't curious?'

'Inspector, I am their commanding officer. If I decide to throw some junk overboard, they do not question my actions.' He laughed. 'I told them it was personal shit that belonged to my soon-to-be ex-wife. Expensive frocks and shoes. Her pet dog. They thought it was hilarious.'

'Whose idea was it to deliver the head to the apartment in Kwakiziwi?'

Sutherland's face fell into a scowl once again. 'Ellen said she had plans for it.'

'You didn't know what she was going to do?'

'Why should I? Listen, if it wasn't already obvious, Ellen has got a lot of issues with her family. I'm just screwing her, I don't choose to get involved.'

68

When Jouma returned to Mama Ngina Drive later that afternoon, he was bone weary. The events of the last few days had crept up on him like a Jamhuri Park mugger and now all he wanted to do was finish up his paper-work, send Mwangi's belongings — which were still in the boot of his car — to his parents and go home for a bowl of Winifred's stew.

But when he got to his office he found he had company. A young African girl in the ill-fitting uniform of a rookie constable was sitting at Mwangi's desk, staring intently at the screen of his laptop. She nearly jumped through the ceiling when he entered the room.

'Who the devil are you?'

'Constable Lucie Mugo, sir,' she said, standing to attention.

Jouma looked at her. She was a tiny figure, even shorter than him, snub-nosed and big-eyed. And she barely looked old enough to be out of school, let alone in the police force.

'What are you doing?'

'Begging your pardon, sir — but Superintendent Simba said you might require some administrative assistance.'

'She did, did she?' He went across to his desk. 'How old are you, Mugo?'

'Eighteen, sir.'

His eyes narrowed. '*Mugo* ... You are not by any chance related to—?'

'Uniform Sergeant Oliver Mugo of Nyanza Province Police is my uncle, yes, sir.'

'*Uniform Sergeant* Oliver Mugo?' The last time he'd seen the old charlatan he had been lording it as a Detective Inspector.

'Yes, sir,' the girl said.

'And you say Superintendent Simba sent you?'

'Yes, sir.'

'Well, she *is* a devil, isn't she?'

'Beg pardon, sir?'

Jouma wiped the burgeoning smile from his face. 'Tell me, Mugo – what are you doing with Detective Constable Mwangi's computer?'

Her perfect mahogany skin flushed with a hint of pink. 'Forgive me, sir. I did not realise it was Detective Constable Mwangi's computer.'

'I asked you a question, Constable.'

'I was using the algorithmic program designed to identify integer similarities in SIM card contact books, sir.'

Jouma sighed. What *was* it with young people these days that they had to talk in an alien language?

'What are you talking about?'

'Superintendent Simba gave me a SIM card recovered from a cellphone at the Chakama Reserve when ...'

'Go on.'

The phone, Jouma knew, had been recovered from the headless corpse of Sergeant Odenga of the General Service Unit. The Sergeant had found it next to the headless corpse of Chipche Molonga, the Headhunter's accomplice.

'Well, sir – I took the liberty of extracting the data from it and running it through the computer program.'

'You did, did you? And what did you find?'

'There was only one number in the memory. A cellphone number.'

'And?'

'Well, sir, I checked with the service provider – and I think there must be some mistake.'

69

Superintendent Simba was enjoying a late-afternoon chocolate muffin when Jouma burst into her office, followed several paces later by Constable Mugo.

'The SIM card from Chipche Molonga's cellphone,' he said breathlessly.

She swallowed a mouthful of muffin and dabbed her mouth with a napkin. 'Yes, Daniel?'

'There was only one number in its memory.'

'Yes, Daniel?' she said, her gaze shifting to Constable Mugo.

'It is the personal number of Dr Nicholas Lutta.'

'Lutta? Are you sure?'

'At first I assumed it was because Molonga worked as an orderly at Kalami Hospital. But then I wondered why an orderly would have the personal cellphone number of one of the doctors. So I despatched Mugo to the filing office to check for any records we might have on him.'

'Yes, Mugo?'

Mugo took a breath. 'There was only one, ma'am: in July 1989 Chipche Molonga was convicted of the illegal brewing of alcohol. At the time of his conviction, he was working as a foreman at a fruit and vegetable distribution business in Malindi.'

'May I ask where this is leading, Inspector?'

'The business was called R M Lutta Ltd,' Jouma said. 'It belonged to Dr Lutta's father.'

Simba rubbed her temples in an effort to process this

information. 'I am sorry, but this has been a long day already.'

'Molonga worked at the factory for more than twenty years – until February of last year, in fact, when it closed down. Or, rather, when it was *forced* to close down. A week later, he was taken on as an orderly at the hospital.'

'So Molonga was a loyal servant of the Lutta family. When the business went bust Dr Lutta gave him a job for old times' sake. I still don't see the point of all this.'

'The business didn't go bust, ma'am. It was acquired by a syndicate of businessmen who immediately sold it off.'

Simba leaned forward. '*Syndicate*?'

'*The* Syndicate, ma'am. Gordon Gould, Eric Kitonga, Justice Banda, Alec Standage. They each made more than a hundred thousand dollars from the sale.'

'You said these men *acquired* the business? How?'

'They won it. In a poker game.'

'How do you *know* all this?'

'Because it was in the suicide note found beside Mr Lutta Senior's body. The old man lost the business in a card game, then he hanged himself. And when Nicholas Lutta and Chipche Molonga found out, they decided to avenge him.'

'But the Headhunter—?'

'A psychopath called Isiah Oulu, locked away in the system for so long that everyone forgot about him. He was Dr Lutta's patient – and Lutta had perfected a way of controlling his mind. With Molonga working as an orderly, it was a relatively simple business to set him loose. Isiah might have believed he was sacrificing apostates, but in reality he was doing Lutta's and Molonga's bidding. They created the Headhunter, ma'am. They created the perfect killing machine.'

Simba flopped back in her chair, her head spinning. 'Where is Lutta now?'

'According to Dr Klerk, he is at a conference in Berlin,' Jouma said. 'Except when I checked with the International Association for Correctional and Forensic Psychology they had no knowledge of a conference in Berlin. Their next gathering in Europe is in Prague in three months' time.'

Simba thought for a moment. Then she looked at Jouma. 'Alec Standage.'

'The only member of the Syndicate still alive.' Jouma nodded. 'And ever since the Headhunter's last attack, he's been living under a blanket of security.'

'But now—'

'But now the Headhunter is dead,' Jouma said, 'he thinks he is safe.'

70

The cleaners had been in his hotel room while he'd been at breakfast. Consequently, it stank of disinfectant and air freshener. They'd made the bed, they'd changed the towels, they'd even folded the first sheet of toilet paper into the shape of an arrow. Why did they do that? Was manicured toilet paper supposed to make you feel better about paying three hundred dollars a night? Was the bouquet garni, the freshly stocked fruit bowl, the sweetie on the pillow supposed to make you feel *good* about being here?

Lutta ripped the sheets from the bed and poured his complimentary bottle of house wine over the mattress. He threw the clean towels on the bathroom floor and tore the toilet paper into tiny shreds.

Three hundred dollars. It was an obscene amount to pay for a room that probably cost ten to maintain over the course of a twenty-four-hour period. His father would have been horrified if he'd known. Hadn't he done his best to instil thrift into his only son?

If only Ranasinghe Lutta had practised what he'd preached. Oh, he'd scrimped and saved to send his son to medical school in the United States. But Nicholas, studying hard for his PhD thousands of miles away, had never thought to question where the money had really come from.

Because he'd never suspected that his thrifty old father was an inveterate gambler who occasionally struck lucky at the poker table.

He was such an innocent man at heart. Such a foolish man. His father had actually believed in the sanctity of the gaming tables, that winning was all down to luck and judgement.

They must have seen him coming a mile off. *His new best friends.* The writer, the dhow owner, the judge, the hotel manager. So respectable. Such good company. Nicholas could almost picture the beaming smile on his father's face when they'd invited him to join their exclusive little club, their self-styled *Syndicate.* No doubt they'd let him win at first. Not big, but enough to whet his appetite. But then, when the snare was baited, they had taken him for every penny. It didn't matter to them that his father had built his fruit and vegetable business from nothing. It was theirs now, a lifetime of struggle transformed into a pile of plastic chips on a baize table.

They had killed him. Not shame or remorse.

And it was the duty of a son to avenge his father's murder.

Isiah Oulu had fascinated him from the very first time they met. The young, ambitious criminal psychologist and the unrepentant, deluded killer.

'Why did you kill them, Isiah?'

'Because they were unbelievers.'

'They were your family.'

'I am Athi, the living god, son of the transcendent Ngai, the Divider of the Universe and Lord of Nature.'

And he remembered how Isiah had flinched involuntarily then, because it was at this point that he would expect to feel 20,000 volts ripping through his body as punishment.

But instead Nicholas Lutta had reached out and taken his hand and said, '*I understand.*'

Their sessions continued for several months while

Lutta gauged the true extent of Isiah's Messiah Complex and, more importantly, the level of his disdain for those he dismissed as mere mortals.

Only then had he begun his experiment.

Deep hypnosis, during which the subject's twisted subconscious was gently unravelled in an attempt to reach and shut down its deep-rooted psychosis. Curing the criminally insane mind by rebooting it. Lutta knew that the technique was radical, but in Dr Klerk he found an enthusiastic advocate. And with Isiah he had found the perfect guinea pig.

Then his father had been found on the end of a rope in his warehouse, with the confessional note stuffed into his urine-soaked trousers – and suddenly everything changed. Lutta began to plot revenge, but his keen mind knew that it would be self-defeating to simply kill the members of the Syndicate himself.

Far better to have someone do it for him.

His first thought was to use Chipche – and the loyal foreman would have done the deed without a qualm. But there had to be a better way. One in which the guilty would suffer while the architects of their death went free.

And then one day, during a routine session with Isiah, the idea had come to him.

'What if it was within my power to free you from this prison? What if I could bring the apostates to you, Athi?'

And, from deep in his trance, Isiah had replied, 'It is the will of Ngai.'

Over the next weeks and months Lutta manipulated Isiah's mind so that his delusions, instead of being erased, were heightened, and the reality of his incarceration buried so deep in his subconscious that he would never remember it.

Then it was a case of arranging his escape, which had proved ridiculously easy with Chipche's help.

Ah, dear Chipche. So unflinchingly loyal. Did any family deserve such a true servant? Because Lutta was not about to let loose a madman who thought he was a living god, not without strict supervision. It was all very well killing apostates – but they had to be the right ones.

And so it was that Chipche the factory foreman became Chipche the witchdoctor, the mortal who had a direct, prepaid line to Ngai himself.

He went to the minibar and selected an ice-cold can of Fanta. He rolled it across his sweating forehead and reflected that his plan had so nearly worked to perfection. Isiah had begat Athi who had begat the Headhunter who in turn had become a living, breathing bogeyman. Everyone was so obsessed by him they never thought to question why he existed or why he killed.

It really was a work of genius.

But he had died before his mission was complete. Three of the Syndicate were dead, but one still remained. And for Nicholas Lutta, the vengeful son, that was unacceptable.

The psychologist made his last preparations, then left his room for the last time, pausing only to put the plug in the sink and turn on the taps full blast.

71

The wicked witch was dead and it was business as usual at the Sandpiper Hotel. The building still bore a few scars, but the bulk of the repair work to the shattered atrium was complete, the bulletholes in the walls and ceilings had been filled in and the bloodstained carpets had been replaced. And, now that he no longer felt like he had a death sentence hanging over him, Alec Standage had dispensed with the expensive army of private security goons.

But the best news of all for Standage was that the guests had returned. It seemed that the hotel's recent travails had not affected advance bookings, and as Jake arrived for his meeting with the hotel manager a fresh coachload of pasty white Europeans was disembarking from the airport shuttle bus and trudging wearily into the cool reception area.

Standage was at the door to greet them all personally, a big smile on his wide face. He looked like a new man, Jake thought – as well he might.

'Mr Moore! How nice to see you again.' He beamed. 'I'll be with you in two minutes.'

In fact, it was more like fifteen as Standage busied himself with the new guests, helping them to sign in, making sure there was a steady stream of porters to take their bags and plying them with fresh orange juice and chilled face towels.

'It's good to see them back,' he said when he eventually led Jake towards his office. 'Between you and me there were times when I thought we were stuffed. First that maniac hitting people over the head, then the business with the gunmen. I tell you, Jake, it would have killed a lot of businesses.'

'I'm pleased to hear it,' Jake said.

They had reached Standage's office now. It was compact and functional, with a desk, a small sofa and various items of English memorabilia on the walls – a framed football shirt, a black and white poster of Keith Moon, a beermat collection, scrawled children's drawings of stick men with potato heads.

'And of course I wouldn't be here today if it wasn't for your friend Mr Bowden,' Standage said with due solemnity. 'I understand you visited his family in London.'

'I went to his funeral.'

'I will never forget what Mac did for me that day. In fact, I'm thinking of having a garden of remembrance in his name built in the grounds. It would be nice to fly his widow and children out for the opening ceremony, don't you think?'

'I'm sure they'd appreciate that,' Jake said. 'In fact, Mac is the reason I'm here today. Last time I saw him, he told me you had agreed to pay him a substantial bonus for the extra bodyguarding work. Danger money, I guess you'd call it.'

Standage's eyes narrowed. 'Is that so?'

'I think the figure you quoted him was an extra twenty thousand pounds on top of the agency fee.'

'I don't deny figures were discussed, Jake – but twenty grand is way off beam.'

'You said it yourself, Mr Standage: Mac saved your neck. You owe him.'

The hotel manager smiled thinly. 'Of course, I would be more than happy to make a donation to Mac's widow—'

323

'Twenty grand, Mr Standage.'

'Any agreement between Bowden and this hotel is none of your business,' Standage snapped. 'I think you've got a bloody nerve to come here demanding money. Who the hell do you think you are?'

'I was his friend,' Jake said.

Standage picked up the telephone. 'I suggest you get the fuck out of my office before I have you thrown out.'

Shit, he thought as he headed back to the atrium. That had gone as badly as it was possible to go. Worse, in fact. And now he had probably obliterated any slim chance of getting Mac's money.

But then he deserved everything he got, Jake thought bitterly, because he was a fucking snake. A snake who claimed to be Mac's friend, but was only interested in the dead man's money because it might help him out of a hole.

He reflected on the long-distance call to Shirley the previous day, how she'd cried with gratitude because twenty grand had been transferred into her account by Colin Ryeguard, and how she'd cried again when Jake told her that Mac was owed twenty more – and that he would see to it that she got it all.

He didn't tell her that he planned to borrow it, temporarily of course. Nor that, if it all went up in smoke, he and Harry had come up with a contingency plan to sell *Yellowfin* and whatever assets they had at the boatyard – because either way Britannia Fishing Trips Ltd was toast.

As he rounded the corner, deep in his own misery, he walked straight into a guest coming in the other direction towards the office. He was small, olive-complexioned, with thick-rimmed spectacles and a baseball cap tugged down over his face – and for some reason he looked familiar, although for the life of him Jake couldn't think why. To his jaundiced eye, the little man looked like a trainspotter. They exchanged curt apologies and continued on their way.

At the reception desk, Jake stopped. This was bloody ridiculous. If he walked out of that door now, then there was no going back – it really was all over. Five years of hopes and dreams and bloody hard struggle down the pan. He thought about freezing London, the Tanner's Arms, smokers shivering on the pavement. *Jesus.*

He turned and headed back towards Standage's office. He had to smooth the waters. The framed football shirt on the wall – it was Leeds United, wasn't it? Jake supported Newcastle United. Maybe they could have a man-to-man chat about underachieving football teams.

The door was shut, but he rapped once and went in.

'Listen, Alec, I think we got off on the wrong foot—' he began.

But Standage was otherwise engaged. In fact, he was writhing in his chair, his face puce, his eyeballs bulging, a vicious-looking steel garrotte biting into his throat. The trainspotter was standing behind him, twisting the wooden handles of the garrotte tightly, his face a mask of concentration. Then one of Standage's flailing hands dislodged the spectacles and the baseball cap and suddenly Jake realised where he had seen the man before.

He sprang across the room and hit him as hard as he could on the nose with his fist. He felt bone splintering on impact and Nicholas Lutta screamed with pain. A second punch sent the little psychologist sprawling against the wall, and it was clear he would not be getting up for a while.

Standage was heaving for air, his hands clutched to his throat where the steel wire had sliced into the skin.

'Are you OK?'

Standage nodded.

'What the hell was all that about?'

'I don't know.' The hotel manager's voice was little more than a papery rasp. 'But thank you ... Thank you.'

72

'One of these days, my friend,' Jouma said, 'a day will pass when you do not get yourself into trouble.'

'I confess I've been thinking of rejoining the Flying Squad, just for the quiet life,' Jake said.

They watched as Nicholas Lutta was bundled into the back of a squad car. He cut a pathetic figure. His hands were cuffed and his nose was purple and disfigured. The door slammed and the car pulled away from the outside of the hotel.

'Where will they take him?'

'Shiwo La Tewa jail. Then it depends how he pleads – and how the judge finds his state of mind.'

'Do you think he's crazy?'

Jouma shrugged. 'Who can tell? Grief can do strange things to a man's mind. In Lutta's case, it spurred him into vengeance against the men whom he blamed for his father's death.'

'There's vengeance and then there's vengeance,' Jake pointed out. 'If you ask me it takes a pretty sick mind to dream up a scheme like that.'

'Or a brilliant one. Lutta was able to rewire the mind of a psychopath to do his bidding. It was murder by proxy, the perfect crime.'

'He created a monster.'

'Yes – but imagine what he might have achieved if he had put his techniques to good use. Imagine if you were able to *cure* the criminally insane mind.'

'Once a psycho, always a psycho if you ask me,

Inspector. You might be able to subdue the urges for a while, but they will always be there under the surface, waiting to come out.'

Jouma sighed. 'Perhaps. And perhaps now we will never know. Not unless somebody takes Dr Lutta's work further. But I doubt that will happen. From what Dr Klerk tells me, the psychological community is conservative by nature. They do not easily embrace change.'

'That's fine by me. One Dr Frankenstein is enough.'

They walked back into the hotel.

'So that's it?' Jake said. 'Case closed?'

'*Cases* closed.' Jouma smiled.

They turned at the sound of a commotion, as somebody attempted to break through the police cordon into the hotel.

'Just tell Inspector Jouma who it is,' Katherine Rapuro exclaimed, waving her press card. 'He'll let me through.'

'You would think Miss Rapuro had had enough headlines to last a lifetime,' Jouma said wearily.

'You know what they say, Inspector — today's newspaper is tomorrow's fish and chip wrapper.'

Jouma looked at him quizzically. 'They say it in your country perhaps, Jake.'

Alec Standage, his neck in a brace, was being pushed in a wheelchair towards a waiting ambulance. As he passed them, he reached out and tugged Jake's arm.

'I know what I said to Mac,' he rasped. 'But the truth is, I don't have twenty grand. Not any more. All that security cleaned me out.'

Jake nodded. 'It's OK.'

'No, no,' Standage said urgently. 'You're right. I owe him big time. I've got a bit of money stashed away — investments mainly. Ten grand all in. I'd like it to go to his wife and kids.'

'Maybe you can do better than that.'

'Anything.'

Jake grinned. 'What are you doing tomorrow night?'

73

In a small room down by the dhow wharf at the heart of Mombasa Old Town, two men sat at a large oval card table and watched intently as the last of five cards was turned face-up on the worn green baize. It was the three of clubs. The game was Texas Hold 'Em, one-hundred-dollar minimum small blind, unlimited ante. The two men were the last remaining players in a game that at the beginning of the evening had consisted of six. One by one the rest had dropped out, their money exhausted. The survivors were now playing for a pot of one hundred thousand dollars. The winner would be the player who could fashion the best poker hand from the five cards face-up on the table and the two cards they had been dealt at the start of the round.

Alec Standage lifted his two cards a couple of millimetres from the table and glanced at his hand. To his left, Tajik ul-Mraq did the same.

Above their heads was a bare bulb in a conical metal shade. Its light filled the table below, but left the rest of the room in darkness. The players could not see the two dozen spectators craning their necks to watch the outcome, but they could smell the tension they generated in the room.

Unlike Harry and Ralph, Jake could not bring himself to watch the denouement. Instead, he stood at a window at the far end of the room, blowing cigarette smoke against the pane as he stared out at the lights of the Old Town shimmering in the muggy heat of the night.

After more than six hours of poker, it had come down to all or nothing on the turn of a single card.

Mac Bowden, he thought, would probably have appreciated the lunacy of the situation.

The easy way was never your way, was it, kimosabe? *Fancy staking your business on a game of fucking cards. You'd be better off sticking the lot on the 3.10 at Wincanton.*

Ah, but, Mac — you have to appreciate that our boy knows what he's doing. Standage was part of a syndicate that raked in thousands of dollars by taking unwitting saps to the cleaners. He knows the game. He understands the percentages.

Yeah — but look who he's playing. If that prick thinks he knows a trick or two, then the Arab knows them all a hundred times over. He was playing poker when he was in his nappies in the souk. And don't forget, at the end of the day it's my hard-earned bonus money you're playing with.

Shirley will get the twenty grand you're owed, whatever happens, pal. *Yellowfin* is worth at least fifty.

Well, that's very gallant of you, kimosabe. *And don't think I don't appreciate it. But at the end of the day it was me that fucked up my job and my marriage, not you. It was me that got killed. If it hadn't been for you giving the old Jimmy Cagney routine to that dwarf lawyer in London, Shirl and the kids would never have got a bean. You did me proud, Jake.*

Well, let's just see how we get on, eh?

Yeah. Let's just see how we get on.

From the table Jake heard the dealer say, 'Mr Standage?'

The hotel owner poured himself three fingers of Pusser's Rum.

'Full house,' he rasped hoarsely, his throat still fucked from the attempted garrotting.

There was a gasp from the spectators.

'And now you, Mr ul-Mraq?'

Jake raised his glass and tipped it towards the glowing city outside.

Cheers, Mac. Whatever happens, I'll always miss you like hell.

Turn the page for a sneak peek
of Nick Brownlee's gripping new novel

Snakepit

coming in 2010 from Piatkus

1

When the crack of the gunshot had faded, and the dead man had finally stopped twitching in the dirt, his executioner hawked with a noise like bubbling tar and spat contemptuously into his startled face. Now there were just two men on their knees waiting to die in the broiling midday sun. They were the men from the fishing boat – and from his perch high on the crumbling ramparts the boy called Jalil waited to see which of them Omar would choose to kill first.

Others were waiting, too. Below in the fortress compound, where the rabble had emerged from the bunkhouses to watch, a frantic exchange of dollar bills had already begun. Jalil could hear their excited jabbering, and he knew that the smart money was on the white English skipper rather than the policeman from Mombasa.

The boy shifted slightly on the warm stones and, not for the first time that morning, he wondered what had happened that meant they had to die.

The ancient fort was built on a rocky spit of land that formed the southern arm of a natural harbour, protected by sandbanks, mud flats and a vicious reef three hundred yards out to sea. There was only one way through the reef, and the wooden skeletons of vessels that had tried their luck still jutted out of the water where they had been ripped apart by the jagged coral.

Jalil had been on watch duty that morning, and he had known something was not right the moment he'd spotted Omar's speedboat cresting the southern horizon. Squinting against the harsh sunlight he could make out familiar figures in the cockpit as the boat neared the shore – stocky Rafael, Omar's right-hand man, at the wheel; Julius and his brother Moses squatting like crows on the bulkheads; and Omar himself, tall and broad-shouldered, his hands gripping the windscreen, *keffiyeh* headscarf blown horizontal in the wind.

But that morning *two* boats had left Kanshish for the border. Now there was only one. Where was Mustafa? Where were his men?

Where was the skiff?

In the compound below Omar now stood in front of the two men from the fishing boat. His gun was in his hand, and as he slowly moved it from one hand to the other the crowd continued to agitate excitedly, because they knew what was coming. So did Jalil, and even though he was no stranger to violence he felt his heart thudding in his chest.

He had been a soldier for Omar since his whore of a mother had dumped him at the gates of Kanshish at the age of five. The bitch had expected payment; but when Omar saw the whip marks on Jalil's back he had put a bullet through her pockmarked face and allowed the boy to feed her corpse to the wild dogs. After that, Jalil would gladly have followed Omar through the fires of hell and back.

He was ten now and short for his age, with a palsied left leg that he'd had from birth – although no one in their right mind would ever mention his deformity to his face, and certainly not within earshot of Omar. Like rats, the men of Kanshish shared an impulse for self-preservation, and they had no wish to die a lingering and unpleasant death like Demus, the fat quartermaster, who had drunkenly blurted out something about Jalil being the right height to suck Omar's cock and had been pegged out in the middle of the compound and left there, screaming for mercy until he expired of sun stroke and dehydration three days later.

Jalil adjusted his withered leg into a more comfortable position. Normally he would wear his calliper; but up here on watch duty he could take it off. He hated the unwieldy leather and metal contraption. Not only was it uncomfortable to wear, it drew unwelcome attention to his disability. Jalil knew he could not walk unaided without it, yet when he wore it he *felt* like a cripple. Up here, on the highest point of the ancient walls of the fort, fifty feet above the compound, was the one place the boy felt free from constraint.

He could see the faces of the two men now and, although there was no mistaking their fear, the boy was pleased to see that they were not reduced to begging for their lives.

Their faces were raised, their eyes fixed on Omar as they waited to die. The boy shook his head sadly, because he had become friendly with them, especially the Englishman.

But if Omar had decreed they must die, then die they must.

This was Kanshish — and in the Snakepit death was simply a way of life.

Bait

Ex-Flying Squad cop Jake Moore's career was cut short by a bullet; ten years on, he runs a game-fishing business that is about to go to the wall. But old habits die hard, and when cerebral Mombasa detective Daniel Jouma – seemingly the only good policeman in a city where corruption is king – asks for his help in solving a baffling murder case, he cannot help but become involved.

The mangled body of a street criminal has been washed up on the beach and a fishing boat skipper and his bait boy have blown up in the water. When Jake and Jouma look closer, they discover that not only are the murders linked, but the conspiracy surrounding them stretches far beyond the reaches of Africa – and has deadly implications for everyone concerned.

978-0-7499-2884-1

Burn

Just when Inspector Daniel Jouma believes calm has returned to Mombasa, all hell has broken loose. Bodies are piling up in the morgue, Jouma's new boss wants answers – and the mayor wants him out.

Meanwhile, bulldozers are hurtling towards Jake Moore's stomping ground. Ever the hero, the maverick cop turned fishing-boat skipper faces up to the might of Kenya's most ruthless – and dangerous – developer.

Then a chilling secret, long thought to be buried in the ashes of a deadly inferno, brings the crime-busting duo together once again. And Jake and Jouma are about to discover that, when you play with fire, someone always gets burned . . .

978-1-84744-359-5